The Pieces We've Lost

The Pieces We've Lost

H.K. GREEN

Editing by Editing by Andrea

Proofreading by Love & Edits

Cover Design and Formatting by H.K. Green

Paperback ISBN: 979-8-9909156-0-2

For the ones who stay strong for the people they love, even when it feels like the world is caving in.

playlist

Me and My Kind | Cody Johnson	2:36
I Drive Your Truck | Lee Brice	3:54
She's a Cowgirl | Midland	3:34
Cowboys & Tequila | Grace Tyler	3:31
Cowboy Scale of 1 to 10 | Cody Johnson	2:55
Baby Blue | George Strait	3:29
The Bottom | Chris Stapleton	4:06
Welcome to the Show | Cody Johnson	2:40
Butterflies | Kacey Musgraves	3:38
On Purpose | Sabrina Carpenter	3:57
peace | Taylor Swift	3:53
It Takes A Woman | Chris Stapleton	4:06
You Are In Love (Taylor's Version) | Taylor Swift	4:27
Best of You (feat. Elle King) | Andy Grammer	3:05
LOVE IS A COWBOY | Kelsea Ballerini	2:42
For The Both of Us | Dan + Shay	2:45

author's note

When I first had the idea for *The Pieces We've Lost*, I knew I wanted to write a story that was representative of the way of life I grew up around: agriculture and rodeo. I didn't want to just brush over the aspects of the western lifestyle, but rather educate readers who are curious about the way of life and the sport.

With that being said, the story is set half in Houston, Texas, during the Houston Livestock Show and Rodeo, and half in Montana, during the Miles City Bucking Horse Sale and the Home of Champions Rodeo. The book is rodeo heavy, with the team roping event being a main focus of several chapters, but there are also discussions of steer wrestling, breakaway roping, bareback bronc riding, mutton busting, and wild horse racing.

In rodeo, the animals are extremely well cared for and that is reflected in my story. Rodeo is not meant to be an act of animal cruelty, and thus no animals are injured (although it can happen) during the events of this story.

Although *The Pieces We've Lost* is a fictional story, it is based on the activities and lives of real cowboys and rodeo athletes. There is also mention of calf branding, although it is brief.

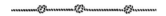

Content/Trigger Warnings:

This book is intended for adult readers and includes mature themes, on-page explicit sexual content, and explicit language.

For closed door modifications, flip to the back of the book right before the acknowledgments.

Additional on-page content warnings include:

- Alcohol consumption
- Alcoholism
- Death of a parent
- Discussions of depression, divorced parents, and grief
- Panic attacks
- Physical violence
- PTSD/flashbacks
- Ranching activities (mention of branding)
- Rodeo events (roping, bronc riding, steer wrestling)—No animals are injured
- Severe injury and depictions of blood
- Sexual assault attempt (not graphic and not by the MMC)
- Trauma after an injury

Readers who may be sensitive to these subjects, please take note. It is my sincere hope that I handled these topics with the care they deserve.

rodeo 101

Advantage Point: The point at which the steer has gotten an adequate head start and the barrier is released for the contestant to follow the animal.

Barrier: In a timed event, the line stretched across the front of the box that the contestant and their horse cannot cross until the steer or calf has a head start.

Box: In a timed event, the box is the area where the horse and rider back into before they make a roping or steer wrestling run.

Breaking the Barrier: Failure to give the animal enough of a head start before a roping or steer wrestling event, resulting in a ten-second penalty.

Bulldogger: A steer wrestler.

Chute: A specialized, narrow corridor designed to hold a calf or steer and release it for a roping run.

Cinch: The leather or fabric band that secures the saddle to the horse.

Dallying: The act of wrapping the rope around the saddle horn for the header to secure his catch.

Hazer: In steer wrestling, another horse and rider, usually another steer wrestling competitor, who travel along the steer to ensure it runs in a straight line so the contestant can jump off his horse onto the steer.

Header: In team roping, the cowboy who ropes first and aims for the horns.

Heeler: In team roping, the cowboy who follows the header and aims for the hind legs.

Honda: The knot through which a rope passes on its way to becoming a loop.

Nodding: A signal that a cowboy gives when they are ready for the gate or chute to be opened.

No Score: Failure to make a qualified ride (8 seconds) in roughstock events.

No Time: Failure to make a qualified run (illegal catch, no catch) in timed events.

NFR: National Finals Rodeo; the premier rodeo event by the PRCA which showcases the talents of the PRCA's top fifteen money winners in each event as they compete for the world title.

PRCA: Professional Rodeo Cowboys Association; the oldest and largest professional rodeo-sanctioning body in the world.

Roughstock: Bareback riding, saddle bronc riding, and bull riding. Other events are called timed events.

Roughy: A person who competes in roughstock events.

Standings: In professional rodeo, a cowboy's success is measured in earnings. There are several sets of standings where cowboys can keep track of where they rank.

prologue

Ladies and gentlemen, this is shaping up to be another great night of rodeo here in Houston. Up next, we've got a cowboy, who you know and love, from our great state of Texas! He was your world champion in steer wrestling last year. From your hometown of Houston, please welcome Levi Merritt!"

Thousands of people from all around the world had gathered to watch my dad compete, and the roar of the crowd filled the entire arena, drowning out the announcer's sentence.

I bounced on my heels in excitement as I looked over at my mom, who watched the chute at the end of the arena intently. Anxiously. Nervously. We'd both seen him perform countless times before, but her expression would always remain the same until the event flew by in an instant. It never took long, and if you weren't paying attention, those three to four seconds would be over before you even caught a glimpse of the action.

Most people would assume her reaction was out of fear, but it was truly because of the love she had for my dad. If you looked past the anticipation in her eyes, you would see the same love I had for rodeo, the love we all had for it.

I looked back just in time to see Dad flash me a confident smile like he always did before a performance. My heart filled with adoration as I watched him back his horse into the box. His horse was antsy, clearly more than ready to run. Dad's attention focused on the task at hand, and he nodded his head ever so slightly to signal for them to open the chute and let the massive steer run free, giving it a head start to sprint down the length of the arena floor.

A memory of me at five years old flashed across my vision, and I smiled thinking about it.

Dad and I sat on the living room floor as I looked at the pictures in a program from one of the rodeos he had been to earlier that year. I flipped to a page with Dad's picture and a bunch of words I couldn't quite understand on it.

"Dad, what is steer…resting?" I pointed to the big words at the top of the page as I tried to sound them out.

"Steer wrestling?" he asked as he looked where I was pointing.

"Yeah, what does that mean?" I asked.

"It's what I do when I go to rodeos. It's my event that I compete in."

"Oh." I nodded my head enthusiastically, but after thinking for a moment, I tilted my head in confusion. "What exactly is a steer?"

"It's the animal that I have to wrestle to the ground when I compete," he explained as he scooted closer to me. "They're like the cows we have on the ranch, except they're only used for rodeos."

My eyes went wide as I tried to picture Dad wrestling one of the huge cows we had on the ranch. "How big are they?" I asked him.

"They're around five hundred pounds." His response had been so nonchalant as he shrugged his shoulders. His attitude toward it was no doubt calming, yet a wave of anxiety still flowed over me.

"Is that as big as you? Or…bigger?" Dad was pretty big.

He laughed. "No, sweetie, they're a lot bigger."

I looked down and fidgeted with the page before looking back up at his big brown eyes. "Whoa, that is big." With how big Dad was, they must have been huge. "Isn't that scary, though? What if one… hurts you?"

"I've never been hurt by one before, Sunshine. You have nothing to worry about." He took the program away to tickle me, and I squealed with laughter, already forgetting about my fear surrounding the steer wrestling. Dad was always right, and so I believed him.

Nothing could hurt him.

He was invincible.

Dad's horse followed a split second after the steer was released, running up next to the animal my dad would take to the ground. Dropping from the horse, he grabbed the steer by its horns, intending to land and slow its movement so he could flip it onto its side. Except, his movement was slightly off, causing his feet to catch the ground too abruptly. A hazy cloud of dust rose to surround his body, and the audience strained to see what was happening.

I couldn't tear my eyes away as I squinted and stood on my tiptoes to try to see what was happening over the heads of all the people in front of me. Within a split second— which felt suspended in time—he flipped over the top of the steer's head, causing the animal to come crashing down on him. The crowd winced when its horn turned directly into his chest, piercing through his shirt. I gasped as red blossomed around the horn.

"I've never been hurt by one before, Sunshine. You have nothing to worry about." Dad's reassuring words repeated over and over in my head as my heart started racing. *"You have nothing to worry about."*

I turned my head toward Mom, looking for

reassurance, but she had shot up from her seat, her eyes wide with alarm. The color had drained from her face, like she'd seen a ghost, and I caught myself holding my breath, tears stinging my eyes as my vision blurred.

He's going to be fine. He's never been hurt by a steer before. He said nothing will ever happen to him. He promised *me.*

The arena, once lively with the chatter and cheers of spectators, turned eerily silent as everyone waited to see if the hometown cowboy would get up. If he would move, even if just an inch.

Waiting to see if he would do *something.*

Anything.

CHAPTER ONE

PRESENT DAY

W e are only a couple short days away from opening night here in Houston, and the energy is electric! You can tell these folks are ready for the action you *cannot* find anywhere else. This isn't the world's biggest rodeo for nothing, and what better place to have it than Texas?"

Voices from the Cowboy Channel droned on in the background, but I wasn't paying attention, instead absentmindedly picking at the split ends of my hair.

That was until, "And this year also marks the fifteenth anniversary of the death of local Texas rodeo legend and former world champ—" I grabbed the remote from the coffee table in record time, snapping off the television before the host could finish his sentence. With the absence of the TV, the whir of the A/C unit was the only noise remaining in the house.

I didn't need to be reminded of what happened fifteen years ago. I dealt with the consequences every single year, and I knew all too well the effect the sport had on my family.

I used to love rodeo. If you had asked me how I felt

about the sport at eight years old, I would have told you that one day I would be a champion just like my dad. I went to every performance with my parents. I was practically raised in the arena, and I watched the ropers and barrel racers in awe, knowing one day that would be me out there.

But then the accident happened, and my entire world split in half.

When you witness an accident like that, one with fatal consequences, you grow up fast. I knew rodeo was the reason I would never see my dad again, so I vowed to never associate myself with it in the same way he once did.

Rodeo only served as a painful reminder of how life, and everything you knew, could be ripped away in the blink of an eye.

The problem was that my mother still loved it. She still went to the one in Houston every single year, despite what had happened. And to make matters worse, she dragged me along with her—call it emotional support from her only daughter.

I slowly inhaled and exhaled, counting to ten with my eyes fixated on the popcorn ceiling in an attempt to slow down my heart rate. When it inevitably didn't work, I swiped my hand across my forehead and headed toward the front door.

Before I could reach the door handle and free myself from the room that had suddenly gotten too stuffy for my liking, my mother came around the corner. "Everything okay, Ells?" she asked, the concern evident in her voice.

"Yeah, Mom." I swallowed the lump in my throat. "I was just leaving."

Hanna Merritt was the glue that held our family

together. She was a ray of sunshine, the light in a world of darkness.

At least that's what it looked like to the rest of the world. Deep down, I knew she was missing a part of herself, the other half of her heart. But she held it together like any strong woman does.

Hanna and Levi were a classic case of opposites attract. She was nurturing and patient and put others before herself, always. When my dad died, she was the one who kept everyone from going under. She didn't allow his death to shut her down, working day in and day out to set me up for whatever future I wanted. She was selfless in that way, and sometimes I looked at her and wondered how in the world we could be related. If one thing was for certain, though, it was that we were soul-connected. You do not—cannot—go through the same thing we've been through and not be.

"Be safe, hon." My mom's tender voice broke me out of my trance.

I looked back at her over my shoulder and gave her an apathetic look, pursing my lips as my fingers grasped the doorknob. *No guarantees there, Mom.* I thought about the way my dad always told me he'd be safe before a rodeo and that nothing would ever happen to him.

And look where that got us.

"Right… Just going to clear my head for a while," I muttered softly, mostly to myself, to keep me from saying what was really on my mind.

I twisted the door handle and stepped outside. Even though it was a bit overcast, I still had to pause for a moment to let my eyes adjust to the sunlight.

The Merritt family ranch sat on 150 acres of land on the perimeter of Houston. After I graduated from college,

I came back home to help my mother. I was worried about her. Although we had family close by to help, I didn't want her to be alone here.

I walked across the yard toward our barn and the large shop that my dad used to work in, taking in the panoramic views of the Texas landscape around our property. To the west were farms and ranch land that stretched for miles. To the south was Houston, and to the north were the hills where my dad was buried.

When I reached the shop, I lifted the garage door to let as much light into the large space as I could. When he wasn't on the road for a rodeo or doing work around the ranch, my dad loved to restore old vehicles. He had done it his entire life, the skill passed down to him from his parents. Rodeo and cars were his focus before my mom came into the picture.

I made my way back through the dusty, dimly lit space, maneuvering my way around toolboxes, farm vehicles, and my dad's old workbenches. The lightbulbs hanging from the ceiling back here had long since burned out, but I knew exactly where to find what I was looking for. Whenever I got stressed or needed to clear my head, I came out here.

My mom didn't know about this coping mechanism— this way for me to feel closer to my dad—and I intended to keep it that way. This was just for me.

In the far-left corner of the shop, under a tarp, was my dad's old 1965 F-100 that he started restoring right after he married my mother.

I pulled the tarp off the old pickup truck and suppressed a cough as a thin layer of dust rose into the air. Once the dust had settled, I ran my fingers over the hood and the baby-blue paint before opening the driver's side door and sliding onto the bench seat. The interior looked almost brand new, despite having a bit of a musty smell from sitting in this shop for so long.

This pickup was my dad's pride and joy. My mother used to joke that he loved it more than he loved her, even though we all knew that was far from the truth. There was nothing he loved more than her.

It took a little bit of maneuvering, but I pulled the vehicle out of the shop and onto the dusty gravel road. After closing the garage door and making sure everything looked exactly like it had before I got there, I drove the truck toward the highway, away from the view of the main house and my mother's gaze.

A photo of my parents from the year they met sat on the dashboard. In it, my dad had his arm around my mom's shoulders and he was smiling at her while she smiled at the camera. I knew I took more after my father, but looking at photos like this one confirmed the two of us were practically clones with our dark hair and athletic build.

My mom and I were opposites when it came to our looks. She had vibrant, strawberry-blonde hair and, unlike my father who always developed a tan while working in the summer, she burned easily in the sun. While my features were sharp, hers were softer, rounder. The one, and only, thing I got from my mother were her eyes. Baby blue.

The radio was set to an old country western station, and the lyrics to George Strait's "Amarillo By Morning" played softly in the background.

I never touched anything in this pickup, never moved anything or gave the impression that the vehicle was being used, but I always admired the photo of my parents. The only things that made it difficult to keep my driving habit a secret were the fuel gauge and odometer, but I held onto the hope that no one besides me came out to the vehicle, and if they did, they just ignored the numbers or never started it.

I rolled down the driver's side window, cruising north down the backroads, and let the cool breeze blow my hair to the side. There were no other vehicles in sight. Although I was still driving on a public road, it was not very well maintained, so no one really used it. I took this route every time I drove my dad's pickup for that exact reason. There was no one who could potentially see me driving the vehicle and report it back to my mother.

It wasn't that I was breaking any laws by driving the truck or that my mother would be mad that I drove it. In fact, I was so cautious that the only law I could possibly be breaking was driving too slowly. I just wanted to keep this ritual a secret. It was special. Sacred. Just me, my dad's favorite truck, which I had continued to restore for him once I was old enough, and the endless dirt roads.

I liked to think I was pretty strong, that I could hold my own and not let my emotions get the better of me. My mom used to joke that I was truly my father's daughter in that way, inheriting every personality trait of his, both good and bad. My dad was determined, confident, and charming, but he was also overly competitive and stubborn as a mule. I didn't mind being compared to him, though, despite the way I rolled my eyes every time she would say it. Deep down, it made me feel close to him in a way that I had longed for since his death. I considered it a compliment in some ways, to bear resemblance to a man so many people still idolized years after his accident.

Sometimes when I drove out here, the tears just fell. It

was almost cathartic, the privacy that allowed me to mourn the man I never really got to know.

I wondered what he would think of me today. If he would be proud of me, or if he would be disappointed in my estrangement from the rodeo community. Part of me thought he would understand how painful it was to watch other people replace his memory and legacy. How much it hurt to think about the sport that took his life.

I swiped a tear out from under my eye as I looked out onto the horizon. The sun peeked out from behind the clouds, creating an ethereal scene on the hills before me.

"Hi, Dad." I sniffed. I talked to my dad all the time, even if it seemed illogical to think he could hear me. I truly wanted to believe he could in times like this, though. "I wanted to take your truck out for a drive again today. I'm taking good care of it, I promise. I know you wouldn't want it to sit in the shop to gather dust." He wouldn't have. He took pride in keeping his "toys" looking shiny and new.

"Mom's holding up. I know she's trying to be strong for us, but I also know the weight that this time of year has on her. I can't believe in a couple weeks it will have been fifteen years. Everyone's been talking about you on the radio and TV. You're still as famous now as you were back then.

"I'm not sure what I'm going to do this year. I want to stay here with Mom, but I know she wants me to go out and experience the world. She says she wants me to make the most out of my twenties because, 'you're only young once.' I worry about her, but I know she worries about me too." I huffed, rolling my eyes a little as I thought about my mom's lectures about being young.

My mother had assured me she was fine, that she didn't want to prevent me from getting out and making memories, from having things to look forward to. But sometimes I caught her wiping a tear from her eyes when she looked out at the arena in our yard. She stayed so strong for others; it didn't seem fair to leave her behind. Even the strongest people needed someone to lean on.

"We miss you a lot down here, Dad, but I'm sure you're up there wrestling steers and having a grand ole time." I sighed.

As if in response, the sun emerged completely, casting a golden glow on the land. The breeze seemed to pause completely, a melodic sound of birdsong filled the air, and I knew he was listening to me.

CHAPTER TWO

"Carson, toss me a beer, will ya!" Mikey, one of the guys I competed with, called out to me from across my front yard.

I reached into the cooler he brought to grab him a cold one and noticed that all that was in there was lager out of the Pacific Northwest. I was pretty sure it had that motorcycle commercial back in the day.

"What the hell is this, man?" I teased.

"It's cheap, dude. And it ain't all that bad," he defended as I shook my head and tossed the can to him.

I was just giving him shit. Truthfully, I didn't mind the kind he brought; it just wasn't what I normally drank.

It was a tradition for us guys to get together at my house before a big rodeo to chill with a couple beers and not worry about work, competing, or anything overly stressful. In addition to Mikey, my roping partner, Reid, was there, along with two other guys, Hayden and Jake.

"Y'all packed and ready to go tomorrow?" Jake asked.

A chorus of "yup" went around our little circle, save for Hayden who wouldn't be coming with us this time.

"I'm ready to get on the road. Not so sure if I'm ready to spend twenty-one hours with you fuckers, though." Mikey slapped me on the ass as I walked by him to go sit down again.

The Houston Rodeo started in a couple of days, and we were driving all the way from Silver Creek, Montana, a small settlement outside of Miles City. We all traveled together, even for events like the Houston Rodeo that had a bracket-style format where we might not be competing on the same days.

I'd been involved with the sport for as long as I could remember. Growing up on a ranch in Montana ingrained the competitive spirit in me. I competed in high school and even in college before graduating with a degree in farm and ranch management, naturally. As much as I would have loved to save money and not go to college, I'm glad my parents made me.

If this rodeo thing didn't work out for me—which it would—at least I had something to fall back on, and that was more than I could say for some of the people I knew in my small town.

"What makes you think we want to spend twenty-one hours with you, Michael?" Reid fired back, unable to keep the smirk off his face.

"Who wouldn't want to spend twenty-one hours with me?" Mikey winked in response.

We all raised our hands.

I met my best friend and roping partner, Reid Lawson, in college. We went to a school in Goldfinch, a small city in central Montana. He was a year younger than me, but we started roping together as a team my sophomore year and quickly developed a friendship. He also grew up in

Montana, in a little town about four hours away from Silver Creek.

Needless to say, Reid was like a brother to me. We'd helped each other through good times and hard times.

"Carson, we need to find you a woman down in Houston." Mikey grinned at me.

Michael Tucker, or Mikey, as everyone called him, was most likely the biggest playboy you'd ever meet. He had a different girl with him every week. But the women loved him, for some odd reason. That way of living wasn't really my style.

My last serious relationship didn't end well. Sophie and I met in college, close to the time I was about to graduate. She was a couple years younger than I was, but the spark was instant. All of our friends thought we were going to get married one day.

And that was the plan. We were engaged for about a year and had our wedding date set for the summer after she graduated from college. But she didn't like the idea of me being on the road all the time while she was still in school. I'm not sure what it was that caused her to have such a distrust in me, but I was raised to only have eyes for one woman. And my eyes were glued on her.

She broke it off via text message while I was out of town for a rodeo in Arizona, and it absolutely crushed me. For about a year, I was in a really rough place. Reid pulled me out of the hole I had dug myself.

I'm not proud of the man I was during that time. I was angry, drank too much, and didn't care about the people around me like I should have. I was better now, at least on the outside. I had to be. If not for myself, then for the people who loved and cared about me.

"You know me, man. I'm not trying to get into anything like that." I shrugged him off.

"Come on, brother. Live a little! Have some fun. When was the last time you brought a girl home anyway? It's not like you'd have to commit to anything. Those girls down there would do anything to say they were with cowboys like us, even if only for one night."

"Not all of us are like you," Reid grumbled as he rubbed his eyebrow. He knew Mikey was trying to get a rise out of me. Reid was observant, had a sharp radar for bullshit, and could sense any issues from a mile away, which made getting a lie past him almost impossible.

"Lawson, you're just as bad as me, the fuck you talkin' bout?" The look on Mikey's face screamed, *"Can you believe this guy?"*

While Reid did have his fair share of flings, he wasn't nearly as bad as Mikey.

"Listen, I'm simply trying to get the job done and win. I'm not the type for one-night stands and you know that. But I also know on the off chance I did find a girl in Texas, she wouldn't like the fact that I'm constantly on the road. Right now, I'm only focused on rodeo and *nothing* will change that." I explained my case for what felt like the billionth time.

"All right, man. I get that. Guess that just means there's more options for me and the boys." Mikey stretched out his arms behind his head.

I couldn't even imagine all of the trouble that man had gotten himself in, especially when he wasn't around us. He was twenty-eight and still acted like a college frat boy.

The rest of the guys rolled their eyes and changed the subject, wanting to talk about anything but Mikey's next sexual conquests.

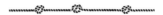

A few hours later, the guys had gradually started to head home. Mikey caught a ride with Hayden because he was drunk off his ass and said he'd come back to get his pickup from my house in the morning.

Jake had also headed back home, leaving me and Reid sitting in front of the house.

"Have you heard anything about Sophie lately?" Reid dared to ask.

It was a touchy subject, but because he was my best friend and I was real with him, he was willing to take that risk.

"Nah, I try to avoid anything related to her." I shrugged. That usually meant avoiding looking at social media, but it also sometimes meant avoiding the spots we used to go together. "Truth is, I'm worried about what I might do when I find out she's moved on and is seeing someone else. I'm honestly trying to avoid what's inevitable."

I was sure she had already found someone else. I might not have seen the breakup coming, but other people had, especially toward the end. According to my friends, she'd always had one foot out the door.

"I'm here for you, man. Whatever you need, you know that right?" Reid's response confirmed my suspicions. He had to have heard something or seen something. Unlike me, he wasn't actively avoiding Sophie and her world, and besides, word got around quickly in a small town. And Montana was really just one big small town.

"Yeah, I know, and I appreciate it. You don't have to worry about me, though. My focus is all on bringing home some more gold," I insisted.

I hated hiding things from Reid, but it was easiest to cover the truth with a hard exterior. To act like nothing was wrong and be the charismatic, friendly face everyone knew and loved. For the most part, the charismatic, friendly face wasn't a facade. But sometimes, it was. That was the cold, ugly truth. It had been two years since the split. I didn't want nor need the pity glances that came my way if I so much as dropped my walls during those moments of vulnerability, and deep down, I still felt guilty for how everything happened. I blamed myself for my relationship failing and had always assumed it was because I wasn't good enough for her. If Reid saw through the mask I put on for everyone, he didn't say anything.

"We'll get it done, buddy." He clapped me on the shoulder as he rose from his chair. "Well, it's getting late. I'd better get back home."

I gave him a nod as he headed toward his truck and then drove away.

I walked into the small double wide I owned and flicked on the light switch on the wall right inside the doorway. I didn't have a whole lot in the house because I was always on the road for rodeos.

After kicking off my boots, I threw my cap onto the kitchen counter and looked into the living room where there was a small couch, a TV sitting on a bookshelf serving more as storage for baseball caps than books, and a dining table with two chairs.

My room had a queen-size bed, a nightstand, and a spot in the corner where I kept a lot of my gear. I wasn't much for decorating, so my array of cowboy hats were the sole pieces of "art" hanging on the walls.

The house was no more than a place where I could lay

my head, not something I would necessarily call "home." But I was fine with that. I didn't need the fancy house with all of the decorations and furniture. I had no one to impress.

The road and the rodeo were my home, the only places where I really felt like I belonged. The people I traveled with were the only people who mattered.

Don't get me wrong, I grew up with a great family in a loving home, at least for a while when it was important. But as I grew older, I gained another one in the guys I rodeoed with. My family, of course, supported me every step of the way, but there was something different about the brotherhood.

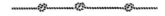

SOPH

I just don't think this is working out, Colt. I hope you can understand where I'm coming from.

I stared at the text I had received a couple hours ago. There was no explanation. No, "I'm sorry," no offer to talk and work something out. Sophie had broken my heart as quickly as she had stolen it from me, all with a single text message.

What do you mean? Please, let's just talk this out.

SOPH

This isn't something we can talk about right now. I need space. I'll talk to you when I'm ready. Please don't call me.

I debated calling her anyway. The devil on my shoulder told me to go off on her for her selfish way of ending our relationship, but I tossed that idea as quickly as it formed. Starting a fight wasn't going to make the situation any better or convince her to change her mind. Burning bridges wouldn't get me where I needed to go.

I had to focus on winning. I was traveling to rodeos to make a living, to provide us with a future, and I needed to remember that. It was all for her. Everything I did, all of the hours I spent away, was to set us up for a comfortable life.

Maybe she'll change her mind, I hoped. After a few hours of thinking, she'll realize we were made for each other. She'll decide that ending the engagement would be a terrible idea.

A week of me giving her the space she had asked for went by, and she never called me. Instead, I opened the door one morning and discovered the ring I had bought her sitting on the doorstep. After that, I decided to call her.

One ring and the call went to voicemail. *"Hi! You've reached Sophie Andersen. I'm sorry I can't make it to the phone right now, but leave your name, number, and a message and I'll return your call as soon as I can."*

The beep of the voicemail system rang in my ear, but I couldn't say anything. I had so much I wanted to say, but I couldn't get the words out, so I hung up.

A couple days later, I tried calling again but immediately received a busy dial tone. It didn't take a rocket scientist to know she had blocked my number. That was when I knew it was really over. What was the point in continuing to fight, in trying to fix something broken beyond repair, if she wouldn't even talk to me? I hated the idea of throwing away everything we had built the last couple years, but the message was received. *She didn't want me.*

I tried to think of the weeks prior to the breakup. Yeah, we had our fair share of arguments, but nothing other couples weren't also experiencing. There was no warning. Right before I left for Arizona, everything had been fine. Better than fine. We seemed happy. I was aware she didn't like how often I was on the road, but I kept reassuring her that she was the only woman I loved. I was doing this for our future.

A car horn blaring outside my window woke me from my dream, or nightmare, about my failed relationship. They weren't as frequent as they had been in the year after the breakup, but I still had them occasionally, usually when there was pressure building on me to succeed. With the Houston Rodeo coming up, it made sense. Even though I didn't feel like I was stressed or nervous, my body probably was.

I groaned as I tapped my phone screen to see what time it was.

04:30

The digital numbers seemed to mock me and my attempt at getting any amount of sleep.

It was still dark outside, but I rolled out of bed and walked over to the window to see what all the ruckus was about. I peered out and saw what no one wanted to see this early in the morning.

I opened the window enough that I could yell through

the screen. "Mikey, you dumbass, what the hell are you doing?"

"What does it look like, Carson? I'm trying to get my damn truck!" he yelled back.

"You couldn't have waited until it was at least light out?" I grumbled as I closed the window and headed to the door to help him.

It hadn't been that long since Mikey stumbled home drunk with Hayden. Just because he wanted to get up early to get his pickup didn't mean the entire neighborhood wanted to wake up with him.

"This piece of fucking trash," Mikey cursed under his breath.

I had gotten outside barely in time to see him kick the side of the door, which set off the alarm again.

"Not sure that's gonna keep the alarm from going off. Where are your keys, man?" That was the moment I got close enough to the pickup to realize the idiot had locked his keys inside. I couldn't help but chuckle at him. "You really thought you could break into your own pickup?"

"Colt, just shut the fuck up and help me, will you?" He rolled his eyes.

About fifteen minutes later, we had successfully broken into Mikey's pickup and he was on his way back home.

I knew I wouldn't be able to get back to sleep after all that, so I broke my rules of avoiding social media and settled for mindless scrolling on my phone. I had nothing better to do, and besides, Sophie had blocked me, so what was the worst I could see?

I opened Instagram—which I hadn't been on in months. If someone needed to talk to me, they had my number or they could come talk to me face to face. Even if Sophie wasn't a factor, I still wouldn't feel the need to share anything on social media. The most important people in my life already knew about the things going on because I'd either told them or they saw them happen.

At first, the mindless scrolling was just that. Mindless. Photos of people I hadn't seen since my college days, some guy I met at a rodeo's new dog, Sophie posing with a guy... *Wait, what the fuck?* I did a double take to make sure my eyes weren't deceiving me this early in the morning. Blonde hair, elegant features, and striking eyes that could make any man drop to his knees. *Fuck. Yeah, that's her.* I had no idea who the guy was, but she had to have unblocked me for the post to come up in my suggested feed. I knew Sophie could be petty, but this seemed like a new low.

This is what I get for breaking my rules, I thought as I threw my phone across the room. It was only five a.m. I still had hours before I could even really do anything, since most of the work around the ranch had been taken care of already, and to top it off, my method of passing the time had been tainted by my ex-fiancée. *Wonderful.*

I had to admit she still looked good, though. I hoped whoever the new guy was made her happy. He probably wasn't a cowboy, judging by the way he looked, and he probably wasn't traveling constantly. She needed someone to be there for her every waking moment. Someone she didn't feel she needed to tie down because she already knew his every move. Someone she could keep a tight leash on.

I think deep down we both knew that man wasn't going to be me—couldn't be me—and that was neither of our faults. It came down to compatibility, but damn, the outcome still hurt.

With my phone sitting on the floor across the room and time to kill, I decided I had to at least try to close my eyes.

At some point, I ended up drifting back to sleep, Sophie still on my mind.

I needed to find something that would take my mind off her. The next few weeks would be hectic, and I needed no distractions.

CHAPTER THREE

ellison

The next week flew by in a blur. I avoided Houston as much as I could while still doing my job around the ranch. There was a lot of work that had to be done. A lot of blood, sweat, and tears went into continuing the family legacy.

In particular, today there was a broken fence on the north side of the ranch that needed to be fixed as soon as possible unless we wanted cattle to get out, which could turn into a shit show really quickly.

I swore under my breath as I reached the fence, getting out of the side-by-side to examine the damage. It was an easy temporary fix—all it would take was splicing in some new wire and stapling it to the post—but eventually we'd have to replace the section.

Television shows and other forms of entertainment romanticized ranches so much that it seemed like everyone wanted to work on one or marry into a ranching family. But they didn't get the full picture of what the lifestyle really required. It wasn't just riding horses all day.

Half of the girls I saw on social media wishing they

could marry a cowboy wouldn't last a week out here. It was hard work. And it was hard work that—most times—wouldn't make you a millionaire, at least not financially. It took a special person to live this lifestyle.

Horses needed to be taken care of, cattle needed to be moved, and there always seemed to be something broken. Repairing things almost always required a trip into the city, but during this particular week I usually was able to pawn that task off to a younger ranch hand. Not my proudest moments, using my dad's death as ammunition to get people to do the things I didn't want to do. But if it meant I didn't have to go into Houston during the rodeo, it was worth it.

After I finished my share of the work later that afternoon, I was planning on going back to the house and taking a nice long nap. But I knew the universe had different plans for me when I saw the familiar gray Honda Civic in my driveway.

I walked into the living room and there she was, helping herself to the food in our fridge. Isabelle Bennett. My best friend.

She was like a second daughter to my mother, so Hanna never minded when Isa came over and raided the cabinets, or the pantry, or the fridge. But sometimes I wished Isa would at least give *me* a heads up.

"Hey, Is. What's up?" I sat at the counter, trying to see what she was getting into.

"I was gonna make Hanna some cookies, but now that you're here I have a way better plan." The corner of her mouth curved up into a smile that could only mean trouble.

"If this involves going into Houston, I'm afraid you're going to be very disappointed," I muttered.

"What? You have to come out with me, Ellie," she whined.

"You know how I feel about going out during the rodeo, Isa. We've been over this before."

The bars during RodeoHouston were a trap, full of fake cowboys and buckle bunnies. I had better things to do than spend my evening fighting off horny college boys.

"Please, one night. I will make it up to you, I promise." She had been begging me to go downtown with her for days now.

The rodeo had started a little over a week ago, and she no doubt was looking to get in on all the action.

"Can't you ask Erin or Jess to go with you?" I suggested. She had other friends, so I didn't know why *I* had to go with her.

"I mean, yeah, but you're my *best friend*. I just want to spend time with you, Ells."

I guess even I didn't get a pass on this one.

"Fine, but you owe me." I gave in because when Isabelle Bennett wanted something, she didn't stop until she got it. That applied to boys, jobs, and apparently getting Ellison Wilson to go downtown during one of the busiest times of the year.

I met Isa at our college freshman orientation when I spilled an iced coffee all over her. I turned around too quickly after grabbing it, and the force of me bumping into her popped the entire lid off, and suddenly my drink was soaking her white tank top.

Instead of getting upset like most would, she simply shrugged and said, "Guess my shirt needed a coffee boost too."

The joke was so awful I snorted laughing, and our friendship only grew from there.

We spent more time hanging out with each other than we spent with our dorm roommates that year, and we lived together for the rest of college.

We were the perfect duo. Isa was the life of the party and I was the rational one. With her blonde curls and bubbly personality, she was always catching people's attention. I was the one who reined her back in when she got a little too crazy, but she also brought me out of my shell.

In the four years since we'd met, we'd experienced it all. Breakups, failed exams, job interviews, bad Bumble dates. You name it, and we probably vented about it over cheap wine or ice cream.

I was there when Isa's first college boyfriend cheated on her and broke her heart. She was there when I got rejected from my dream internship. She was also one of few people who knew about my dad and the upcoming anniversary of his death.

Going out was no doubt an attempt to distract me and make sure I had a little bit of fun, which I appreciated, but at the same time I questioned why we *had* to go to the bars and couldn't just do a movie night with wine or something.

"Okay, so I'm thinking we get downtown a little before nine so we can find decent parking, especially since most people will hopefully be going to the concert first and then the bars after, so that means we should start getting ready by at least six o'clock." She eagerly started planning out the night.

"Isa, that's right now. You couldn't have given me at least a day or even a few hours to prepare?"

"You and I both know that if I had given you that much time, you would have backed out and made some excuse about how you can't come." Isa crossed her arms and gave me a knowing look.

"Okay, okay, you're probably right." I rolled my eyes.

"Of course I'm right, Ellie. When have I *ever* been wrong?" The corners of her lips curled up in a devilish grin as she flipped her hair over her shoulder and disappeared around the corner.

I followed her into my bedroom and flopped down on the bed. She was already digging through my closet.

"Where are all of your sexy clothes?" She had resorted to tossing clothes out of the closet after she realized she wasn't finding what she wanted.

A T-shirt hit me in the face, and I rolled my eyes as I stood.

"Wow, first you force me to go downtown with you and now you insult my clothing choices?" I scoffed, holding my hand to my chest in mock offense. I pushed her aside and pulled out a pair of light-wash Wrangler jeans and a simple black crop top, holding them up for her to see. "Here. Is this good enough for you?"

"Not exactly what I had in mind, but I'm not going to change yours, am I?" Isa pouted.

"Nope. It's called compromise. Besides, you would have been looking for something all day if I had let you, and we definitely don't have time for that with how long it takes you to get ready." I grinned.

If you thought typical girls took a long time to get dressed and do their hair and makeup, you would be amazed Isa was even able to make it out of the door on time. I had never met someone who took as long to get ready as her.

I sighed as I lay down on my bed, watching as Isa continued to dig through my closet for God knows what. I was slowly starting to accept the idea of going out because I had to admit, being able to take my mind off the looming anniversary of my father's death was nice. This week had been tough on both my mother and me, and it was all leading up to tomorrow, aka the worst day of our lives, so why shouldn't I go out and let off some steam?

colter

My ears pounded with the clapping and screaming of fans in the arena. Reid and I weren't set to compete until the second week of the rodeo and the days had gone by painfully slow. I ached for the rush of competition, and our time was finally here, whether we were ready or not.

There were five different groups with eight competitors in each, all competing to make it into the semifinals and championship rounds. The first week had consisted of us watching the competition we could potentially see if we moved on and practicing as much as we could without getting fatigued. This time also allowed us to get into a winning mindset. We were in the company of some of the best cowboys in the world.

I lived for this atmosphere, the expectations to perform well and take home prize money rising with every success. Many men crumbled under this kind of pressure. Not me, though. My focus was on one thing—throwing the rope with perfect timing and catching the steer's horns so Reid could come behind me and finish the job by roping the legs.

The time to beat this round was six-point-five seconds.

Attainable.

Very doable.

"Ladies and gentlemen, your next team comes from way up north in the Treasure State. We've got two young cowboys from Silver Creek, Montana, tonight. Colter Carson and Reid Lawson!" The announcer called out our names. "Let's give them a big ole Texas welcome, shall we?"

"You ready for this, bud?" I looked over at Reid.

He nodded, but it looked like his nerves were getting to him a little.

If I got nervous, it was generally only for a moment and went away the second I stepped into the arena, but the pressure affected Reid a bit more than me. I was always there to help ground him and keep his mind locked on the task at hand, though.

We guided our horses into the boxes on opposite sides of the chute and backed them up, Reid positioned on the right side and me on the left. My horse, Faster Than a Silver Bullet, aka Bullet, had been with me all throughout college and my professional career. He knew exactly what to do and lived for this as much as I did. Maybe even more.

The worst that could happen during this run would be to break the time barrier and get a ten second penalty. While it wouldn't put us in last, it sure wouldn't put us in first. The next worst thing would be to get no time for failing to rope the steer, but that wasn't going to happen. When Reid and I were on a roll, we were like a well-oiled machine—perfectly in sync, movements smooth as honey.

It had taken a couple years of roping together to develop the type of chemistry we had as header and heeler. When we first started out, Reid was working on his confidence as a freshman roper, even though he was damn good, and I admittedly was a bit arrogant coming off my first season. My former partner and I had made it to the College National Finals Rodeo and placed in the top three for team roping. We could have been first, but my heeler at the time was much slower than Reid.

I took a deep breath and glanced over at Reid to make sure he was ready. I was the one who would give the signal for the steer to be released from the chute. Our timing had to be perfect.

Reid tilted his chin up, letting me know he was ready, so I nodded and the chute opened. The steer ran perfectly straight out of the gate and once it had reached the advantage point, my horse and I took off with Reid following behind a couple moments after. A rush of adrenaline went through me as I swung the rope over my head and focused on the honda, locking in on the perfect timing to throw the rope and legally catch the steer's horns.

There were three ways you could legally catch a steer's head: around both horns, around the neck, and a half head, which meant the loop went underneath the horn on one side of the head, either under the chin or neck, and on top of the horn on the other side of the steer's head.

"There's Colter Carson on the head," the announcer chirped in the background.

Once I caught both the steer's horns, I jerked the slack out of the rope and immediately dallied to restrict the steer's movement and turn it so Reid had access to rope its legs.

"And we've got Reid Lawson on the heels, folks."

Reid came behind the steer and expertly roped the hind legs. With ease, we both guided our horses backward to face each other and remove slack from the ropes. That was when the time stopped.

"How about a five-point-seven for the cowboys from Montana?" the announcer called. "Let's give them a round of applause, shall we, and then we'll move on to our next event."

While it wasn't our fastest run, it was still enough to put us in first place for the round and a great position going into the group championship round the next day.

"Reid, Colt, my boys. What a great run!" Mikey clapped us both on our backs after we had exited the arena.

"Thanks, man." Reid acknowledged him, but I stayed quiet. I was wondering what he was about to get us into.

"Listen, a bunch of us are going downtown to the bars tonight. You should come with us," he suggested.

I generally didn't like to go out the night before a competition. There was too much risk of either a hangover the next day or someone doing something they would regret. With how crowded it would be, I wasn't sure I was convinced.

Before I could protest, Reid answered for the both of us. "I think that would be fun, right, Colt? Have a little fun. Destress before tomorrow?"

I thought about it for a moment and weighed the options of going out versus doing nothing at the trailer.

"Yeah, all right, let's do it." I conceded. What harm would going out do, realistically? Besides, I could make sure I left at a reasonable time.

CHAPTER FIVE

ellison

Despite us arriving downtown just before nine o'clock, the bar Isa wanted to go to, duly named the Ace in the Hole Bar, was packed. And when I say packed, I mean *packed*. When we arrived, there was hardly any room on the dance floor, and you could clearly tell who *thought* they knew how to swing dance but obviously didn't. They were the guys who were swinging their partner into everyone else and weren't doing their job as a lead: watch the dance floor and protect your partner.

We ordered our drinks, a Malibu lemonade for her and a tequila soda for me, and found a table across from the bar. I knew I would end up sitting alone for a bit later on while Isa made her rounds. It didn't bother me. I was fine on my own. Besides, this was normally how going out went.

Between the two of us, Isa was the flirt, the girl who caught everyone's attention, and I had zero interest in any of the men here. They were either fake cowboy frat boys who only wanted one night or they were actual cowboys who were here for the rodeo. And I wasn't trying to get roped back into that lifestyle.

"Did you hear about what happened between Maddie and Logan?"

When I said no, Isa gave me the inside scoop of the breakup between two of her friends. Apparently, Logan got caught cheating on Maddie with Maddie's cousin. I didn't have a big friend group like Isa did. I also didn't get involved with the gossip mill or drama as much as she did. It wasn't that I was anti-social, I merely chose to keep to myself. It was easier that way.

"God, Houston is always so busy. I seriously can't believe they're still letting people inside the bar." I observed the bouncers glancing at peoples' IDs and letting them through without even considering capacity limits. The air was starting to feel as sticky as the floors.

"I know, the rodeo always makes downtown so packed. Speaking of which, how are you holding up?" she asked as she sipped on her drink.

"It honestly doesn't feel real," I admitted. "It never does. Fifteen years later, and I still expect to come home to see him in the living room dancing with my mom and getting ready to go to a rodeo."

"I'm sorry, El. You know I'm always going to be here for you, though."

She tapped her hand over mine as she gave me a knowing smile, one I had gotten way too often from people. I knew Isa meant well, but it was hard to separate any kind of sympathy from pity.

I attempted to reciprocate her smile, but I knew mine didn't reach my eyes. "I know. You're one of the few people who I trust with this. If I had it my way, I wouldn't even be going tomorrow. But everything I do these days is for my mom." I shrugged and took another sip of my drink.

"I'm sorry." She pouted, drawing out her apology. "I didn't mean to kill the mood. This is supposed to be a fun night! Come on, let's go find some guys to dance with." Isa pulled me to my feet. I groaned but allowed her to drag me onto the edge of the dance floor.

The DJ was playing an old George Strait song, one of his many number one hits. The song ended shortly after we got up and the intro to a line dance started to play. Everyone started lining up, and Isa handed me her drink so she could join.

I'll admit, I wasn't big on line dances or dancing in general. I mean, I knew how to. Everyone who grew up in a small town in Texas knew how to dance. It was kind of a requirement. But dancing always seemed to have the expectation of a conversation, and conversation was the gateway to something more.

Isa gestured for me to get out into the crowd with her, but I shook my head laughing and held up our drinks with a shrug, as if to say, *"Sorry my hands are full."* It was her fault for handing me her drink in the first place, and I already could see people struggling with the choreography. It was a more advanced dance with lots of steps and turns.

"Okay, that was so hard," Isa gasped after she ran off the dance floor in the middle of the song, choosing to bail out instead of suffering through the rest of the dance.

"There's a reason why I wasn't going out there." I handed her back her drink.

"You should have at least come out there with me. Make fools of ourselves in solidarity, you know." She held back a laugh as someone messed up a step somewhere in the middle of the floor and caused an entire group behind them to trip up.

Those poor people.

The song ended a couple painful minutes later and the hardwood cleared up. Another old country song started to play and people were already filing back onto the dance floor.

"Would you like to dance?" a guy asked as he approached Isa.

I looked over at him. He seemed nice enough, and Isa was instantly charmed.

"Sure!" She put her drink down on a table nearby and grabbed his hand as he led her out onto the dance floor.

This was my cue to leave. I didn't want to hurt someone's feelings by saying no if they asked me to dance, but I also didn't feel like getting my toes stepped on or elbowed in the head by another couple. I had seen that happen one too many times already.

The table we originally sat at was still open, so I quickly made my way over to sit down, wanting to snag a seat before the group of college girls in neon-colored tops and pink cowboy hats could get there.

I was still nursing my drink when a new song started playing and I spotted Isa on the dance floor with a new partner: a lanky guy with dark, messy hair, slick with sweat, presumably from all of the body heat radiating on the dance floor. He was stumbling over his feet and I couldn't tell who was leading, her or him.

I chuckled to myself and turned my head just as a blond in a silverbelly sauntered up to my table. I could tell right away that this dude was all hat and no cattle. On the cowboy scale of one to ten, he'd probably be a two. His hat also desperately needed to be shaped. It didn't even seem as if it looked like that from use. It looked like he had left it on his pickup dash for a couple days to make it seem worn. It didn't quite have the effect he was probably looking for.

"Hello there, darlin'," he drawled as he swayed back and forth, grabbing the edge of the table to help balance himself.

I looked up at him and saw that his eyes were glassy and he couldn't seem to focus on my face.

Oh wonderful. He's plastered too, I thought to myself. I resorted to ignoring him, his advances, and his desperate attempts to take me home. He wasn't doing a very good job.

He set his hat brim down on the table. *Rookie mistake.* You never set your hat down on the brim otherwise it would start to lose its shape. It was a well-known fact, just like putting your hat on a bed was an invitation for bad luck. Any *real* cowboy would have known that. I rolled my eyes as he invited himself to a seat at my table.

"Aren't you gonna answer me, buttercup?" He raised his eyebrows at me.

"Hello," I muttered before I took a long swig of my drink. Damn, it was almost gone and I knew he was about to ask to buy me a new one.

"Your drink looks a little low. Let me buy you a new one."

Called it. There was no way I was letting him bring me a drink without me seeing the bartender pour it, though. I did not trust him to not slip me something.

"That's all right, thank you," I politely declined.

"Name's Tyler. What's yours, darlin'?" he slurred, not bothering to offer to shake my hand. He knew what he was trying to do and there was no room for formalities in his eyes. But I wasn't susceptible to his "charm" and corny fake accent.

"Emerson." I gave him a fake name because it wasn't too far off and my parents almost named me that so it wasn't like I completely made something up. I wasn't going to waste that much effort on him.

"Pretty name for a pretty girl. You know, I think you'd look damn good in my hat there. Why don't you put it on for me?" He gestured to his poorly placed Resistol.

I was past the point of annoyance at his idiotic attempt to pick me up. Rolling my eyes, and narrowing them, I answered him slowly. "I'm not touching your damn hat. I know the rules." Wanting to really drive the knife in, I added, "I am not stepping within a mile of your bed. And while *I'm* not against fighting you, I know damn well you wouldn't hit a woman. And if you would, well, you aren't a real cowboy then are you, *darlin'*?" I challenged him with an icy glare, putting an emphasis on darlin' to mock him a little.

"Bitch." He gave me a look of disgust, grabbed his hat, and wandered off to his next victim. Probably a poor, unknowing buckle bunny.

I needed a shot of something strong after that exchange. Then I needed to find Isa so we could get out of here. I wasn't sure why I had agreed to this. Okay, I mean, of course I knew why I agreed; roping the wind was easier than saying no to Isabelle Bennett. But looking back, I definitely should have known something like this was going to happen.

I pushed through the crowds of people, not making eye contact with any of the men who were undoubtedly staring at me as I walked past them, and made my way to the bar.

"What can I get you?" the bartender asked as he walked up to me.

"Just a tequila shot." I handed him my card and told him to close the tab.

He came back a moment later with my favorite man, Jose, and I welcomed the burning sensation of the liquor as I knocked back the straight shot and tossed away the lime. I already felt warmer, lighter, but I also knew I had even more bite when I was buzzed. I was like a wasp, and anyone who messed with me was going to get stung.

I scanned the room for Isabelle. It was a little bit like trying to find a needle in a haystack with the amount of short blonde girls here, but I eventually found her. I started walking toward her with a purpose. My eyes were locked on her location, and I was stopping for no one.

That was evident when, in my determination to get to Isa and get out of here, a decently tall cowboy—he had to be about six-foot-one—stepped directly in my way. I was too distracted to see him and it was way too late to do anything about it.

He turned his head in my direction, looking like a deer in the headlights, right before I crashed into him.

CHAPTER SIX

colter

The girl who bumped into me backed away, a little bit flustered. She looked up at me and the first thing I noticed was her eyes.

Baby blue. Huh, kinda like the George Strait song.

"Excuse me?" She raised an eyebrow, panic flashing in her eyes for a split second.

Fuck, did I say that out loud?

Judging by the way she narrowed her eyes at me, waiting for a response, I apparently did.

I racked my brain, trying to figure out what to say to her. What do you even do to recover from voicing an internal thought like that? I came up short, settling for an introduction because it was polite and how could I fuck that up?

"My name's Colt. Er... Colter." I stumbled over my words trying not to look like an absolute creep. Did I stare at her too long?

Oh, God, she probably thinks I'm trying to hit on her. Nice, Colt.

"I don't have time for this." She rolled her eyes and pushed past me, bumping my shoulder in the process, and started to march away, shaking her head a little bit in annoyance.

"Wait, I'm sorry I—" I started to apologize, but she was already gone, lost in the sea of people crowding the dance floor.

I debated going after her, but decided that would raise more questions from the boys than anything. I was already pretty far behind them because I had gotten caught up in a crowd of girls in pink cowboys hats when we walked in. One of them had grabbed my arm and insisted on buying me a drink, which I declined several times. I was honestly surprised Mikey hadn't stopped to talk to one of them.

I made my way over to the bar to catch up with Mikey, Jake, and Reid, still thinking about the interaction with the girl. Something about it caught her off guard. I could see it in her face.

"Carson, what happened to you? How'd you get so far behind us?" Mikey asked when I found a spot next to them.

"I ran into this girl, no big deal," I replied. *Please don't ask questions. Let me get away with this, just this once.*

"What? Well, where is she?" He threw up his arms expectantly.

"No, I mean literally ran into her. Or I guess she ran into me. I don't know where she went. She disappeared." I looked around, but my attempts to find her were futile.

I wished I could find her in the crowd, though. There was something about her that drew me in, intrigued me. Maybe it was the intensity in her eyes or the way she had her sights so focused on where she was trying to go. Most people would consider her rude, that she wasn't being aware of her surroundings and had a bad attitude, but I didn't see it that way. For some reason, I kind of admired her determination and that made me curious. The majority of women here, clearly demonstrated by the group of girls from earlier, would have seen me as a trophy and tried to flirt—save a horse, ride a cowboy or whatever —but not her. I wanted to know more about her.

"Man, that's too bad." Mikey sighed and turned to order from the bartender.

It is too bad.

"All right boys, here's to ridin' and ropin' and bringin' home the goods, however you see fit." Mikey handed us all shots of Pendleton whisky and raised his glass.

I raised mine in acknowledgment and shot it back.

"Back to that girl, Carson. Did you get her name?" he asked.

"Yeah, what did she look like?" Jake added.

"Did you get her number? What did you say to her?" Reid asked.

The boys kept firing questions at me, not giving me any time to answer.

"She have any friends here?" Leave it to Mikey to be thinking about that.

"Guys, I told you, she literally ran into me. We didn't talk. I didn't get her name. I told her mine, but I had blurted something about her eyes and she didn't want to talk to me." I finally got a word in, but I started rambling.

"Wait, what did you even say, man?" Reid chuckled.

"Nope. No, I'm not giving you guys any ammo." I denied them the opportunity to hold this over my head for the next five years.

"It's just like you to scare off a woman, Carson," Mikey teased. "Wait, how did you even manage to run into a girl but not get what she looked like?"

The problem was I *did* get what she looked like. The

image of her carved itself into my brain, refusing to leave my head. Words couldn't do her justice, and I also wasn't about to give Mikey any ideas. Knowing him, he would go look for her and then either hit on her or embarrass me, and I wasn't on board with that.

"It doesn't matter. She's not even here anymore. Let's just get on with our night." I was bluffing, hoping they would change the subject.

"Man, Colter, you're no fun." Mikey loved to get involved with everyone's personal life. I was starting to think he needed a new hobby. Maybe he could take up bird watching or something.

"Jake, you're competing in a couple days. How're you feeling, buddy?" Reid changed the subject, thank God.

Jake was a bulldogger and also did tie-down roping, but for this specific rodeo, he was only competing in tie-down.

"I'm just ready to get out there, you know," he replied.

That was the general consensus among the guys who hadn't competed yet. Waiting was the worst part about rodeos like this.

The boys kept talking about their schedules. Jake was competing in a couple days, and Mikey had ridden early in the week, during the first group. He made it to the semifinals round for bull riding so he had been hanging out the past few days.

I tried my best to be present in their conversation, but all I could think about was that girl. I had so many questions. Where did she go? Why did she react the way she did? Was it something I did? I remembered the way her eyes softened for a moment as she looked at me, like the way the sky clears up after a storm. But that was before I fucked it up and they went back to the icy glare I earned when she ran into me.

I thought about what it would be like to brush the curls out of her face, to really look into those baby-blue eyes and then to—*What am I thinking?* I just met this girl. Met was an overstatement, actually. I hadn't even gotten her name. The chances of me seeing her again in this city were slim to none. I needed to focus on roping and not on the way my name would sound coming off her lips.

"Carson, are you even listening?" Mikey punched me in the arm.

"Ow! What?" I snapped out of my daydream about the girl.

"Brother, you were the one who wanted to talk about something else and you aren't even paying attention?" He raised his eyebrows at me.

"Sorry, I was just thinking," I muttered.

"Well, stop thinking and start listening. Anyway, what we were saying was that when you and Reid win this whole thing, we need to truly celebrate. I'm talkin' a *big* celebration. Maybe we hit up the strip clubs when we get to Vegas," Mikey droned on, talking about things I didn't care about.

We talked for a couple more hours, about rodeo and work, and *not* about the mysterious blue-eyed girl, before we decided to call it a night and go back to our trailers.

CHAPTER SEVEN

ellison

I rushed away from the cowboy right as he started to apologize. Before I took off, I had taken a moment to look at him. A few pieces of his chestnut-brown hair curled out of his baseball cap, and his eyes, kind of a hazel color with blue mixed in, had looked into mine with fascination and intrigue. He looked nice and was probably a decent person, but it was too late, the damage was already done. I'd acted like a complete and utter bitch, but it was for the best.

I had far too much baggage to explain to a complete stranger about how and why he caught me off guard when he simply uttered the words baby blue. I hadn't heard those words spoken together in fifteen years. Not since I heard my dad call my mom that name for the very last time. I couldn't even listen to the George Strait song he got it from. It was too painful, and I had to skip it every time.

I quickly found Isabelle at a corner table with some friends she was catching up with. I hated to take her away from her night out, but I wasn't in the mood to stay.

"Is, we need to go," I said, giving an apologetic look to her friends.

"Oh, is everything okay?" she asked.

"Everything's fine, I just want to get out of here." I would explain everything to her later. Right now, I was determined to leave so I wouldn't have to potentially run into Mr. Resistol or Deer-In-The-Headlights dude again.

"Okay. Bye, guys! I'll see you later." She waved at her friends and followed me out to the car.

Since Isa was driving, I knew she only had one drink. Usually I was the designated driver, but tonight was the exception.

"So, are you going to tell me what happened?" Isa looked over at me as she turned onto the main road to head out of town.

"I love you, but going out is always a shitshow," I admitted. "There was an incident involving someone trying to get me to put on his cowboy hat."

"Oh, God. Please don't tell me you punched him or something."

Isa knew how I could get sometimes when a man went too far. There had been way too many times I left a bar with bruised knuckles. Honestly, I was a little shocked the cops had never been called on me. Probably because the men I punched knew they were in the wrong. Besides, I wasn't just going around punching men like Rocky. I had my reasons for doing it.

"No, of course not. I just told him off," I defended myself. "Then I ran into someone."

"Who? Wait, was it one of your exes?" Now she was intrigued.

"No, nothing like that. I mean I *literally* ran into someone. I don't know who he was. But he said something that completely threw me off," I explained. "He was like, 'baby blue. Like the George Strait song.'" I mimicked his voice the best I could, even though it came off more as mocking him.

"What! Ellie, that's cute! And you wanted to leave after that?" Isa had always been a hopeless romantic, constantly thinking about "meet cutes"—or whatever they called them in the romance novels she was always reading.

She tried to get me to read one of them once, saying it might help with my unrealistic standards for men. I read it, but I didn't think men like that even existed. There was no way a real man actually thought the way fictional ones did.

I was fairly certain men either thought about nothing or the most random shit. They didn't think about the way "the sunlight reflected in a woman's eyes like the light hitting a pool of water perfectly at sunset." No, they were thinking about how your ass looked like a peach in the jeans that perfectly hugged your hips, but in a less eloquent way.

Realistically, if a man spoke to me in the way some fictional men spoke to their fictional women, they would have a fist to their nose before they could get another word out.

"Yes, I wanted to leave! I didn't know what to say to that? That's what my dad called my mom all the time. I told him I was busy and then went to find you." I knew I was probably in the wrong. But I wasn't going to admit that. I did what I had to do to protect my heart and prevent a potentially disastrous situation involving my knuckles, or at least a lot of harsh words.

"Oh, Ells. What if you missed your chance at *true love*?" she fussed.

"I'm not going to find 'true love' with a cowboy,

Isabelle." I made air quotes as I spoke. "Besides, that's messy. There's a greater chance of a cowboy knowing who my dad was. There will be questions. Pity. I don't need that."

"If you say so." She wasn't going to argue with me, even if it broke her little romantic heart. We had been over this enough times.

But what if there could have been something there? No. Not in a million years. I pushed aside the thought of me falling in love with a cowboy. It was their lifestyle that cost my dad his life. If love was real, I'd be better off finding it with someone who lived in the city. Someone who had no interest in riding or roping for a living. Or taking down 500-pound animals for that matter.

Isa pulled up to the house to drop me off. "Hey, if you need anything tomorrow, let me know."

"I will, thanks." I waved her off and watched her drive away.

I walked into the house and saw that my mom was still awake, laying on the couch with an old Western movie on in the background.

"You're back early," she said on a yawn.

"Yeah, well, the bars aren't all they're cracked up to be." I shrugged as I sat down on the couch next to her.

"I can't say I miss those days." The corners of her eyes creased. "I still hope you had a good time with Isa."

"It was fun. Isa always knows how to have a good time. Bars just aren't as much my scene as they are hers. I guess that's something we have in common." I smiled back at her. "I wasn't expecting you to be up this late, though."

"Oh, well, you know me. I just wanted to make sure you got back home safe. Besides, I don't anticipate waking up as early tomorrow," she replied simply.

"Right, with the rodeo and everything," I murmured.

"Thank you for going with me, Ellison. I know that—"

"It's really nothing, Mom. I—" The sadness that crept into her eyes made me stutter. "I'm sorry, I'm just tired. I think I'm going to head to bed." As much as I hated interrupting her, I wasn't ready to talk about the rodeo and the implications of the day. What I needed was a good night's rest. Tomorrow was going to be a day, and I didn't even know the half of it.

CHAPTER EIGHT

colter

I got into the arena around eight the next morning. This allowed me and Reid to not only practice before we competed tonight but also gave us the ability to watch our competition practice. Besides, if we weren't at the arena, we'd most likely be hanging out at the trailers and I wasn't exactly in the mood to deal with Mikey this morning, especially after everything that happened last night at the bar.

As if the boys giving me shit about the mystery girl wasn't bad enough, Mikey started hitting on one of the college girls in the pink cowboy hats right as we were leaving. I did not want to stick around long enough to see how that played out, but knowing Mikey, he probably had her in his trailer right now.

A few people had the same idea of going to the practice arena. Sometimes the difference between a winning time and a no time was getting in a couple runs the morning of the performance.

Reid and I had to wait a little while before we could get out there and practice, as they had set times for each event, but that gave me time to tack up Bullet and make sure everything was adjusted correctly for later. I wasn't going to overwork him by riding too much this morning, just enough to find the sweet spot of getting him warm without him being too tired tonight. But to be fair, Bullet would go all day if he had the choice.

I was walking to the corral to grab him so I could take him to the trailer when Wyatt, one of the other team ropers here for the rodeo, stopped me.

"Hey there, Colter, how's it going?" he asked. Wyatt was admittedly one of our biggest competitors, but overall he was still a great guy and a friend of mine.

"Hey, man," I greeted him. "Oh, not too bad, just ready to get out there tonight."

One thing about the rodeo community was that it really was a big family. Sure, you were all competitors at the end of the day, but it was mostly friendly. I knew several men here who would give me the shirt off their back if I needed help.

A couple years ago, a saddle bronc rider's family home burned down and they lost everything. The entire rodeo association banded together to help raise money to get them back on their feet. These were good men and women.

"I feel you there. I don't even have my first performance until the fifth series. But we came down here pretty early because Cora's family wanted to make a little vacation out of it."

Cora was his wife. He had a great family. They let me and Reid crash at their place when we were up in Colorado once.

"How is the family doing?" I asked, not wanting to be rude.

"They're good! The little one has been pretty fussy lately, but our oldest, Jackson, has loved spending time with the grandparents."

"That's good to hear. Well, I'd love to chat longer, but I've gotta get my horse. Let's catch up another time, though. Good to see you." I patted him on his shoulder. If I hadn't ended the conversation, we would have been talking there for hours.

About ten minutes later, I had made it back to the trailer and tied up Bullet. Tacking up a horse properly was essential. If any of your equipment was damaged or ill-fitted, it could cause discomfort for the horse when competing and, in the worst case scenario, serious injury.

I brushed Bullet starting from his neck, working my way down to his back and girth and finally his hindquarters and legs. This ensured the horse didn't get sores from either the saddle or cinch.

After getting the saddle pad on, I set the saddle on top of it and fastened the cinch. This step was important to get right. You didn't want the cinch to be too tight, but you also didn't want it to be too loose or the saddle could slip. Finally, I attached the breast collar and undid the halter so I could put on the bridle.

It had only taken about five minutes to saddle up, but with Wyatt stopping me, Reid and I wouldn't have to wait anymore to do our practice runs. He had already tacked his horse and was almost certainly waiting for me.

I got into the practice arena and did a couple laps. Cattle companies provided steers and calves for the competitors to practice with. There were also staff there to help so teams didn't have to find someone to open the chute for them when they practiced.

Reid and I ran a couple times so we could make sure

we were synced up. Reid missed the first time, but the second time was a perfect run. We clocked six-point-two seconds, which wasn't terrible. We'd need to be faster tonight, but for practice, it was a good time.

"Looking good out there, boys," a familiar voice called from the side of the practice arena.

"Well, I'll be damned. Coach Aaron, what are you doing here?" Reid waved at our old college coach, Aaron Sawyer, with a big grin on his face.

"I was in the area with the family. Thought I'd stop by and support a couple of our own." He shook Reid's hand and pulled him in for a hug.

"It's good to see you here, sir." I tipped my hat to him.

"Come here, Colter, and none of that 'sir' bullshit." He chuckled at me and extended his arms for a hug from me too.

I knew Aaron hated being called sir because it made him feel old, so I mostly did it to mess with him.

"How's everything been with you two?" he asked.

"We've been good. It's been a pretty successful year so far," Reid answered.

"I saw you both were in the top ten in the world standings, that's great. I always knew you two were going to go far." He sounded like a proud father. In a way, he was comparable to a father, or at least a father figure in the way that coaches often were.

"We've been working hard this year," Reid added. He wasn't wrong. We spent as much time as we could perfecting our craft. When we weren't working, we were roping.

"I can see that. Well, if you boys have any time in the next couple of days, we should sit down together for dinner. Talk about how you can be involved with the team in the future, if you want to at least," he offered.

"Thank you, Aaron. We'll definitely keep in touch with you. I'm sure we'll have some time." I nodded.

"Good luck tonight. I'll be watching." He gave us a parting wave.

"Do you think you'd ever take up coaching?" Reid asked me once Aaron was out of earshot.

I had never really thought about coaching. But eventually, I wouldn't have as big of a career in professional rodeo. It was never too early to start thinking about the future. At the same time, though, thinking about a life where I didn't travel for rodeos was terrifying.

"I don't know. It's hard to even think about not having a career at this point," I admitted. But then I chuckled thinking about my college days. "I also know how I was in college and I don't know if I want to have to deal with that."

"It might be good for you. Get a little taste of your own medicine," he kidded.

"If I go back and coach, you know you'll have to come with me, right? Aaron's not going to be happy with one of us. He wants the duo," I pointed out.

"Eh, I'm sure he could live with having only one of us." Reid playfully rolled his eyes.

Aaron was always trying to get alumni to come back and coach. Probably because he eventually wanted to pawn off the job to one of us so he could hang up his coaching hat and retire, even though he was only in his late thirties and we all knew cowboys never really retired.

"All right, let's get out of here before someone yells at us for still being in the arena."

We led our horses out of the arena, but put them in

one of the corrals off to the side of the practice arena so we didn't have to untack them quite yet. I wanted to watch a few other people practice first.

There was a specific team that wasn't in our group that I felt would be our greatest competition in either the semifinals or the championship, if we made it that far. Dash Kingsley and Wayne Marlow were a duo from Oklahoma and they had been one of the best last year, barely losing the NFR average championship to a team from Idaho. They both had a few years on me and Reid, nearing their thirties. Dash was tall and muscular, with more of an athletic build than Wayne, who was shorter than Dash but not stocky like some of the other cowboys I'd seen.

I wasn't sure if they would be practicing at all today, but then I saw Dash tacking up his horse when I first took Bullet out. Their horses were surely restless from not being able to compete yet.

Reid and I found a spot in the stands among the few people there. Very few people, if any, came to watch practice runs. They were either out shopping or doing other things related to the rodeo. But some of the athletes who wanted to assess their competition would watch to see what they were up against.

We had to wait for a few other teams to practice before the team we were waiting to see went. While watching the other teams didn't necessarily hurt, it wasn't as important. They were decent, but they weren't as good as Kingsley and Marlow. They were clocking in around six to six-point-five seconds. Still, you never wanted to underestimate the competition. They might have a great run on the day you have your worst.

Finally, the team from Oklahoma got ready for their

first practice run. Dash was the header and Wayne was the heeler. And damn, were they good. Good was an understatement. There was a reason they were the runners-up for the NFR average last year. Their timing was flawless, with no hesitations or mistakes. They clocked an impressive five-point-two on their first practice run.

If we made it to the championship, we would have our work cut out for us.

CHAPTER NINE

My mother and I walked side by side into NRG Stadium like we were walking into battle, or at least that's what it was like for me. This day would never get easier, but every year I put on a brave face for my mother. I ignored the glances that lingered a bit too long— the ones that questioned who the girl with Hanna Merritt was.

No one recognized me because I practically dropped off the face of the Earth after my dad's death, at least to the rodeo world. I started going by my mother's maiden name, Wilson, eventually changing it legally, and stayed away from anything that would bring attention to me being Levi Merritt's only daughter.

The fact I went to only one event a year helped me keep my anonymity. Besides, I looked different enough from my mother that no one read into it too closely and I was still a child when my dad died. My dad would have to be alive and physically standing next to me for strangers to notice our resemblance enough to put together the pieces. And well, he wasn't.

Even if people did recognize us, they didn't dare confront us about it. Not today.

Everyone knew about the accident. And if they didn't, they either didn't pay attention very well or they weren't a member of the community. It, ironically, was a favorite topic for rodeo news and radio stations. You'd think they'd want to talk about people's successes, not the ultimate failure.

We found our seats right as the rodeo was about to begin. They had started to parade the sponsor flags around the arena and the national anthem and prayer would be next. A prayer was said at every single rodeo. It wasn't so much about religion, but more about wishing safety on the athletes and animals.

"Lord, thank you for this opportunity to allow us and these athletes to participate in one of your greatest events. Please look after our athletes, both two-legged and four-legged, as they compete tonight. Also, please protect those in the armed forces who gave us the freedoms that we sometimes take for granted. Watch over our law enforcement, firefighters, and medical first responders." The entire arena was silent as the announcer prayed. "Lastly, thank you for keeping us, our friends, and our families healthy, and bringing us all together here tonight for one of the greatest sports in the world. In your name we pray, amen."

A chorus of amens went around the crowd as he finished, and then the crowd went wild.

"Houston, Texas, are you ready for some rodeo?" the announcer cried.

A roar emerged from the crowd in response, people clapping and cheering and whistling.

"We've got a great lineup for y'all tonight. We're kicking it off with bareback riding!"

The events would go in the order of bareback bronc riding, saddle bronc riding, tie-down roping, breakaway roping, mutton bustin', team roping, steer wrestling, barrel racing, and bull riding.

The rules of bareback were simple. As a roughstock event, it was similar to bull riding. The contestant had to stay on the back of the bucking horse for eight seconds to receive a score out of 100. There were two judges. Each judge's score was based on a cumulative total of up to fifty points, twenty-five for the rider and twenty-five for the bronc. Points were awarded based on how the horse was bucking and the style of the rider. Saddle bronc riding was basically the same as bareback as far as rules go, except you also had a saddle.

The first bareback rider had a rough time; he didn't make it to eight seconds.

Watching the cowboys scramble to get out of the way of broncs or bulls always made you hold your breath a little until they were safe. That was the way rodeo worked, though. It was a thrill, almost an addiction to the danger of it all, both for the spectators and the riders. They all knew the risks and most of them left the arena without a scratch, even if they didn't make it the full eight seconds.

"That was a tough one," my mom murmured as she marked her day sheet with "NS," or no score, by the rider's name. The day sheets had the competitors for every event listed plus a space where you could keep track of the scores.

I glanced over at her score sheet and noticed a name that seemed vaguely familiar. Colter Carson/Reid Lawson, team roping. At the moment, with all of my thoughts on the rodeo and my dad, I couldn't place why the name was familiar or why I had heard it before, but there were probably so many cowboys named Colter that I brushed it off.

The competitions went by fairly quickly. There were forty total competitors in each event throughout the rodeo which made it even larger than the National Finals Rodeo that took place in December. But the competitors were split into five groups of eight with the top four from each group moving on to one of two semifinal nights. From there, the top five from each semifinal competed in the championship. It was an interesting format but it worked. Having an event that lasted for over two weeks was a huge money maker for the city of Houston and a great way to build hype for the sport.

For a brief moment during the breakaway roping, one of the two women's events, a pang of grief shot through my chest. One of the girls competing was nineteen. She was younger than I was and an incredible athlete.

I momentarily pictured myself in her shoes. She was a teenager with so much potential and a whole career ahead of her. That could have been me out there. I pushed those feelings down, though. It was my own choice. I had made that bed and would lie in it.

My mother had tried her hardest to get me to compete. She knew how much I loved it. How riding was as easy as breathing for me. But I was stubborn—*thanks, Dad*—and every time she asked me, I said no. Eventually she stopped.

Perhaps a small part of me wished she had continued to try, continued to push the subject, and had been one of those mothers who didn't give their child a choice in the matter. Wished she had said, "You are going to do this whether you like it or not, Ellison," and dragged me into the arena, even when I had kicked and cried and fought against her.

Maybe I wouldn't feel an ounce of regret. Or maybe I would have given up after a year. At least if she had forced me to do it, I would have known.

That wasn't in her nature, though. She never wanted to be the type of parent that tried to control her child's entire life. She wanted me to make my own choices, but she made it very clear that I would have to live with the decisions I made. A "sure, you can eat bags on bags of candy and sweets, but when you have ten cavities and have to get them all filled at the dentist, don't come crying to me," type of thing.

"Folks, we've got a fan favorite coming up next." The announcer's voice cut through my thoughts. "If you didn't get the chance to sign your child up to compete in the mutton bustin' during the actual rodeo but they want to try their hand at it, take them over to The Junction, where they can participate in mutton bustin' all day."

Now, mutton bustin' was a fan favorite for a reason. It very well could be up there with bull riding because it was highly entertaining and a lot less dangerous. Picture a child, between the ages of five and seven, riding on the back of a sheep trying their best to hold on and you had mutton bustin'. It never failed to get the crowd laughing and was a great break between events. It was almost like a halftime show for the rodeo.

I'd done some mutton busting when my dad was still around. He took me with him to a lot of the local rodeos where they would have it, or some kind of activity, for kids to participate in. The kids rarely got hurt during the event and the only tears that might have fallen were from getting a big mouthful of dirt. For the most part, these kids were built tough.

My mom and I watched as a little boy named Emmett held on for dear life as the ewe sprinted across the arena. After his turn, another one named Payton rode the sheep facing backward, his helmeted face bouncing into the wool on its back as the crowd cracked up.

For some kids, this was how they would get their start in the sport. Some of them would go on to be great bull riders or ropers. Others, though, might end up like me, jaded and alienated. That was life.

My mother and I didn't chat much about the rodeo. It was hard to talk about something when one person still loved it and the other didn't. But that didn't mean she didn't try.

"Those girls looked good out there during the breakaway roping." She tried to start a conversation.

"Mm-hmm," I replied, unsure of what to say. This was so hard for me.

"I remember the first time you got on the back of a horse when you were little." She reminisced. "You loved it. You could tell some of the other kids were terrified, being so high up, but not you. You always were such a brave girl."

"Thanks, Mom." I gave her a weak smile. I knew she was trying her best. We all had different ways of coping. This was hers. I did the best I could to stand by her and support her, but there was only so much trying I could do and I hoped she saw that.

A wave of cheers interrupted whatever conversation we weren't having. Turned out a little girl had held on to her sheep for the entire six seconds without falling off and everyone was going crazy for her.

CHAPTER TEN

A fter that run, we have a new leader on the board. Six-point-two seconds is the time to beat tonight, folks. Remember, the top four teams who have earned the most prize money over the past three days will have the chance to compete in the semifinals next week."

I soaked in the announcer's words.

Reid and I had already punched our ticket to the semifinals. If we won tonight, we'd be the top team in our series. If not, we'd be either second or third and would still move on.

Of course, neither of us wanted anything but first. We wanted to take home as much prize money as we possibly could from the round. But if we didn't win, we'd still have the opportunity to compete, which was more than other teams could say.

The pressure increased with every win. There was no room for mediocre at this level. Once you got into a rhythm, you had to ride that momentum all the way to the end. You couldn't afford to lose it in this sport. No time for mistakes. No room for distractions.

I mounted my horse and took a few practice swings over my head to keep my arm warm. They already had the next steer—our steer—in the chute.

"All right, ladies and gentlemen. These two cowboys are currently sitting second in the standings for the past three days. If they can beat six-point-two seconds, they'll move into first place and take home $3,000 tonight. Let's make some noise for Colter Carson and Reid Lawson!" the announcer boomed.

Our routine was the same every time. Some might call it a superstition, but I wasn't about to break my habit and risk a loss. It always involved Reid backing into the box first, almost a reverse order of how we'd leave it. We also followed the classic superstitions: never wear yellow, don't eat chicken before a competition because "you are what you eat," and never carry change in your pockets, unless that was all you wanted to leave with.

I took a deep breath as I guided my horse back into the box. *Exactly as you practiced. You've got this. Muscle memory.* I went over my affirmations in my head before I finally gave the signal and the steer was released from the chute.

We roped the steer swiftly like we had done a million times. The run felt amazing. It felt even better when the announcer called out, "Five-point-nine seconds for the Montanans! We have a new series champion, folks! Colter Carson and Reid Lawson! They'll follow the Boot Barn sponsor flag as well as the Montana flag around the arena for the victory lap."

I took off my hat and waved it as I rode around the arena during the victory lap, soaking in the cheers from fans that came from all around the country, the world even, for this. And to think, this was only the series championship. We had secured our spot in the semifinals round and had a shot at a championship gold buckle and $50,000. That was something to be proud of, but the work wasn't finished yet.

We wouldn't compete for another week, but that didn't mean we were going to kick back and relax. No, we would still be practicing and keeping ourselves ready.

They would announce all of the winners again tonight after the bull riding, so I wanted to take the opportunity to take care of Bullet and get him untacked and in the corral while I had time.

"I'm going to take Bullet to the trailer and get all his equipment off," I told Reid.

He nodded and said he'd be behind me with his horse shortly.

As I was walking my horse back to the trailer, I caught a glimpse of her—the girl from the bar who hadn't left my mind since I saw her. She was sitting next to an older woman with red hair and the same bright-blue eyes, who I could only assume was a relative. She was deep in conversation with a radiant grin on her face. It was magnetizing, and I had to force myself to break my stare and continue walking.

This was my one chance to redeem myself. I guaranteed if I fucked this up, I would never see her again. And that wasn't even taking into consideration the fact I was only going to be in Houston for a little over a week. I hadn't felt this instant attraction to someone since Sophie, and that was either a good thing or a sign of inevitable failure.

Focus on getting your horse back to the pen for the night. There are more important things than that girl. Remember your future. I tried to focus on rodeo and toss the memory of her face out of my mind, but everything kept going back to her.

Fuck it. Maybe if I just have a conversation with her, made up for the other night, I'll be able to move on with my life.

It was decided. I would take Bullet back to the trailer, take care of everything that needed to be done for him, and then if I happened to see her again, I would talk to her. I would do whatever it took to just have a conversation with her.

CHAPTER ELEVEN

ellison

Realization hit me like a semitruck when I put two and two together. Of course the guy I ran into at the bar would be here and of course he was good at what he did. I just couldn't get away from him.

It's okay, I thought. The stadium was so large and filled with thousands of people, so the odds of me actually seeing him again, face to face, were extremely low.

I brought my attention back to the rodeo. Steer wrestling was next. This event was always stressful for us.

My hands started to get clammy, and the arena seemed to rise in temperature despite it being such a large space. Even though I had no ties to any of the cowboys here, steer wrestling always made me nervous.

The idea of steer wrestling was to start on the back of your horse and chase the steer, kind of like roping. Except the horse came up right next to the steer, allowing the rider to drop from the right side of his horse and reach for the steer's horns. Once the cowboy had grabbed the steer's horns, he dug his heels into the ground to slow the animal and enable the rider to turn the animal, lifting up on its right horn and pushing down with his left hand. The clock stopped when the animal was on its side with all four legs pointing in the same direction. The goal was, of course, to get the fastest time.

"Ladies and gentlemen, our first cowboy comes from your hometown of Houston, Texas," the announcer called out, and I stiffened.

It was all way too familiar, a film I'd seen a million times before. Except even though I thought I already knew the ending, the outcome was different every time.

The first steer wrestler successfully took down the animal in four-point-two seconds. Not a horrible time, but it wouldn't win him any big bucks.

The announcer called the next steer wrestler's name, a cowboy from Arizona. He started out great, his horse running alongside the steer, perfectly synced. But when it came time for him to ease down from his horse, he overshot the landing and went over top of the steer. Images of my dad's accident flashed through my mind, and I realized I had squeezed my eyes shut without knowing. My breath caught in my throat and a lump started to form.

You're not going to cry. It's not the same, it'll be fine. I reassured myself subconsciously, but at the same time I couldn't bring myself to reopen my eyes for fear of what I would see.

When I finally stopped holding my breath and looked again, the steer was running down the arena, but the cowboy was okay. He ended up getting a no time instead. Everything was normal, spectators were chatting amongst each other and clapping and cheering for their favorite competitors, but I couldn't ease the feeling of dread that rose in my stomach.

"I think I need some air," I mumbled to my mother.

She gave me an absentminded nod and continued to watch the event.

I planned to walk around the arena a couple times, maybe step outside for a moment then go back to my seat. Anything that would take up enough time so I wouldn't have to watch the rest of the steer wrestling. Otherwise my dinner might end up on someone's back, and nobody wanted that.

I went out to the area that had the concessions and walked through the current of people trying to get their hot dogs and popcorn. Little kids pulled their parents toward the stables, desperate to get an up-close look at the horses, and then their faces turned sad when their parents ultimately told them no.

No one noticed me as I walked through the crowd without my mother, as if I were a ghost. I was just one of them, another face in the crowd, and that was comforting to me. I didn't want attention brought to me. I would've rather coasted through life than been in the public eye all the time.

Bullet did not want to be at the trailer. He didn't want to be tied up, so he resorted to being a major pain in my ass. He kept moving parallel to the trailer so I couldn't get around him and, to make matters worse, he kept pawing at the wheel well. He was restless and wasn't ready to be done. He wanted to keep going, to run.

"Knock that shit off," I scolded him, trying to get this done as quickly as possible. I managed to get an arm between him and the trailer so I could push him away from it. He grunted in protest but eventually moved. *Asshole.*

"Help me out here, buddy. You're supposed to be my wingman, not an obstacle," I muttered at the horse.

If horses could roll their eyes, that's what Bullet did.

A few minutes later, I had all of the equipment removed and back in the trailer. I took Bullet to one of the corrals and told him I would deal with him later. I had a girl to find.

It wouldn't be that hard to find her, right? Right?

Fuck, Colter, you are in over your head. What are you doing, man? I was starting to think I was going delusional. But then I turned the corner and there she was.

She was walking right toward me and I was able to get a real glimpse of her, actually see what she looked like this time. I thought she was pretty last night when we ran into each other, clearly enough that she had been on my mind since, but I realized now she was beautiful. But it was a subtle kind of beauty. Like the way the sunlight hits the mountains perfectly in the morning. Soft and elegant, yet blazing at the same time.

As she met people that walked by her, she gave them a small, polite smile. One that made me wonder how it would feel to get a real smile out of her. She was both day and night, sunlight and shadow, with her warm features, yet cool, intense eyes. Eyes that could burn holes through a man's heart. I was a goner.

I continued to walk toward her, silently begging that I wouldn't fuck it up this time.

CHAPTER TWELVE

ellison

I froze in my tracks as I saw Colter Carson, the cowboy from the bar who was one hundred percent here for the rodeo and one hundred percent not my type, walking toward me.

Nope. Not dealing with this.

I spun on my heel to turn around and started to make a hasty escape, but the clunky sound of boots increased in speed and I realized this man was literally running after me.

"Wait! Please, wait!" He caught up to me and matched my pace.

"What do you want?" I rolled my eyes and kept walking, picking up my stride, trying to go fast enough that maybe he would give up.

"Listen, I think we got off on the wrong foot last night." The words tumbled out of his mouth as he tried to get me to stop.

"It's really no big deal. We both weren't watching where we were going. Water under the bridge." I shrugged him off.

He wasn't giving up, though. He kept walking with me. "Can we at least try the conversation again before you walk off into the sunset like last time?"

What is this guy's deal?

I stopped in my tracks and turned around so I was facing him. "That was probably the worst line I have ever heard." I crossed my arms over my chest. "But tell me, cowboy, in the case I actually did have a conversation with you, what could you possibly want to talk about?"

I had to hand it to him, he was bold. Most men would have given up or called me some crude name at that point. Either I needed to up my game, or he was immune to my attitude. I was starting to worry it was the latter.

"Let's start with names. I'm Colter. Colter Carson." He extended his hand.

I accepted his handshake with an exaggerated sigh. "Ellison Wilson. My friends call me Ellie."

"Well, Ellie, it's a pleasure to meet you." He smiled, a dimple on the right side of his mouth appearing, and for a second I thought this might be okay. I could get to know him and there would be no consequences. But reality came back to me.

"It's Ellison to you, Sparky. We aren't friends, don't push your luck. And as much as I would love to stand here and make small talk, I came with my mother and I need to go find her. And you should probably get back to being a little show cowboy, don't you think?" We knew each other's names now and that was enough for me. I wasn't quite sure what he was attempting to do, but I wasn't going to stick around long enough to find out.

If calling him a "show cowboy" bothered him, he didn't let it show in his expression. "No problem, Ellison." He paused, and I figured I was in the clear.

I smirked, feeling satisfied with myself and ready to get on with my night.

But then he continued. "Hey, before you go, how about this? Tomorrow, will you meet me at the coffee shop on the corner of 23rd and North at ten? Continue our conversation? No pressure, of course."

He could see right through me. He knew exactly what I was doing and could tell I was trying to dodge an actual conversation. But why wasn't he just letting it go?

Colter Carson was like a boomerang. Every time I tried to get rid of him, he just kept coming back. He wasn't exactly guilting me into this...date? No, this was merely a conversation, but turning him down outright would be rude, and my parents raised me better than that.

"I'll think about it." I shot him one last look and then walked away to find my mother.

I texted Isa on my way back to my seat.

> You will not believe what just happened

ISA

brad and angelina got back together?

I scrunched my nose at her message. Classic Isabelle. She was always thinking about the latest celebrity gossip. It was usually entertaining, but this time I was having a crisis.

> What? No

> The guy from the bar who I ran into? He's here. And I just saw him again

ISA

OMG WHAT

He wants me to meet him at The Corral
tomorrow at ten

ISA

you HAVE to go ells

it's a SIGN

i mean what are the ODDS

I ignored her last texts.

"Oh, good, you're back. I was worried I was going to have to come look for you," my mother joked when I got back to our seats.

"I would have found my way back eventually. Don't worry about me, Mom," I reassured her. I knew she would worry about me anyway; I was the only one she had left.

"The energy in this place hasn't changed. Every year, it's so consistent," she murmured.

I couldn't tell if she was talking about the rodeo itself or about the night of the accident. The hardest part of the night was over. We had watched the steer wrestling, well I had seen part of it at least, and there were no injuries. The only events left were barrel racing and bull riding.

I didn't have anything to say to her, so I stayed quiet. I was just trying to get through tonight so I could get back to my normal life, sans rodeo and sans cowboys who couldn't take a hint. Especially cowboys who couldn't take a hint.

I thought about Colter's invitation. It would be rude not to go, right? But also, what business did I have getting to know a cowboy from Montana who was going to leave in a week? Then again, maybe if I did go meet up with him and talk to him for a half an hour—tops—then I wouldn't have to see him ever again. Surely, he wouldn't keep bothering me. He would go about his business roping cattle and I would go about mine.

My mom would tell me to go. She thought I kept myself cooped up in the house enough as it was. I could hear her now. She would say, *"Ellison, life is too short to not get out and live. I'll be fine here for a couple of hours, go enjoy yourself."*

"All right, I'll go," I grumbled to myself, not realizing I said it out loud.

"What was that, Ells?" my mother asked.

"Nothing. Someone just invited me to go get coffee tomorrow morning," I told her.

"Oh, you should go. Life is too short to not get out and actually live."

After the competition was over and I was back home, away from the prying eyes of fans and my mother, I texted Isa.

> My mom also thinks I should go

ISA

you actually told her about the cowboy?

> Of course not. I accidentally started talking out loud and she asked me what I was saying so I kind of had to tell her that someone asked me to get coffee

ISA

i mean you could have just lied

> Yeah, but what kind of daughter would that make me?

ISA

a normal one...

I groaned and lay back on my bed as I thought about my impending coffee…meeting with Colter, also known as my own personal hell.

All you have to do is give him thirty minutes of your time. That's all. Then he will be out of your hair and out of your life.

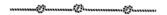

The early morning sunrise emitted amber rays on the ranch, making the hills look ablaze, and the katydids chirped in the grass. The birds sang a cheery melody and the wind rustled the tree branches, creating an entire symphony that only the earliest risers would experience. It was a rare peaceful moment before the ranch hands arrived and started working.

We had several horses, but my dad's horse, the one he had competed with, had passed a couple years prior. His name was Blue Eyes Crying in the Rain. My horse was a little Palomino named Lucille, after the Kenny Rogers song. She didn't have a fancy registered name like my dad's horse. Some of the ranch hands also had dogs they would bring onto the ranch to run around. My favorite was a good old boy named Smokey.

I went for a quick ride around the ranch, walking the perimeter along the fence-line. While the broken fence got fixed earlier in the week, I wanted to make sure there weren't any other damaged spots. A small part of me hoped there was a weak spot so I could have an excuse to take a rain check on coffee, but the rational side of me knew canceling wouldn't solve the issue. He'd probably just find me again somehow.

The longer I put off going, the less time I would have to get ready—not that I was trying to impress Colter. I was thinking of it as more of a courtesy to other coffee shop patrons to not smell like a barn.

I rode Lucille back to the stables where I got all of her equipment off and put away, set her loose in the pasture with the rest of the horses, and then ran back to the house to make myself at least presentable to be in public.

"Oh, Ells! You're up early." My mother was in the kitchen making breakfast when I got back in the house.

"Took Lucille for a ride to double check the fence," I explained.

"Would you like something to eat? I'm fixing some things for the boys to come by and pick up," she offered, holding up the spatula that she was using to scramble eggs for the ranch hands.

"No, that's all right. Thank you, though." I squeezed her arm as I walked by her.

"You're still going to go into town this morning?" she asked.

"Yeah. Just meeting up with a, uh, friend." I wasn't going to tell her who I was actually meeting. She'd either be shocked or excited. Or both.

"Okay, well, have fun. Keep your phone on you in case I need you to pick something up," she instructed.

"Yes, ma'am." I smiled at her before I disappeared down the hall to the bathroom.

I stripped down and started the shower, the hot steam rising and enveloping my body in the small space. When I stepped in, the scalding-hot water burned, causing me to hiss and turn it down slightly. My plan was to take a quick shower, in and out, but I found myself taking my time. Making an effort. Definitely not because I was going on a…hangout. Not a date. It was *not* a date. My brain already knew it wasn't a date. There was absolutely nothing that was going to come out of this. We were two people redoing a really bad first conversation. So then why was I nervous?

This was really no big deal. Just strangers meeting for coffee. *It sure sounds like a date*, the voice in my head told me. *It's only a date if you make it a date*, I reassured myself. *And you will not make it into a date.*

The drive into Houston could take a good hour or more with heavy traffic. Luckily for me, there wasn't a lot of it so I had less time to overthink.

I tried to make my mind blank, to not think about anything, but I've never been good at that. My mind was constantly in a state of planning. I was always thinking about how to prevent situations in which I would be vulnerable or defenseless. Not just physically, but emotionally. I would have rather bottled up my feelings than dished them out to a stranger like a buffet. My personal life was just that. Personal.

I would gladly be perceived as a coldhearted bitch if it meant my heart and emotions were protected. I wasn't going to be a pity project, or someone to psychoanalyze. This was how I had lived the past fifteen years, and it worked just fine for me. I had my inner circle, my mom and Isabelle, and that was enough.

I pulled onto the street where The Corral was located. There was a practically empty parking lot across the street, and I debated turning around instead of parking. I considered wasting the gas and never looking back, but I drove around the block a couple of times instead. I'm sure I looked idiotic, judging by the confused glances the group of people eating outside on the patio at one of the restaurants gave me each time I passed. But I wasn't ready to potentially put myself and my heart out there for someone to see.

Fuck, Ellison. Come on. You're not a fucking chicken. It's just coffee. You're not marrying the guy. I gave myself a pep talk in my head as I parked, grabbed my bag and keys, and then headed in the direction of the coffee shop.

CHAPTER THIRTEEN

colter

I sat at a table for two by a big window in the coffee shop I asked Ellison to meet me at. I faced the door so I could see her when she walked in. I had done what I could, and now the ball was in her court. There was nothing I could do except hope she showed up, and God was I hoping.

I arrived twenty minutes early. I was a creature of habit, and I was always taught that if you weren't fifteen minutes early, you were late. I can attribute fifteen of the twenty to that, but the extra five? I was getting restless sitting around, and I wanted to be there before her in case she showed up early too.

I tapped my heel against the ground repeatedly, my leg shaking.

What if she doesn't show up?

I couldn't remember the last time I was so stressed over a girl.

It was nine fifty-eight when I spotted her across the street in the parking lot. She seemed to be contemplating whether to cross the road or turn around and never look back.

She sighed and made the decision to cross the street. My heart was racing with nerves, even more than the nerves I got from competing. At least roping was something I knew how to control. I had no idea how this conversation would go.

The bells on the door of the coffee shop chimed as she walked in. She looked around for a moment, as if trying to figure out her next move, but then her eyes landed on me. She gave me a small wave in acknowledgment and then walked up to the counter to order.

I hadn't gotten anything yet because I wasn't sure if she would show up.

Should I get up and get something or is that weird? Maybe I should just wait for her to get her stuff and then I'll go?

I was grossly overthinking this. I ruffled the hair on the back of my head and decided to stay in my chair.

A couple minutes later, she walked over to the table and took a seat. Her hair was pulled up into a ponytail, but a few strands fell around her face, framing it perfectly like a work of art.

"Hi," she greeted me politely.

"What did you get?" I asked.

"I got a white chocolate mocha." She seemed as nervous as I was, which was reassuring.

We sat there for a few moments, not speaking, the grinding of coffee beans, baristas frothing milk, and light chatter of the other coffee shop patrons the only noise. I noticed her look away, scanning the room instead of meeting my eyes.

"I'm really not that interesting." She laughed, finally

breaking the silence. "I don't know what it is about me that you want to figure out."

Everything. I want to know everything about you.

I didn't just want to know her favorite color. I wanted to know why she loved that specific shade of blue or green. What she thought about when she heard her favorite song on the radio. If she sang along or just felt the music.

"Anything. I want to get to know you. Like, if you were a pie, what kind of pie would you be?" I asked the most ridiculous question I could think of.

"What kind of a question is that?" She smiled—really smiled—and in that moment I wanted to do everything in my power to keep that smile on her face.

"It's just a question. Personally, I'd be an apple pie. It's classic and everyone loves it," I offered.

"I don't," she responded flatly.

"Well, then you'd be the first," I joked. "Come on, what would you be?"

"Peach, maybe. Or coconut cream." She puckered her lips and looked up, deep in thought.

"Ellison?" the barista called out.

She got up to get her drink, taking a sip of it as she walked back. A soft smile appeared on her face as she closed her eyes for a heartbeat, like she was savoring the taste. Her mood instantly changed, and I made a mental note to make sure she always had coffee.

"Anyway, sorry about that. Back to your question. I thought about it and I'd definitely be a peach pie," she concluded.

"I can respect that, even if you are an apple hater," I joked, and she blushed a little.

"So, you're from Montana?"

"Yep. Born and raised. Have you always lived here?" I continued the conversation.

"Yes, I was born here. I left Houston to go to college, but I didn't go too far. My mother is from Wyoming, but my dad grew up here," she explained, not getting into too many details.

"Do you think you'll ever leave?"

"I'm not sure. My mother always tells me I should get out and see the world. That there is so much more out there than this little corner of Texas. But I think I'm happy here."

The problem was, she didn't seem happy. I could tell there was something holding her back, keeping her here, but I didn't know what it was. I wasn't going to pry, though.

"Do you go to the rodeo every year?"

She stiffened at the question, and a wild look flashed through her eyes. "Yes. Just for one day," she answered curtly, her eyes narrowing a bit at the subject.

Okay, don't talk about rodeo. I could take a hint, even if it seemed like most of the time I ignored them. *Change the subject, Colt. Come on.*

"Uh, do you like cars?"

Her demeanor immediately changed, and her eyes lit up. "Well, I don't like cars, specifically. I like classic pickups." She bit her lip a little. Now this. This was something I could talk about.

"Okay, okay. So, tell me then. What's your favorite brand?" I asked.

"Ford. One hundred percent Ford," she responded.

"Great answer."

She had great taste. All my family had ever owned was

Ford trucks. They were reliable and great for work around the ranch.

"Thanks." Her cheeks flushed a little.

"I prefer old vehicles, though, too. Cars just aren't built the same way anymore. I preferred when they actually lasted ten years," I joked.

"Well, unless you leave them to sit for over a decade," she murmured a little sadly, leaving me to wonder what had happened to the girl that was in front of me a few moments before. The one who had seemed overjoyed to talk about classic vehicles.

That felt oddly personal. Or am I imagining it? I was really striking out here so far. I didn't want to upset her. That was the last thing I wanted. I had to think of something we could talk about that wouldn't make her retreat.

"What is your number one interest?" I decided on.

"That's very broad." She was toying with me. But I wasn't going to fall short here. I could also play this game.

"I just want to know what you're interested in. What makes you, you." I shrugged. Was it weird that I was trying to get to know her? I mean, sure, I was leaving, but didn't that mean there was nothing to lose in this situation?

"Fine, I really enjoy collecting stamps," she deadpanned. "My collection is sitting at about seven hundred right now. I have American flag stamps, flower stamps, Christmas stamps, all of the stamps."

"Really?" I was kind of intrigued but a little confused at the same time. It was a fucking weird hobby, but I wasn't going to judge her. I mean, I asked her what she was passionate about, so I wasn't going to make fun of her, no matter how weird it was.

"No." She raised her eyebrows and broke her poker

face, her expression transforming into one of amusement. "I don't fucking collect stamps."

"I thought you were serious." I tried my best to hold my laughter in. "I mean, I definitely thought it was weird but I wasn't going to judge." It was good to see this side of her personality. It was a stark contrast to the coldness from the bar.

"I'm a great actress." She looked up through her lashes. "My main interest is hard to explain. It's a really long story to be honest."

"Well, I hope to hear about it someday." It slipped out of my mouth before I could catch myself: the idea of a future with Ellison. Not necessarily a *future* future, because even the idea that we could talk more after today was probably wishful thinking.

"Yeah, maybe." She tried to hide the small curve of her lips, a small twitch of a smile. "So, what is your number one interest then?"

"I mean, roping is obviously one of my favorite things to do. It's hard to picture myself not competing, but outside of rodeos and ranching, I always try to head back to my alma mater during football season. It brings back really good memories being in the stadium with all of my friends. We used to get pretty wild." I chuckled, thinking about all of the trouble we used to get into.

"I loved going to football games when I was in school too. The atmosphere at UT Austin was always so fun. My parents always tried to go to NFL games when I was younger too. I'm definitely more of a college sports fan, though." She added to the conversation, her face lively once again talking about something she loved to do.

I could talk about sports with her all day. I could

honestly talk about anything with her all day if it meant she lit up like she did just then.

"I'm more of a college sports fan too. We don't have any professional teams in Montana, so I think growing up with only college teams being close made my love for them grow that much more," I explained. Growing up, I never went to a professional football or basketball game. Our weekends were always spent going over to Goldfinch for the Sapphire Gulch University games.

"So, besides your cowboy exhibitions, what's your favorite sport?" she asked—her tone much more teasing than when she called me a show cowboy—her elbows perched on the table.

"Football for sure," I answered. "What's yours?"

"Basketball. I played all throughout middle school and high school. I don't play anymore, obviously, with coming back to help my mom, but it was fun at the time. I was always a little bit too competitive, though." Her face turned slightly pink at the confession. I could definitely see how she would be competitive. She had a type of fire and determination in her.

"My parents tried to get me to play basketball when I was younger. I was horrible at it." I cringed at the memory of me trying to shoot hoops.

"Now, I'd pay to see that." She looked away as she bit the bottom corner of her lips, presumably holding back a giggle.

"By chance, could I get your number?" I asked as we got up to leave. Even after a short conversation talking about stupid things like pie, I knew I wanted her in my life.

"I'm not giving you my number, Sparky," she replied, and my heart dropped. Before I could say anything else to ease the blow of the rejection, she stopped me. "I won't give you my number, but you can give me yours. That way I'll get to be the one to decide if texting you is worth my time."

This girl. She was keeping me on my toes.

"Oh, yeah. Sure. Here." I listed off the numbers for her to put into her phone. There was a chance she was bullshitting me and wasn't actually writing down my number. But I wanted to give her the benefit of the doubt.

"Can I walk you to your car?" I asked her.

She thought about it for a moment and then nodded. I let her walk in front of me until we were close to the door. Then I slightly stepped around her to reach for the door and open it for her.

"After you." I gestured for her to go ahead.

"Thank you." She looked at me, possibly a little surprised.

We walked outside, and she started heading in the direction of the crosswalk. Before she got too far ahead of me, I moved onto the street side of the sidewalk, so she was on the inside. She gave me another confused look, and I just shrugged. It was the chivalrous thing to do. You never let a woman walk on the side closer to the street.

The light at the crosswalk was still red when we got there, so we had to wait. We hadn't said a word since we left the coffee shop, and I wondered what was holding her back. How one moment her face could light up with excitement and the next she was reserved with her emotions locked up. I didn't think she was shy either.

"Thank you for inviting me," she finally spoke up.

"Thank you for coming. Seriously, I really enjoyed

getting to talk to you, and I hope this time I made a better impression." I smiled, and she smiled back. At least we had reached a mutual agreement that the conversation went better this time.

The crosswalk signal turned into the walk symbol, so we hurried across the street to the parking lot where her car was.

"Well, this was nice." She unlocked her car. "I guess I'll see you around?" She didn't sound one hundred percent confident, but at least she wasn't ruling out the possibility.

"Yeah, Ellison, I'll see you around." I waved as she got in her car and closed the door. The engine roared to life as I was walking away, and I glanced over my shoulder just as she pulled out of the parking lot and drove away, leaving me wondering if I would hear from her or never see her again.

CHAPTER FOURTEEN

ellison

I drove away from Colter and the coffee shop with a whirlwind of thoughts going through my mind. Why did I tell him I would see him around? That was my first mistake because now he'd probably be expecting me to text him, and if I didn't he'd be upset and—*ugh*. Since when did I care so much about the feelings of a cowboy?

You literally never have.

So why was this one any different?

This one actually spoke to you like you were a human being and not a trophy. He didn't pressure you to talk about anything you weren't comfortable with, but he didn't give up on trying to get to know you either. My heart was telling me to take a chance on Colter. My brain wasn't sure what to do.

Stupid, stupid, stupid. This was the last thing I needed right now. I took a deep breath. *Think, Ellison, think.* How could I get myself out of this mess? Feelings were messy. There was absolutely no way I was even thinking about catching feelings for Colter Carson.

It didn't matter that he cared about my interests and asked me questions that made absolutely no sense but also made me feel lighter, happier. That, even for a moment, he made me forget about the world around me and my internal struggles.

It didn't fucking matter. We could never work. A cowboy like Colter and a woman like me were like oil and water. Fire and gasoline. You didn't dare mix them, lest you wanted something disastrous to happen. We were twin flames, threatening to consume one another until we eventually burned each other out.

When I got home, I immediately texted Isa.

> SOS

ISA
> what's wrong? what happened? how did the date go?

It was NOT a date. I rolled my eyes as I typed out my reply.

> It wasn't a date.

> But it was...fine

Almost immediately, her next messages popped up on the screen.

ISA
> i need DETAILS

> SPILL

> actually you know forget that. I'm coming over.

Isabelle pulled into the driveway in record time. She had to have been breaking so many laws on the way here, but it was nice to know she'd risk a speeding ticket and hefty fine for me.

"All right, Ells, I didn't drive twenty over the speed limit for nothing, so spill." She hugged me as she walked in the door.

"So, we met for coffee," I started.

"Well, obviously. Get to the good stuff."

So impatient.

"He was nice. He asked me the weirdest questions, but it was kind of sweet. He also didn't push me to talk about anything if I didn't want to. There were a couple of times my dad almost came up and I felt awkward, but I think he could sense that so he changed the subject."

"We love a self-aware man." She grinned.

"He asked me for my number…" I trailed off.

"And? Did you give it to him?" She was excited now. Leave it to Isa.

"No…"

"Ellison Jo Wilson. What the fuck?" Her mouth gaped. "You're telling me that this man is essentially *perfect* for you and you *didn't* give him your number?"

"If you'd let me finish." I laughed. "I didn't give him my number, but I told him he could give me his."

"Okay, that's better than nothing. But did the romance novels I made you read teach you *nothing?*"

I didn't have the heart to tell her that her romance novels might have caused her to have even higher standards for men than I did. And mine were near impossible in a place like this.

"Give me your phone," she demanded, her eyes wide.

Uh oh. When Isa had an idea, she was not going to give up.

I didn't like where this was going. "What are you going to do with it?"

"Trust me, please." She gave me puppy dog eyes.

"Sorry, I don't know about—" Before I could even finish my sentence she was already in full-blown attack mode, her target: my phone. I never should have given her my password. I needed to remember to change it.

She snatched it out of my hand and scrolled through my contacts. When she inevitably didn't find his name there, she searched my notes app instead.

"Seriously? Why haven't you added him to your contacts?"

"I was going to wait so I could decide if it would be worth it," I explained.

"Yeah, right. That's just Ellison code for 'I'm never going to text this poor guy,' and now he's going to forever wonder what could have been," she scoffed.

"Remind me again why I let you come over?" I rolled my eyes.

"Because, deep down, you know the right decision is to text him too, Ells."

Was it the right decision, though? I didn't see the point in starting a relationship, friendship, whatever this was between me and Colter, when he was just going to leave. Not only did texting him break the main rule I had set for myself, it also ran the risk of me being dragged back into the world I had so desperately wanted to leave.

"Hypothetically, if texting him was the right thing to do, what's the point? He's not from here, Isa. After this week is over, he'll leave. He'll eventually go back to Montana and forget all about me anyway. What if he's just playing the nice guy card to have a chance? It won't end well." I didn't actually think Colter was faking being nice to have a leg up. I was picking at straws, trying to justify why I didn't want to text him, when the real reason was simply that I was afraid.

"You'll never know unless you try." She handed me the phone, putting the power back into my hands.

Isa was letting me make the decision, but, just like my mother had taught me, I knew I would have to live with whatever I chose to do. Take a risk and potentially have my heart broken, or spend forever wondering.

"Fine, I'll do it. But if this blows up in my face, I'm blaming you." I copied his number from my notes and opened up a text message.

> Hi it's Ellison.

"See? That wasn't so hard. You act like I'm trying to pull all of your teeth out." She gave me an encouraging smile.

I added his name to my contacts as "Ace in the Hole." It was enough of an identifier for me, but no one else would have known who it was if they happened to glance at my phone. It might have drawn questions, but I would deal with that when the time came.

ACE

Hey! That was fast. I guess you decided texting me was worth your time after all?

> Don't get your hopes up too much. I'm giving it a test run

ACE

Well, I hope I exceed your expectations and you don't decide that you made a huge mistake.

> We'll see

"What is he saying?" Isa poked her head over my shoulder to look at the texts we had exchanged. "Why are you being so…"

"Honest?"

"I was going to say cynical but sure, honest works too." She pursed her lips, deep in thought. "Let me have that." She grabbed my phone again without warning, this time not giving me the opportunity to try to take it back. "Ace in the Hole? Never mind, I'll address that later." She started typing a few things. "There."

> I meant that I really enjoyed talking to you earlier. and I was wondering if you wanted to get together again sometime soon

ACE

> …

"He's typing. Thank me later. But you're welcome by the way." She grinned.

I groaned internally. That was literally not how I sounded. I had never texted someone anything remotely like the message she sent Colter, who was still essentially a stranger.

ACE

> Did an alien take over your body?

> I mean I'm not turning down your offer, I just…

> That didn't really seem like something you'd say is all.

I laughed at his alien comment. That's basically what Isabelle taking over my phone was.

> You mean, actually say something nice?

> But you're right. No, I did not send that message

ACE

Oh? So you did get taken over by an alien. Or?

> My best friend. Isabelle. She's kind of a hopeless romantic

ACE

Ah, so you told your best friend about me. That seems like progress in my favor.

> Again, don't get your hopes up too high

ACE

So, I might be grasping at straws here, but maybe you're ready to tell me the story behind your real interest?

I had to hand it to him. He was brave. But it wasn't a story that I could convey through a text message.

> Hmm. Nah I'm good.

> Let me rephrase. I just don't want to talk about it over text

ACE

Well, there's an easy solution to that.

> Oh really?

ACE

Let me take you up on your, or I guess your best friend's, offer to get together again. Then you can tell me all about it.

Maybe not tomorrow, but the next day? I'll let you pick the place.

How am I supposed to say no? Sure, that works I guess

The Legless Cow. One o'clock

ACE

Legless Cow? Why did someone name a restaurant that?

They sell burgers

ACE

Ok and?

You know, legless cow? Ground beef?

It was stupid joke. I actually cringed every time I drove past the place, but they sold the best burgers made from local beef. The joke seemed to be right up Colter's alley, though.

ACE

Haha that's funny!

I knew he would appreciate it. It was a fairly decent marketing strategy, too, naming your business something ridiculous that would make people ask questions and get them talking. The Legless Cow had been there forever. But when you made food as delicious as theirs, it wasn't hard to keep people coming through the doors.

"What are you smiling about?" I had almost forgotten Isa was with me.

Wow. Never thought I'd be that type of girl, so engrossed in a conversation with a man.

"The Legless Cow." I snorted.

"I love that place. Great marketing strategy too. Wait, why were you talking about The Legless Cow?"

"We may or may not be going there in a couple of days." I chose my words carefully.

Isa squealed and started jumping around excitedly. "See! I *told* you texting him was a good idea! I *better* be the Maid of Honor in y'all's wedding."

"Whoa, hold on. Nobody said *anything* about getting married. We're two friends, if you can even call us that, getting lunch." That was it. Isa was absolutely *delusional.* I loved her, but she was crazy. She had no problems attracting dates, so of course she chose to expend all of her hopeless romantic energy on me, the girl who avoided relationships.

"I'm calling it right now. Whether you believe me or not is up to you, but I have a good feeling about this." She giggled.

The Legless Cow was a small burger joint in the suburbs on the way out of Houston toward the area where my family lived. It was started back in the thirties by a husband and wife who were both ranchers. When they died, they passed it along to their kids, and it has stayed in that family forever. It had an old diner type feel with its candy apple red booths and homey, welcoming atmosphere. It was my parents' favorite place to take me as a kid.

I slid into a booth near the back corner. Not for

romantic reasons. I simply didn't need people to overhear our conversations.

I shot Colter a text.

> I'm here. At a booth in the back, but no rush

Less than a minute after I sent the text, he walked into the doors of the diner and spotted me. He gave me a goofy grin and walked up next to the table.

"This seat taken?" He winked.

Such a charmer. Classic cowboy. I playfully rolled my eyes and gestured for him to sit. He slid into the booth next to me.

"What are you doing?"

"I need to sit facing the door," he replied simply, as if it was the obvious answer.

"Let me get out then. I'm not sitting on the same side as you." When he didn't move, I glared at him. I tilted my head and gestured for him to move. All I got in response was a couple blinks.

"Oh my God. You're insufferable." If he wasn't going to move, I would take matters into my own hands. I slid under the table and popped up on the other side with an annoyed look on my face.

"All you had to say was please, and I would have moved." He shrugged, his eyes glinting with mischief.

If looks could kill, Colter Carson would have keeled over right there in that booth.

"Hi, y'all! Welcome to The Legless Cow. My name's Lauren, and I'll be taking care of y'all today. Do you know what you'd like to drink?"

Perfect timing. If she had waited three more seconds to

come over, I might have strangled Colter, and that probably wouldn't have looked good for business.

"Ladies first." He nodded at me.

"Could I get a water, please?" I smiled sweetly at our server while Colter ordered an iced tea.

"Absolutely, I'll be right back with those drinks."

"So, what's the best thing to get here?" Colter was reading his menu intently. The specialty was obviously the burgers, but they also served all day breakfast, had the best milkshakes, and had a variety of options for people whose preference wasn't beef.

"I always get the Breakfast of Champions Burger." It was a 1/3-pound burger with bacon, a fried egg, and whatever other toppings you wanted. "I also always get a chocolate milkshake."

"All right. I trust you." He snapped his menu closed and set it down on the table.

"Just like that?"

"Just like that."

Lauren came back shortly with our drinks and to take our order. Exactly like he had said he would, Colter ordered the Breakfast of Champions Burger and a chocolate milkshake. The difference between us was he ordered his with onions, tomatoes, and no pickles, and I ordered mine without onions or tomatoes and extra pickles.

"So, how did you find this place? Or, why did you choose to come here?"

I figured he would ask that. I mean, after all, who chooses to meet up for lunch at a place called The Legless Cow? It was a pretty unique place. Kind of a hidden gem.

"This place is pretty significant to me. My parents would always take me here as a little girl. They were pretty much royalty whenever they stepped through these doors." I smiled, thinking about those days. We had a lot of happy memories here.

The owners were practically family. They even let me pick up a few shifts here while I was in high school. *"Anything for Levi's girl,"* they would say. They respected my privacy, though, and didn't tell the world who I was. They told me they didn't feel the need to because it wasn't their story to tell. And that's why I loved them.

"That's really sweet. You mentioned your dad grew up here. What's he like?"

What seemed to be such an innocent question to most people was one of the hardest ones for me. I debated brushing off the question and changing the subject, but part of me felt like opening up to Colter wouldn't be the worst thing in the world. I'd kept my grief and feelings about my dad buried for so long. There were things my mom and Isa didn't even know. Maybe if I talked about him, despite my fears of letting people in, a small weight would be lifted off my shoulders.

"It's kind of a hard subject for me to talk about," I admitted.

Colter looked like he was about to stop me, to tell me that I didn't need to say anything, but I took a deep breath and continued. "My dad died when I was young, but he was larger than life. He was my hero."

This was the part I dreaded the most when I told people about my dad. I waited for the pity to come like it always did. But instead, a glimmer of understanding flickered across Colter's face.

"I'm sorry to hear about your father." Even though he was offering his condolences, it didn't come across as him feeling sorry for me. It felt real, genuine. "I understand what it's like to have people look at you with pity, like you're broken and in need of fixing."

It was almost as if he read my mind, and I wanted to get a glimpse of what was going on inside his head, what had happened to him for his reaction to be that way.

I opened my mouth to say something of the like, but before I could ask, Lauren came up to our table with our food.

CHAPTER FIFTEEN

colter

Our server dropped off giant plates of food and our two milkshakes, along with the metal containers of leftovers that didn't fit in the glass. It reminded me of the burger joint we had back in Goldfinch. Reid and I would always go there after practices and college football games.

I took the initial bite of the massive burger and groaned. "This is one of the best burgers I've ever had. I'm so glad I trusted you on this."

She smiled at me before she took a bite of her own.

We ate slowly, making small talk here and there between bites and sips of milkshake. She was the type of person who dipped her fries in the ice cream. She said she got it from a TV show she watched as a kid and it just stuck.

We finished eating, and Lauren brought around our check. I put my credit card down before Ellison could reach for her wallet.

"Let me get this, please." I didn't realize I had instinctively put my hand on top of hers, so I pulled it back quickly.

"Oh, thanks." She blushed.

Lauren ran my card, and I signed the receipt, giving her a twenty-five-percent tip.

"You ready?" I asked Ellison.

She nodded, and we got up to leave. I opened the door for her but when she got outside she stopped abruptly.

"There's something I need to tell you," she blurted.

I gave her a confused look, and she started explaining.

"The night in the bar when we ran into each other was the night before the anniversary of my dad's death." She took a deep breath. "He used to call my mother Baby Blue, because of her eyes. It was quite endearing, actually."

Realization hit me. That's why she reacted the way she did. "I'm so sorry. You don't have to tell me what happened." I wasn't going to push the subject because I knew how difficult talking about her dad was for her. I would let her tell me as little or as much as she wanted.

"He died when I was eight. Rodeo accident," she continued. "He was a steer wrestler. One of the best in the world. Rodeo was his life. It used to be mine too. I remember wanting nothing more than to be just like him. That accident didn't just cause me to lose my dad. I lost my entire world with him."

My heart dropped a little at her confession. The truth was, Ellison Wilson and I weren't all that different. We had both lost someone and with it, felt like we had lost a piece of ourselves. I fully intended to help her get that piece back.

I didn't know the person she was before today. But I wanted to. I wanted to learn every aspect of her. I wanted her to know that she didn't have to build up her walls to keep me out.

"A couple days ago, you asked me what my main

interest was. Well, if you really want to know, you also have to know *why* it's my main interest. That involves knowing what the most important things to me are." She gestured for me to follow her to her car.

We drove out of the city and the skies began to open up. I had no idea where she was taking me, but I was along for the ride. I would figure out how I would get back to my truck later. About twenty minutes later, we pulled through the wooden entrance of Merritt Ranch.

Merritt. Why is that name so familiar? I knew I had heard the name before, but my memory was failing me.

Then it hit me.

"Your dad was Levi Merritt." It was more of a statement than a question. Merritt was one of the greatest cowboys of his time. He was in the peak of his career, with no sign of it slowing down. Until his tragic accident.

"The one and only," she confirmed, never once turning her head to meet my eyes.

Now that I was looking at her and thinking about it, she was a spitting image of the famous cowboy.

"You never wanted to compete?" I asked.

"No. How could I? Rodeo might have been the one thing my dad and I both loved, but it was also the thing that took him away from me." Her hands gripped the steering wheel tighter, her knuckles turning white.

She parked her car behind a large workshop, the building blocking the view of the main house. When she got out to open the garage door, she gave me an expectant look to follow her.

We had walked through racks of tools, ranch equipment, and four wheelers when she finally stopped in the back corner by a large tarp.

"I've never told anyone about this before," she

confessed as she pulled the tarp off of the baby-blue F-100. "My dad bought this pickup after he married my mom. Said the color reminded him of her and he would have been a fool not to buy it. He was restoring it. I remember he'd bring me out here when I was young and I'd sit on the floor while he worked on the truck.

"When he died, the pickup sat here for years until one day, when I was in high school, I came out to grab something for one of the ranch hands and remembered it was here. I've been working on it ever since. Trying to completely restore it. Sometimes I'll drive it around and I swear I can sense my dad in the passenger seat beside me. Nobody knows about this. Not my mother, not Isa, no one."

I was honored she trusted me enough to tell me this secret, to be so vulnerable about the thing that brought her comfort. But I could also sense she was giving me a warning, that she would know if I broke that trust.

"Thank you for showing me this." I didn't know what else to say, but the thank you was sincere.

She shrugged. "Like I said, if you want to really know me, you have to know what's important to me. My family is everything, and this is the only piece of my dad I have left. Come on, we're going for a drive."

The pickup ran amazingly well despite all of the years it had sat in the shop. Ellison must have done some really good work on it. We drove off the ranch property, heading out the back way instead of by the house.

"Every time I miss my dad, I take the truck out for a drive. It's become a bit of a ritual these past few years. No one ever drives these backroads, so it feels like it's just me and my dad out here." She had rolled down the windows, and the wind was blowing through her hair. She looked peaceful, carefree, like all of her sorrows had been left behind at the wooden gates of the ranch. I loved hearing her talk about the things that brought her comfort, the ways she dealt with stress and her grief.

"What about your family?" she asked.

"I love my family. They're very supportive of me and my career. I don't see them a lot, though, because I'm always traveling. I try to make an effort to go visit them as much as I can, but it gets difficult when I'm always on the road." Our schedules hadn't been lining up very well lately either. I would be on the road and then the few days I was home, my mom would be visiting my siblings in Bozeman or Washington and my dad would be off doing who knows what.

"Do you have any siblings?"

"I have an older brother and sister. Caitlin lives in Washington and is three years older than me and Clay lives in Bozeman and is five years older."

"I don't have any siblings," she replied.

"Do you ever wish you did?" I asked.

"I don't think so. I've always been content on my own. Besides, it was probably for the best with all things considered. My mom had enough on her plate when my dad died. I think having more kids would have made it more difficult."

We kept driving until we made it to a clearing in a field. She pulled off the road and turned off the engine. I followed her out of the truck and sat next to her on the tailgate.

"What is your favorite place in the world?" She stared off into the distance. There was a light breeze that caused the grass to sway, but the sun was out, shining on the landscape ahead of us. There wasn't a cloud in the sky either. It looked like a scene straight out of a movie.

"Probably the rodeo arena."

"Really? Not a city or the mountains? The rodeo arena?" She laughed a little like I was making a joke.

"No, I'm serious. The arena feels like home to me. It's where I get to do the thing I love with the people I care about the most. The guys that I compete with? They're family to me. We may not be blood, but we're brothers. I wouldn't trade going on the road with them for anything. My roping partner, Reid, especially. He's done so much for me."

"That makes sense, I guess. Especially if that's all you've ever known. Reid sounds like a great guy." She paused for a moment. "I think this might be my favorite place in the world."

"Houston?"

"No, just this field. This is the place I always go when I take my dad's truck out. And maybe it's not so much the specific place, kind of like how arenas are everywhere, but it's the people you're with, or in my case, the pickup."

I looked at her, noticing the faint freckles on her nose, and I wanted to lean in and see what she tasted like. She met my eyes, and for a moment I thought maybe she was considering the same thing. I couldn't tell, but I didn't know how many chances I would get for this moment, so I was going to take it. I shifted my gaze from her eyes to her lips and back again and slowly started to move, closing the gap between us.

"Is it okay if I—" The sound of my phone ringing cut me off.

What the fuck?

She pulled away from me abruptly, and I dug my phone out of my pocket and saw that Reid was calling.

"I'm sorry, it's Reid," I apologized. I didn't want to be rude by answering my phone, but when Reid called, I always answered. It's what he would do for me. "What's up?" I answered the phone.

"Where are you, man? We need to meet Aaron in an hour, remember?" *Oh shit.* I had forgotten all about Aaron.

"Sorry, man. I forgot. I'll be there, don't worry." I hung up before he could say anything else. "I'm so sorry, I forgot I had plans with Reid and our old coach," I apologized to Ellison, feeling a little foolish for forgetting but also a little ticked off that Reid interrupted our moment.

"We should probably head back into town anyway." Ellison was already hopping off the tailgate and heading toward the cab.

CHAPTER SIXTEEN

ellison

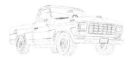

W e drove back into town in silence. I had to take Colter back to his truck, and I was questioning why I had him ride with me. This time, the silence was awkward and uncomfortable. It wasn't even remotely similar to the silence at the restaurant. No, this time there was silence because of the elephant in the room…well, car.

Colter Carson had almost kissed me. And I had almost *let* him.

The only thing that had stopped it from happening was his roping partner calling him. It was both a relief and a disappointment, and I didn't know how to feel about that. So here we were, driving the thirty minutes back into town in complete and utter silence. I hadn't turned on music or anything, and it felt too late to do it now, like I was trying to distract myself from what had happened.

We were playing a dangerous game, both waiting to see who would be the first to bring it up. I already knew it wasn't going to be me. And if and when he did bring it up, I would act as though it was nothing. It was better that way —for both of us.

"Ellison, I…" Colter awkwardly started, and I knew he was about to bring up the almost kiss.

I had two choices here. I could either cut him off and pretend I knew exactly what he was going to say, or I could hear him out. The rational thing would be to hear him out, but since when had I ever been rational?

"It's not a big deal, Colter. We almost kissed but then we didn't. It was probably for the best." The last part was a low blow, judging by the way he flinched. It was true, though. He had no idea what he was getting himself into by falling for me and I was just saving him from it.

Hurt flashed across his face, but then he pursed his lips and nodded.

A twinge of guilt rose in me, but I pushed down the feeling. I was doing what I had to do to protect both of us. Perhaps it was a mistake opening up to him so much about my father, but it happened and I couldn't take it back. I wasn't sure what had possessed me to show him the vehicle in the first place. Maybe it was because I felt like I could trust him. More likely it was because of a selfish, ulterior motive. One that granted me less guilt for keeping it a secret.

But it wasn't too late to let him down easy and let him go on with his life in Montana. Chalk it all up to being lust, a moment of weakness. That's what I wanted, wasn't it? Hurt was inevitable in this situation, so one of us had to be the one to pull the trigger and get it over with. That's all I was doing.

We pulled up to the diner where we had gotten lunch, and I parked next to his truck. He looked like a sad golden retriever puppy as he glanced at me before opening the door to my car.

"Thank you for showing me the pickup, Ellison. It

meant a lot to me." He shut the door and left me alone to wade in my pool of conflicting feelings.

We had just met and we were friends, nothing more. Shit like this happened all the time. It was normal. We talked a couple times but ultimately we wouldn't be right for each other, even as friends, so I cut him loose. So why did I feel like I had made a mistake?

I could practically hear Isa's voice in my ear, *"That's because it was a mistake, you idiot. You clearly had a good thing, great even, but then you pushed him away like you always do. What are you so damn afraid of?"*

CHAPTER SEVENTEEN

I got out of Ellison's car and gave her one more look before getting in my truck and watching her peel out of the parking lot. I shouldn't have felt so disappointed by her comment. After all, we weren't together—hell, we had only gone on two dates. But I thought I was getting somewhere, especially with her opening up about her father and showing me the pickup, something she had never told anyone else about.

I didn't want to keep bothering her if that was how she really felt, but part of me didn't believe her when she said it was for the best. A wave of embarrassment came over me, as I thought about how many times she had rejected me. It reminded me of Sophie, and the deep fear of not being enough threatened to resurface and drag me back down with it. Stressing over it wasn't going to help me, though. I was conflicted between letting go—giving her the choice to come to me if she wanted to—and refusing to let my fear overtake what could be a good thing for both of us.

I had six days before the first semifinal round and nine days before I left Houston. It was both plenty of time and no time at all. I was going to prove to Ellison that whatever we had would be worth it; this cowboy wasn't just going to ride away in the end. Whether she believed me or not was out of my hands.

Reid and Aaron were already waiting for me. I was only a little bit late. I hadn't realized how much time had passed when I was with Ellison. What had seemed like minutes of talking was actually a few hours, and it was already almost five o'clock.

The plan was to go to dinner, but since I had already eaten a late lunch, they decided they wanted to go to a hole-in-the-wall bar, away from downtown Houston. Aaron wanted to catch up with us, maybe grab a beer or two, and then go to the rodeo with his family.

"Oh look, it's the man of the hour. Nice of you to show up." Aaron winked as I walked up to the table they were sitting at.

"Sorry, guys. I was out doing some things." I gave as vague an answer as possible. Reid kind of knew what was going on but he didn't know everything.

"Well, I'm glad you made it anyway. So listen, you boys were two of our school's best. Coachable, talented, not to mention you went on to have a great start to your career."

Here it was. The real reason why Aaron had wanted to get together. He no doubt wanted us to think about coming back to Sapphire Gulch University to coach.

"Athletics and I were talking about the future. Don't look so scared, Colter. I'm not asking you to give up your career. Yet." He chuckled as heat rose to my cheeks. "I know it's too early to think seriously about coaching, but how would you two feel about coming back this fall to do some clinics with the team and maybe also some youngsters in the community?"

Clinics? Huh, that was not what I was expecting. That was easy. Go over to Goldfinch for a couple of weekends in the fall, help teach kids the proper techniques, and then get back on the road again.

"That sounds great, Aaron." Reid nodded enthusiastically. He had always been more of a teacher than I was. It came naturally to him from taking care of his younger siblings. Not that I didn't love working with kids, but they could be a lot sometimes and I didn't know if I was the best teacher.

"Colter? What do you think?"

Honestly, I wasn't sure. But it was a great opportunity to give back to the community that had given us so much during our college careers. It would be foolish to say no to the man who had done so much for us.

"All right, I'll help you out, old man," I joked with him.

He gave me a look of mock offense, but it was fleeting. "Thank you boys. I, and the team, appreciate it more than you'll ever know."

We spent the next thirty minutes or so chatting about life. Aaron's oldest, Mason, was in middle school and his youngest, Mackinley, had started fourth grade. I remembered when his daughter was only a toddler and he'd bring her around to practices, carrying her on his shoulders. I knew I wanted that someday, even if I didn't know how to handle kids right now.

"All right, boys, thanks for this chat. It was great to see you, and good luck out there. I'd better get back to my family or my wife will have my head." Aaron waved goodbye.

Once he had left, Reid turned to me with an expression I couldn't read. "What's going on with you, Colt?" he asked, the concern evident in his voice. "You seem distracted."

"Nothing's going on," I lied.

"Come on, Colt, I know when you're lying. Your face does this stupid twitching thing. Is this about that girl?"

"We almost kissed and then your dumb ass called me. She said it was nothing and probably for the best that we didn't." I shrugged. I was downplaying how I felt, big time. Hiding my emotions was what I did best after all.

"Is that how you feel about it?"

Since when had Reid become such a therapist?

"I mean, I don't believe her for one second, if that's what you're asking. I just don't know what to do about it. I'm not exactly Prince Charming in her eyes."

"Listen, man, I've never known you to be someone to back down from a challenge. If you want her, which it's clear you do, go get her."

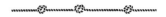

I was fucked. And once Isa heard about what happened, I would be in even more trouble. I paced my room, trying to come up with a solution. I could move back to Austin where I went to college. I could change my name again. Anything that would save me from facing the consequences of my actions. *Or, you know, you could just text him.*

I grabbed my phone and typed out a message.

> Hey, I'm sorry about what happened earlier.
> I was being weird. I didn't mean that it was
> a mistake, I just have a lot of trauma from,
> you know, having a dead father

Oh, good lord. I choked out a laugh because if I didn't, I would cry instead. *Scrap that immediately. That sounds awful.*

> Hi. I'm sure you hate me right now but

What the fuck is wrong with you?

> I'm an idiot

Well, at least that one is true.

I groaned and deleted my last pathetic attempt at typing out a text.

I had never had such conflicting feelings for a person. Other people were easy to forget. They always did something that immediately turned me off, or they didn't understand me and why I was the way I was. Colter Carson was not easy to forget. In fact, lately I had trouble getting him out of my mind. And that was terrifying.

CHAPTER EIGHTEEN

I had a plan. It was not a solid plan, but it was a plan nonetheless. It involved some…questionable research, but I was sure that could be looked past in the name of romance. After all, Ellison did say her best friend, Isabelle, was a hopeless romantic.

A few days had come and gone since I had last seen her, which meant I didn't have a lot of time left. It had killed me not to text her, to ask her to let me make it up to her somehow, but I felt like there was a greater chance she would have outright rejected me again if I had done that. I had to be patient about this because I believed it would be worth it in the end. I just had to find a way to contact Isabelle first.

Trying to find the right Isabelle with no last name or any knowledge of her appearance proved to be nearly impossible. I had spent the last forty-two minutes looking through different profiles on social media. A Google search did me no good either. You wouldn't believe how many Isabelles there were in Houston.

I was about to throw in the towel and give up on my

grand gesture when it came to me. *How much of an idiot am I? Why didn't I think of this forty-two minutes ago?* I already knew Ellison's last name and exactly what she looked like. It was almost a guarantee that she was following her best friend on social media.

It still took me a couple of minutes to find the profile, there were a few more accounts with the name Ellison Wilson than I thought there would be, but eventually I found her and—by the grace of God—her profile was public.

She didn't post often. It was evident she kept her personal life private in all aspects. There were only a few photos of her, but I could have looked at them all day. I had a mission to accomplish, though. I went to her following list and typed in "Isabelle." Only two profiles came up. What a relief. *I have a fifty-fifty shot here.* I clicked on the first profile, Isabelle Ramirez, hoping for the best. It was a private account. *Fuck, okay, hopefully the second one is public. At least help me narrow it down here.* The second profile was Isabelle Bennett. *Fuck.* They were both private.

You are a fucking idiot, Colter. But you're in too deep to back out now. There was no way I was going to get it right on the first try, so why not kill two birds with one stone? I opened my messages and typed both of their usernames into a group chat.

isa.bennett, bellaramirez

> Hi. I know this is weird that you're getting a message from a guy you don't know, but my name is Colter and I know one of you is Ellison's best friend.

> She talked about you but she didn't tell me your last name. After 42 minutes of searching I found you two but now I'm at a deadlock and I need help. Sorry.

> Also, please don't tell Ellison.

ISA.BENNETT

ah the famous colter carson

BELLARAMIREZ

I have no idea who you are.

bellaramirez left the chat.

Well, that was easier than I thought. Not the greatest method, but it got the job done.

> I need your help.

ISA.BENNETT

oh?

> What has Ellison told you?

ISA.BENNETT

why cowboy? what'd you do to her?

Sweat started to pool on my brow.

> Well... It was more that I almost did something and then it didn't happen. I almost kissed her.

ISA.BENNETT

WHAT

> But then my best friend Reid called me so I didn't. And then she told me it was probably for the best. But I think she's lying?

ISA.BENNETT

of COURSE she's lying. she's hiding from her feelings again 🙄

> I really like her. And I want to prove to her that I'm not just going to leave Houston and forget about her.

ISA.BENNETT

oh i have just the idea

And that was how I had a—hopefully—foolproof plan to prove to Ellison how much I wanted this. How much I cared and that opening up about her dad wasn't for nothing.

I had done everything I could for the moment, and it was up to Isabelle to pull through. I just hoped it was enough.

CHAPTER NINETEEN

ellison

I t had been four days since the almost kiss. Four days since I had even heard from Colter. Maybe I had finally gotten rid of him. Still, it felt weird to not even hear from him. He had been so adamant at the beginning, so what changed? *Probably because he felt scorned after all of the times you rejected him.*

I still wasn't sure how to feel or what to do about the situation. The me from a week ago wouldn't have given this a second thought. But the me from a week ago also would have never met up with him for coffee in the first place, much less show him my dad's pickup.

The first semifinal round was in two days, and Colter would be gone in four. We would no longer be in the same city and then maybe I could breathe a little better, knowing he was out of sight and out of mind. I could delete his number and never think about the cowboy from Montana again. But even my cold heart knew that wasn't going to happen. He had come into my life and knocked down a large chunk of my walls, and I knew I'd spend the rest of my life trying to build them back up.

I wished it was as easy as reaching out and apologizing. Asking how I could make up for it. But that wasn't in my nature, and I had never been good at expressing how I felt. I had tried going to therapy once, but they always assumed my feelings or told me how to feel, instead of helping me work through my emotions and teaching me how to vocalize them in a healthy way.

The only person who had really understood me and didn't look at me like I needed to be fixed was Colter. And I had already lost him. All because of my stubborn attitude. I was good at pushing people away, though. I had been doing it most of my life.

I hadn't told Isa what had happened and she hadn't asked, which was odd for her.

ISA

hey we should get out and do something tomorrow

I don't know

ISA

i know something happened. you need to stop feeling sorry for yourself and do something fun

How do you know something happened?

ISA

i'm your best friend. i know you. come on, at least come with me to dinner tomorrow. no bars

Alright fine. No bars though

At least I had Isa. As much as I tried to hide things from her and downplay my emotions, she always knew what was going on and she always knew what to do or say. I was lucky to have her.

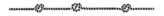

colter

ISA.BENNETT

okay, cowboy. i've done my part. don't mess this up

I read the message she sent with all of the details. I owed Isabelle Bennett big time. I hadn't even met her, yet she still thought I was good enough that she wanted to help me win over Ellison. Even if she simply wanted to look out for her best friend, she still deemed me worthy of Ellison's attention when she could have turned me away and told me to get lost.

You have no idea how much this means to me.

ISA.BENNETT

yeah yeah. just don't make me regret it later

You have my word.

This was the best news I had gotten since I found out Reid and I had made it to the NFR last year. There was almost as much pressure riding on this too, if not even more. The NFR would come and go; there was an opportunity to make it every year. A girl like Ellison Wilson? Now, that was rare.

ellison

Isa had promised me we wouldn't be going out to the bar after dinner, but we ended up there anyway. We were at the same bar we had been at the night I had bumped into Colter, and I was nervously looking around, making sure no one I had seen before was there, especially not the drugstore cowboy who tried to get me to wear his hat. I didn't see anyone I immediately recognized, so I relaxed a little. Tonight was going to go smoothly. It would be fine.

We were sitting at a table, watching people struggle with the line dances we weren't even going to attempt to try. We hadn't talked about Colter at all—at least not yet. I knew she would eventually ask, though.

"Hey, so when are you going to tell me what happened between you and Colter?" Isa asked, almost like she knew exactly what I was thinking.

"What do you mean?" I frowned.

"You haven't talked about him and you haven't been texting him. Come on, I'm your best friend, Ellie."

"I'm just embarrassed I guess. After the diner, we went

for a drive and we talked. Everything was fine, but then he was about to kiss me and we got interrupted by his roping partner."

"And then?" She was practically on the edge of her seat, waiting to hear about my drama.

"I told him it was probably for the best that we didn't." A twinge of shame came over me as I thought about the way I had handled it. I wasn't ready for Isabelle to give me a talk about romance and how I should have gone about it. I loved her, but our minds operated differently. "I need to go to the restroom. I'll be right back."

I got up from the table and walked toward the hallway where the restrooms were. Right as I was about to open the door, a hand blocked the way. *What the—*

I turned, looking straight in the face of the owner of the hand.

"Well, hello again, darlin'," the cowboy from a week ago drawled. He was still wearing his god-awful misshapen cowboy hat, but he had a hard look in his eyes, one I'd seen too many times. "I saw you from the other end of the bar and I wasn't going to let you get away from me again."

"Uh-uh. No. That's not happening." I tried to turn around, screw the bathrooms, but he grabbed my wrist, pulling me back to him, his body flush against mine.

"I'm not taking no for an answer this time." His breath was hot on my face and reeked of alcohol. I tried to throw a punch at him, but he grabbed my other wrist, pinning me to the wall, moving so I couldn't even knee him in the groin. He was stronger than he looked, I had to give him that.

The hallway was far enough out of the way that no one would see us back here. No one would hear a struggle either with how loud it was and how many people were here. He was going to get exactly what he had wanted the first night, and I had no defense this time. I had offended him, and he was getting back at me.

I squeezed my eyes shut, trying to disappear through the wall, not wanting to know what was about to happen. But before he could carry out his plan, a low, familiar voice came out of nowhere.

"I'd advise letting go of her right now."

"Chill, man, she wanted this," the silverbelly cowboy claimed, still pinning me to the wall.

No. No, I didn't.

Maybe my silent plea was loud enough because suddenly the weight was lifted off of me and all I could see was a dark figure punching him.

What the hell?

I tried to step away from the scene and get away while I could, but then the creepy guy was gone and it was Colter in front of me. He was panting, his hand covered in blood.

"I'm sorry I wasn't here sooner. I saw him follow you. I was so scared about what would have happened if I hadn't gotten here." He sounded genuinely scared for me, like he knew something would have happened had he not been paying attention to me.

"What are you talking about? What are you doing here?" I was so confused. How did he get here? I never saw him walk into the bar and I was paying attention to the door. I was racking my brain, trying to think of how this could have happened, but at the same time I felt this abnormal pull to him, making all of my rational thoughts and questions disappear like magic.

"I wanted to make sure you were okay. You're safe now." He pushed a strand of hair out of my face, cupping my cheek. A fire burned through me, the heat making its way all the way down between my legs.

"Colter, I—"

"Shhh. I know. It's okay." He placed a finger over my lips. When he lifted it, sparks lingered in the spot where it was a moment before. His touch was electric. I wanted more of it. I'd wanted him since our moment in the back of my dad's pickup, I could admit that now. I looked up at his eyes, my heart beating faster and faster.

This was really happening.

He moved his stare from my eyes down to my lips, one hand pressed against the wall behind me, the other finding its way up my thigh, the tips of his fingers sliding under the bottom of my dress, like he wanted to explore more. He leaned in, his eyes hungry, and then—

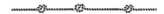

I jolted awake, sitting up in my bed. My heart was racing and there was no denying my arousal as it soaked my underwear. The room felt unreasonably warm as I processed what had happened.

I just had a fucking sex dream about Colter Carson.

I took a deep breath, running my hands along my scalp. *What has gotten into me?* I needed to get the image of Colter out of my brain. And I needed a long shower. A cold one.

Isa was going to have a heyday when she heard about this tonight.

The last place I wanted to be again was downtown Houston, especially after that dream, but Isa was adamant on us going to this specific restaurant, Nectar & Vine. She also insisted on me driving by myself, instead of us going together. I was unsure why, we had never gone anywhere separately, but I was too tired to ask. I had worked practically all day on the ranch, trying to keep my mind off of Colter, but even manual labor couldn't force him out of my memory.

I parked my car in one of the parking garages close to the restaurant. It required me to walk a couple blocks in heels, since Isa also insisted I dress up for this, but I would have done anything for her just because she was my best friend.

She told me the reservation was under her last name, so I checked in at the host stand in case she was already here.

"Looks like your party is already here. Please follow me." The hostess started to lead me back to one of the more private areas of the restaurant.

What is going on? I furrowed my brow but followed along. Isabelle never booked a table in one of the dining rooms. Those were romantic. And expensive.

I was about to tell the hostess that I think she made a mistake. There had to be multiple Bennetts on the list and I would just text my friend, but we were already near the back of the restaurant. I shrugged, knowing I would have it out with Isa for spending so much money on me.

Everything made perfect sense when the doors opened up to the private dining room and I saw him sitting there. Colter Carson, aka the man who never gave up.

CHAPTER TWENTY-ONE

colter

She walked into the room, and my breath hitched as I took her in. Her chocolate-brown hair cascaded down her back in soft curls, and she wore a burgundy dress that hugged her curves in all the right places. She was a vision, and I felt underdressed for a moment, in my black pearl snap shirt and starched jeans. I stood up, holding the bouquet of flowers Isabelle had told me to buy.

Carnations and baby's breath are her favorites. I drilled it into my head over and over until I got to the florist earlier that afternoon. I wanted to get every detail right.

"Hi." I tried my best not to let my voice crack as she walked over to the table. I quickly pulled out her chair for her before she could do it herself.

"What is all of this?" She looked at me with a gleam in her eye. Whether it was out of happiness or amusement, I wasn't sure. I was just glad she was there with me, that she had actually come.

"I couldn't just let you go after that day," I admitted. "I kicked myself for getting out of that car and not telling you how I felt."

"But why? What makes me so special?"

God, I wished she could see herself the way I saw her. I didn't see her as the guarded girl who had lost her dad in a tragic rodeo accident. Yes, it was a huge part of who she was, but I knew that wasn't all she was. She was so much more.

"From the moment I saw you, I knew you were special. I'd never met someone who didn't immediately see me as a trophy. Granted, you didn't see me as anything." I laughed, thinking about the very first time we had met. "But then I got to know you. I got to see the side of you no one else sees. And I like it. I like you, Ellison. I can't tell you how to feel, but I want to believe you see that there's something here too. I'd show up for you a million times if that's what it takes. All I'm asking for is a chance."

I watched her eyes narrow as she thought about what I was saying. I braced myself for her to reject me, knowing this time if she did I would finally let her go. I would accept that I had failed again—that maybe the voices in my head telling me I wasn't good enough were right—and go back to Montana and try my hardest to forget about the girl I had met by chance here in Houston. The girl who made my heart race after feeling like it would never beat for someone again.

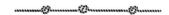

No one had ever made such an effort for me before. My jaw practically fell on the floor when I walked through those doors and saw him sitting there. What had I done to deserve that? I hadn't done anything. I *didn't* deserve him. And yet, there he was, asking me for a chance when *I* should have been the one on my knees begging for one.

I was still terrified, there was no denying that, but if Colter could risk his heart for me, then I would be willing to risk mine. I knew it would take time, my walls wouldn't come crashing down overnight, but Colter had already been slowly chipping away at the stone around my heart, piece by piece, brick by brick.

"Okay," I whispered. I watched his shoulders relax, the tension melting off of him. He thought I was going to tell him no again and that alone caused a pit to form in my stomach. What was going to happen when I couldn't be enough for him in the end? I could hardly fix my own heartbreak; I didn't want to be responsible for another person's.

"Hey, look at me."

I looked up at him, his pleading hazel eyes meeting mine.

"I'm not going anywhere. Let me prove that to you."

I wanted to believe him, but the last person who had told me he wouldn't leave was my dad.

But the least I could do was try. "Okay. I'm not either. But I need to know something. Why try so hard for this? Why me?"

He inhaled a deep breath, his eyes dropping for a second before he looked me in the face again. "My parents are divorced. They divorced when I was in college and everything I knew about love came into question for me. I also failed someone before and it destroyed me. I never wanted to be like my parents and I've blamed myself for it every single day since. It made me question myself, my

133

feelings and whether I did enough, whether I was enough. I don't want that to happen again. I don't want to have any regrets or think about how I could have done more."

Realization hit me with his confession. Yes, Colter was a cowboy, and the last person I thought I wanted to be around, but he was so many other things too. He was a son, a brother, a human being. And I had been so hard on him. I had been so focused on my own loss that I never once considered his side and the things he had been through.

"I'm sorry. I had no idea." I bit my lip.

"How could you have known? It's not your fault." He took my hand and just held it. We sat like that for a few minutes, existing in the same space, not needing any explanations or confessions. I had so many questions, but now wasn't the time.

CHAPTER TWENTY-TWO

colter

I had told her one of my deepest secrets—well, kind of. I didn't exactly tell her about my engagement, but I alluded to it. I couldn't bring myself to tell her everything, about the aftermath of the breakup. How I felt so unworthy of love and inadequate that the only thing I could do to quiet the darkness in my mind was to turn to the bottle. How sometimes my demons still took over my mind and made me feel like nothing. Which was what I would have to do if I told her about Sophie.

You couldn't have one without the other, they were both a part of me. The year after we split had been one of the worst of my life. I never wanted to be the person I was in those twelve months again.

I took another pull from the bottle of whiskey on my bedside table. I was still thinking about Sophie and the breakup. It had happened more than three months ago, but I still couldn't get past the pain.

She didn't want me, us. If I—the man that loved her with every fiber of my being—wasn't good enough for her, how could I be good enough for anyone?

Self-loathing echoed through my subconsciousness. That was my cue to drink more. I would drink myself into a coma if it meant I didn't have her on my mind anymore. It was the only coping mechanism I could think of. I couldn't sleep because she haunted my dreams, and I couldn't stop drinking because she haunted the waking hours too.

Someone knocked on the front door, but I didn't get up. I couldn't. If I got up, I knew I would have ended up on the floor and I would have stayed there. My bed was far more comfortable. I wasn't sure if I was imagining it or not, but then whoever was at the door started pounding on it.

The pounding got louder and louder, so I yelled, "Go the fuck away!" and eventually it stopped. Either the person had left or the alcohol was actually doing its job and numbing everything around me.

I took another drink and realized I was almost to the bottom, but the pain still hadn't subsided. Fuck. I wanted to scream. I wanted to throw something, or punch a wall, cause myself pain in some other way so I wouldn't feel the heartbreak anymore. I should have fought harder for her. I should have done something to make her stay. Why did I just let her go like that?

I finished the bottle. I had been sitting here for hours, taking shot after shot, pull after pull, but nothing was working. I didn't even know how much whiskey I had gone through in the last week. I had lost count, but I knew it had to have been a lot. I wanted to get up, no, I needed to get up to find another one, but I couldn't.

September came, and I still went to rodeos and competed, but everyone knew I wasn't at my best. It was only a matter of time before my career suffered too. I stayed sober to rope, but the moment I got back home or back to my trailer, I started drinking again.

We had just finished roping in Idaho. We received a no time that day and it had hit me hard. A no time meant no money earned, not that it mattered because I was spending it all on gas and alcohol. But it affected our standings and affected Reid, maybe more than anyone.

This was his future too, and I was ruining it. Not to mention we were essentially taking a loss financially, because of entry costs.

After five months of drinking and isolating myself from everyone, Reid finally figured out what was going on and was able to intervene. I was halfway through another bottle of Pendleton when Reid barged into my trailer. He didn't yell at me or make a scene like I had assumed would happen when the truth about my drinking came to light. He only said one thing and that was the moment I knew I needed to get my shit together and be better.

He looked at the bottle and then looked at me. "Hey, buddy. I know what's going on and I'm here for you. No matter what. Through the worst and the best, I'm always going to be there for you and I hope you know that. I want to help you. Please, let me help you."

I blinked away the memory, doing my best to keep a neutral expression so she wouldn't suspect something was wrong. Everything was better now; I wasn't in the place I was back then. And since I met Ellison, I hadn't had nightmares—the ones I knew were a result of the breakup and events that followed.

I'd noticed over the past few days that I'd been sleeping through the night and waking up well rested instead of in a pool of sweat in the early morning hours. There was something calming about her presence, or perhaps my mind was so occupied with her that it didn't have room to throw my trauma back at me, but I still didn't feel strong enough to reveal the darkest parts of my past.

I didn't want her to see me differently, to prove that my fears were true. I was weak, selfish, and I knew that. A stronger man would have told her everything. But I wasn't ready. I could hardly talk to my best friend about it. I still hid things from Reid, especially the fact I still had nightmares and occasional panic attacks.

CHAPTER TWENTY-THREE

I found myself back in the last place I ever thought I'd be this week: the grandstands, watching the first semifinal round of the Houston Rodeo. Colter hadn't asked me to come, but I wanted to show up for him like he had for me. I had swallowed my pride and I was here, even if it brought up feelings I didn't want to address.

I sat alone in the bleachers, not worried about anyone approaching me. Without my mother here, it felt like a small weight was lifted off my shoulders. I told her I was out with Isabelle tonight.

It wasn't something that she expected of me—more a testament to our mother-daughter relationship—but I always let her know if I was going somewhere in hopes that she wouldn't worry too much about me. She never really asked questions about my whereabouts and I knew it was because she trusted me—hell, I was twenty-three years old, so there was no reason for her to be suspicious. Besides the fact that I had been lying to her for the past week, something I'd never felt the need to do before.

Sometimes my guilty conscience caught up to me. *How*

could you lie so easily to your mother? I didn't think it was so much that lying was easy. I thought of it more as self-preservation. The less people who knew about Colter, the less hearts would get broken in the end.

I was watching the performance when a woman sat next to me. She couldn't have been much older than I was and she was holding a baby girl who didn't look more than a year old. The child was fussy, thrashing around, a toy in hand. Moments later, the toy flew out of the child's hand and landed on the ground, causing her to wail.

Before the woman could attempt to hold her child and also pick up the toy, I grabbed it for her.

"Oh, thank you," she said to me.

"Of course, it's no problem."

"I really appreciate it. This little one is a handful. I'm Cora." She introduced herself with a smile.

"Ellison. It's nice to meet you." I smiled back at her.

"Are you here for anyone?" she asked, while trying to settle her baby.

"Kind of." I didn't exactly know how to answer her question. Technically, yes, I was here for Colter, but I wasn't necessarily with him. "I'm a friend of Colter Carson."

"Oh, Colter is a sweet man."

"Yes, he is very sweet," I agreed.

"You're very lucky." She smiled at me, seemingly understanding what "friend" meant.

A feeling of jealousy washed over me for a moment, but I snapped out of it as my face flushed with embarrassment.

She has a kid.

Before I could say anything else, she let out a small laugh. "That look on your face tells me that he may be a little more than a friend." Her tone wasn't accusing at all, just slightly amused as I fought to make my expression more neutral.

"So, you know him pretty well?" I asked, changing the subject.

"He's friends with my husband, Wyatt. He and his roping partner, Reid, have stayed with us in Colorado before when they've been on the road. He's been through a lot in the past few years." She paused and lowered her voice a little. "Between you and me, I know it's hard for him to trust people, to really open up about his feelings and not only be the high-spirited personality that everyone sees at the rodeos, so you must be really special to him."

I let her words sink in for a second. I never once thought of Colter as being unable to trust people. Every time he'd been around me he had been open and honest, as far as I knew, but he did say his parents' divorce really affected him. So hearing it from someone else, that I was special to him, really solidified everything for me.

"Thank you. He's a great person, and I feel lucky to have met him. I want him to know how much it means to me that he cares. I want to be there for him too." I surprised myself by saying that out loud, but it was true. If other people could see what he saw, then maybe I could see it for what it was too. Colter liked being around me, and I liked being around him.

"He needs someone like that in his life. I'm glad he has you."

I tried to hide a smile. It felt nice to have everything validated. If a complete stranger could see my feelings for Colter, I wasn't going completely crazy. I could stop worrying about what might happen and just live in the moment for once. Relax.

I learned that her husband was also a team roper competing tonight. They had two kids, but the older one was hanging out with his grandparents. The younger one, the baby girl whose name was Olivia, was too fussy to be away from her mother for long periods of time, hence why she was with Cora.

"You never know, maybe taking her to rodeos all the time will inspire her to be like her dad one day," I found myself saying without a hint of sadness.

"Maybe." She smiled at the thought, looking at her daughter with all of the love in the world.

"Trust me, if you keep bringing her to these events, she will fall in love with it. She'll never want to leave the arena. Her dad will be her hero."

I thought back to my days as a kid, following my dad around in my cowboy boots and snap shirts. There were still happy memories, if I searched hard enough for them, dug through the pain and trauma. Seeing Cora and her daughter gave me hope that maybe one day I'd love rodeo again and I'd bring my kids here. Coming here today, without feeling an obligation to my mother, was a start. Baby steps.

CHAPTER TWENTY-FOUR

colter

W e were gearing up to rope in the semifinals after a brutal morning of waiting. Our semifinals group was good. There would be big competition tonight. Luckily, the team from Oklahoma was in the second semifinal group tomorrow, so we wouldn't have to compete against them. There was a good chance, though, that they would make it to the championship round, so if we advanced, we would have to be on our game in two days.

Wyatt and his roping partner had also made it to the semifinals and they were competing against us tonight. He had caught me earlier today before the rodeo had begun and wished me luck. If there was any competitor to have in your corner, it was Wyatt.

We were competing in the fourth spot out of ten today, early in the lineup. This meant we needed to do our absolute best because we wouldn't have an idea of what times to beat. This usually stressed me out, not having a goal time, but today I was calm and relaxed.

The events flew by, seemingly much quicker than

normal even though there were more competitors this round, and the announcers were preparing to start the team roping.

Bullet was restless. He hated waiting.

"It's almost time, buddy. Be patient." I gave him an assuring pat.

The first two teams had already taken their turns. The first duo, a couple of cowboys from Austin, clocked a five-point-six, a respectable time. The second team's heeler missed, giving them a no time and no shot at the gold buckle.

The third team was preparing to go, backing their horses into the boxes. They looked determined. I'd never seen them before and wasn't sure where they were from.

"Ladies and gentlemen, we've got ourselves a couple cowboys from Kansas just starting their rookie season. Let's give 'em a hand, folks."

Well, that explains it. It was rare for cowboys and cowgirls in their first season to compete here. They had to be decently good to get an invite.

I watched as the header gave the signal to open the chute and then his horse took off. They roped the steer quickly and easily. They were smooth, I had to give them that.

"Five-point-eight for the cowboys from Kansas!" the announcer called out. "Oh, but I've got some bad news for y'all. It appears they broke the barrier. Unfortunately, that's going to be an extra ten seconds added on to their time. Let's not let them leave without anything, give them a hand as they exit the arena."

Cheers and whistles erupted in the arena. That was one thing about rodeo, you never left with your head hung too low. People always cheered you on, win or lose, catch or no catch.

"Let's do this, buddy." Reid clapped me on the back as he walked past.

We had work to do. I gave him a nod of acknowledgment before mounting my horse and following Reid to the box.

"This next team comes from Silver Creek, Montana. If you missed them in the third series, you'll want to be paying attention to them tonight. They may be young, but they've got a lot of fire. Colter Carson and Reid Lawson, folks!" The announcer introduced us as I backed into the box.

Deep breath. You've got this. I controlled my breathing, steadying my heart rate until it was merely a light drum in my chest.

I nodded and the chute opened, the steer sprinting ahead. I kicked Bullet twice, his signal to get going. I swung the rope over my head three times, waiting for the perfect moment to throw and... *Catch! Yes! C'mon, Reid,* I thought. I turned the steer for Reid to have access to the hind legs, and he threw his rope perfectly, legally catching both.

"Clean! These boys are hot, *hot*, HOT!"

I looked up at the clock as the announcer boomed, "Five-point-two seconds! How about we give a great big round of applause for these cowboys from Silver Creek, Montana!"

The last six competitors' runs wrapped up before I could even comprehend what had just happened. It was one of our best runs yet and it was still so early in the year. I genuinely believed that by the NFR, we could be running in the three-second range. The record for team roping was three-point-three seconds, which was incredible. I wasn't trying to break any records today, though, so five-point-two was all good with me. I knew we had won the round, so Reid and I prepared to do our victory lap.

"Your semifinal round winners for tonight are Colter Carson and Reid Lawson! Let's help them as they take a lap around the arena, folks!" The announcer called us out as our horses took off running.

I was coming around the far corner of the arena when I saw her in the stands, standing up and cheering like she didn't have a care in the world. Like she belonged here.

Ellison. My girl.

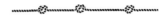

ellison

He was so natural out there, smiling as if he had been doing this his whole life. That smile was magnetic, and every girl here knew it. I was starting to remember why my parents loved rodeo so much, why I loved it so much.

I was watching the steer wrestling, praying nothing bad would happen, when Colter ran up to the spot in the stands where I was sitting. Cora had already left. Olivia was fussy and Wyatt was done roping, so she decided to call it.

He pulled me into a hug. "You came?" He sounded akin to a little kid.

"Of course I did. I wanted to be here for you."

His eyes softened for a moment as he pulled back and looked me in the face. Then he leaned back into the hug.

"That means so much to me." He released me from his arms. "Listen, I need to go back, but stay?"

I nodded. I wasn't planning on going anywhere. He flashed me a grin and ran back down the steps.

I sat and watched the remainder of the events—what was left of the steer wrestling, barrel racing, and then everyone's favorite, bull riding. I admired the wives of bull riders. It took a lot of strength to watch the person you love risk their lives every time they performed. Bull riding was obviously a dangerous sport, but could be extremely rewarding when you looked at the net worth of some of those cowboys.

After the bull riding was finished, they brought all of the semifinal winners down to the arena floor for them to be recognized and receive their prize money.

Colter and Reid had clinched their spot in the RodeoHouston Championship and they stood on the arena floor smiling like they had just won the Super Bowl.

I couldn't help myself. I smiled with them.

I waited for Colter after the rodeo, when the spectators started to file out of the stadium and all that was left were staff, livestock, and cowboys. The arena had a different feel without all the people surrounding it. It made me wonder who those cowboys and cowgirls were. When all the lights went out, who did they have to go home to? Where did they consider home? Was it the arena itself, or the comfort of someone's arms?

From what I gathered from Colter, rodeo was basically his life. I didn't know if he had someone to call when a day went badly, and I considered for a moment what it would be like to be that for him. To be someone's shoulder, someone's rock that they clung to when the waters got too rough. Someone to keep them from being pulled under. But then I wondered if I even had someone like that. Other than Isa and my mom, not really. At least not before Colter.

CHAPTER TWENTY-FIVE

colter

C heers, boys." Mikey raised his glass.

We were once again in the bars in downtown Houston. I had invited Ellison to come with us, but she said she couldn't go. Something about a dream she had and a guy in a really bad silverbelly hat. I wasn't about to ask, so here I was, hanging out with the boys instead.

"Hey, who was that girl you were talking to?" Jake asked me.

"Girl? And she's not *here*, Carson?" Mikey practically spit out his drink.

"No, she's not here." I rolled my eyes. *Were we really doing* this *again?*

"I'm starting to believe that this so-called 'girl' doesn't even exist." Mikey shrugged.

"Oh, she definitely exists. Haven't you noticed how wound up Colter's been lately?" Reid smirked.

I gave him a death glare, and he chuckled. He was just rubbing it in that he knew about my growing interest in Ellison and how much I thought about her. How her name seemed to echo in my thoughts and the sound of her voice ran circles around my brain.

Tomorrow we would be watching the second semifinal round, seeing who our competition would be when we competed again in two days. I should have been thinking about the championship, but the only thing on my mind was when I could see Ellison again.

"You must be right, Reid. I've been trying to get his attention for the last three minutes. You okay there, bud?"

I looked over at Mikey, who had his arms crossed over his chest and an amused grin on his face.

"Give me a break, will you?" *God, I need new friends who aren't so invested in my love life.*

"Come on, Colt, it's all in good fun. We haven't seen you this hung up on a girl in years," Mikey teased.

Yeah, because no girl after Sophie had ever captured my attention like Ellison.

"I guess I need to work on hiding my feelings better then, if you can see so clearly through me," I joked, and Reid winced a little. He knew what happened when I hid my feelings too much. When I shut everyone out. No one else knew, so they didn't think anything of it. They all thought I was being funny.

"I don't know about you guys, but I'm ready for a little break from being on the road." Reid changed the subject.

"What? You got a girl back home that we don't know about too?" Mikey nudged him a little.

"Nope, and don't even go there." Reid gave him a side-eyed look, quieting Mikey real quickly.

We continued to chat for a while before Mikey decided he wanted to go to another bar because he heard there was a mechanical bull. Not like he already rode bulls for a living.

"You coming with, Carson?" he asked as we started to file out of the bar.

"Nah, I think I'm going to head home. Hit the hay." I'd already stopped drinking for the night, anyway. I always made a conscious effort to know—and be mindful of—my limits when drinking so I didn't fall back into unhealthy habits.

"How about y'all?" He looked at Jake and Reid.

"Ah, fuck it. I'll come." Jake shrugged.

"I'm good, man. I'm gonna head back with Colt." Reid tilted his head toward me.

"Suit yourselves. We'll see you tomorrow morning, then."

We parted ways with Mikey and Jake and started to walk toward our trucks.

"You really like her, don't you?" Reid put his hands in his pockets as he walked alongside me.

The city was still very much alive, despite it being almost ten o'clock. The sound of people filing in and out of crowded bars and traffic in the distance filled the air.

"Yeah, I do. She came to the rodeo today. I didn't even ask her to, and I know it was a lot for her." I explained as much as I could without revealing the secret about her dad. That was Ellison's story to tell, not mine.

"I know how much it means to you to have people show up for you," he replied, understanding what I meant.

"She's special, Reid. She doesn't look at me with pity or like she wants to fix me. I feel like I can trust her, tell her about the parts of me that the world doesn't see."

"So, have you told her about Sophie, then?"

Fuck. I knew he would ask this.

I sighed. "That's the one thing I haven't told her. It's not that I'm worried about Sophie and the fact I was engaged, it's the stuff that happened after." The drinking, the anger. The feeling that I wasn't deserving of anything, anyone. It wasn't just an elephant in the room. It was a ticking time bomb, waiting to destroy everything I'd rebuilt for myself since I pulled myself out of the darkness.

"If she's really like you say she is, Colt, she won't judge you. You said it yourself, she doesn't want to fix you. But you'll have to tell her sooner or later."

"I'm not ready to fail again." It was a terrible thing to say, I knew that. But no matter how often people told me that Sophie leaving wasn't my fault, I couldn't bring myself to believe them. In my eyes, there was always more I could have done, more I could have said. I carried the weight of the breakup like a cross on my back. I might not have had physical scars from our relationship, but the cuts ran deeper than anybody realized.

"I know, buddy." Reid had been through this with me before, and I knew I could count on him to stand by me now too.

I had plenty of time before the second semifinal round tonight. There wasn't an urgency to practice right now as we would be able to get in one last run tomorrow morning before the championship. I had a few different options. Hang out with the guys, do something on my own, or try to see Ellison again.

The answer was obvious. I pulled out my phone to send her a message, but she had beaten me to it.

BLAZE

Hey Sparky. Dying to get off the ranch.
You in?

You read my mind. Where to, Blaze?

BLAZE

There's a park fairly close to the stadium

I'm in the mood to just walk. But I don't
want to be out here right now

Works for me.

I'd arrived at the park far before Ellison did. It was also conveniently next to the Houston Zoo. I hadn't been to a zoo in years. Billings had one and my parents took us once as kids, but I couldn't say it was something I sought out in the cities I traveled to.

I waited in my truck until I saw her pull into the parking lot. She looked so focused when she was driving, more serious than she normally did. I was sure I looked weird to people walking by, with a huge, goofy grin plastered across my face, but I couldn't help myself. I noticed everything about her, it was hard not to smile.

I stepped out of my vehicle and walked over to the parking spot she had pulled into. She was looking in her rearview mirror and fluffing an eyelash when I got next to her car. Careful not to startle her, I tapped lightly on the window. She whipped her head around to face me, but once she realized it was me, her face relaxed.

She opened the door and I grabbed the handle, pulling it open the rest of the way for her.

"You know, you probably shouldn't just tap on people's

windows like that." She gave me a cheeky look as she got out of the car.

"Why? Did I scare you?" I teased.

"No." Her eyes narrowed.

"Are you sure?" I enjoyed pushing her buttons.

"Yes, now get out of the way so I can get out and close the door." Although she rolled her eyes, there was a small glint of playfulness in them as I kept my hand on the door and extended the other to her. She sighed out of her nose and grabbed my hand, accepting the help getting out of her car. I closed the car door before she could try to and soon after she locked it.

"So, what do you want to do?" I asked.

"I already told you, I wanted to go for a walk. Get some fresh air." She looked at me but kept walking.

I looked in the direction of the urban park and then toward the zoo.

"You keep looking at the zoo. Is there something you're not telling me, Sparky?" She bumped into me as we walked next to each other, purposely crossing into my path.

"I just haven't been to a zoo in years. I was surprised to see one," I admitted.

"Do you want to go to the zoo?" she asked softly, lowering her eyes a little.

"Was this your plan all along, Blaze?" I teased her, using the nickname that I'd come up for her shortly after we'd met.

"No, I didn't think anything of it. And what's the deal with the name? You called me that earlier too."

"Well, you call me Sparky," I offered.

"And? What does that have to do with anything?" Her steps paused, and she looked confused as ever.

"If I'm a spark, then you're the blaze that keeps me feeling alive. You fuel my fire."

It was true. Sure, rodeo gave me a purpose for my life, but meeting Ellison had made everything I'd gone through leading up to this point worth it. Before her, I'd only been going through the motions and everything was solely based on habits. But with her, everything had changed.

"You're so cheesy." She scoffed, but I could see her trying to hide the smile on her face. "Let's go to the fucking zoo then." She laughed, a real laugh, and it was music to my ears.

The line to get tickets was long. A couple times, I debated grabbing Ellison's hand and dragging her away. We could find something else to do—all I wanted was to spend time with her—but then the line started moving a bit quicker and we were almost to the window.

"Good morning, folks! What can I do for you today?" the employee at the window greeted us.

"Just two adults." I handed my card through the small hole in the window in exchange for two tickets. I handed Ellison the tickets, and she grinned like a little kid on Christmas.

We walked through the gates and were welcomed by signs pointing us toward different exhibits, vendors selling food and T-shirts, and hundreds of people.

Ellison pulled me over to a larger map of the zoo. If we went right, we would be heading toward the more aquatic animals, including the sharks and penguins. If we went left, it was elephants and monkeys.

She looked up at the map, one hand up to her face, her index finger tapping her lips as if she couldn't make a decision.

"Which way are you thinking?" I stood next to her and looked down at her face, still in complete focus.

"I have no idea."

"Flip a coin. Heads we go right, tails we go left."

"All right. Do you have a coin?" She took her focus off the map for a moment.

I dug in my pockets, looking for any loose change, but I came up short.

"There goes that plan," she muttered, obviously amused.

"Well, what's your favorite animal?" I asked, trying something different.

"Probably a giraffe."

I traced the map to where the giraffe exhibit was. It was located near the back of the zoo, so we'd have the chance to go by other exhibits first.

"Looks like we're going right." I brushed my fingers against hers, testing the waters, waiting for a sign to interlock them with hers. She didn't pull away from the touch, but I noticed her cheeks flush a little.

I tried to move my hand away from hers, but instead of letting me, she laced her pinky around mine, keeping our hands entwined.

We turned toward the aquatic exhibits—the penguins, sea lions, and sharks.

"You want to know a fun fact about penguins?" I asked.

She was leaning on the railing in front of the glass that blocked the penguin exhibit from patrons and looking at the animals as they dove into the water and then popped back up to shore.

"Sure, go for it."

"They don't pay taxes."

"Oh my God." She elbowed my ribs at my bad joke attempt. She was unable to keep the grin off her face, though, as she turned back to the glass. It was hard not to notice how happy she looked. I liked this side of her, the carefree, easy going side.

I was so deep in thought that I hadn't noticed she was no longer next to me. Slight alarm rose in my chest. What if someone had grabbed her? I knew she was a grown adult and could no doubt take care of herself, but it didn't stop me from worrying about her. I looked around, trying to spot her, but she was nowhere to be found. I started walking toward the next exhibit; maybe she had kept going. I was scanning the tunnel ahead, not really paying attention to anything else. I turned a dark corner and a hand reached out and grasped my arm, causing me to jump.

"Got you!" Ellison stepped out into the light, a wicked grin on her face, her eyes lighting up.

"Watch yourself, Blaze. I'm going to get you back. It may not be today or tomorrow, but I will," I joked around with her, not considering the weight of my words and the silent prayer I was sending up to let me keep her around.

ellison

After the jump scare in the penguin exhibit, we continued walking, going through the underwater tunnel and watching the sharks and fish swim above us. Colter wrapped his arm around my waist as we walked, pulling me closer to him.

I was confident that, to other people, we looked like a real couple—a happy one at that. And if anyone asked, I didn't think I would correct them. I was more than happy to pretend, even if it was for the day. I was content in this little bubble we were living in.

It was funny how quickly my mindset could shift. I don't think I could have felt this way with anyone else, though—any other cowboy. Colter was different. He was special.

We made our way around the zoo, stopping at exhibits we thought were interesting.

"If you could have any wild animal as a pet, what would you have?" Colter was always full of weird questions, or at least questions that people didn't normally ask.

"You know those tiny little African cats? Black-footed cats, I think they're called. The ones who are the size of domestic cats but are still deadly? I'd have one of those." I had seen a few videos of them. "How about you?"

"I'd have a bison. I know they're basically murder cows, but I love them. They're just so…large."

That checks out for a cowboy. I suppressed a giggle. "You wouldn't have a lion or a gorilla?"

"Nope. Where would I even keep a lion or gorilla in Montana? At least having a bison would make sense."

"What, you'd keep him in your arena?" I teased.

"That's exactly what I'd do."

We had taken our time, but we finally made it over to the giraffe exhibit.

"Why do you love giraffes so much?" Colter asked me as we approached the exhibit.

"I don't know, I kind of always have. They're gentle and quiet, living and getting by pretty simply, but they can also be dangerous if they choose to be, you know?" They were kind of like me, besides the gentle part. I also loved giraffes because my dad always took me to the zoo to feed them. He'd lift me up onto his shoulders and hold me there while I let the giraffe lick the food out of my hand.

We stayed and watched the giraffes a little longer, but opted out of feeding them. Though I loved doing it as a kid, the idea of letting a giant giraffe eat out of my hand now as an adult felt kind of strange.

A couple of hours later, we had walked the entire perimeter of the zoo, taking in all of the exhibits and enjoying each other's company. I wasn't ready for the day to be over. It was one of the most fun days I'd had in a while.

"It's about three-thirty now." Colter checked his watch

when we had reached the entrance gates again. "I'll need to be back at the trailer around five, but I'm all yours until then." He had read my mind. Or perhaps he also wasn't ready to say goodbye yet.

"I know just the spot." I smiled and instinctively grabbed his hand, pulling him along behind me. It was a short walk from here, so there was no need to drive.

When he had matched my stride again—it had only taken him about three steps—he laced his fingers with mine, and I let him. I could still let myself pretend this was real. Let it be a distraction from the reality that Colter was leaving in two days.

"So, are you going to tell me where you're taking me?" Colter asked, still holding my hand and walking in sync with my steps.

"Have a little patience. We're almost there." I was giddy with excitement. I hadn't been to this place since my dad was still alive. Normally, it would have been weird to go here, but something had changed in me. I wanted to make new associations and memories of this place—with Colter.

"All right, but if you're planning to murder me, at least let me call Reid. He'd probably be a little disappointed if his header died."

I laughed, thinking about how confused his roping partner would be. I'd never met him, but Colter had talked about him a bit and said good things.

"Tell me more about Reid."

He knew so much about me, but I was curious about him too.

"We met in college. I'm a year older than him, so we started roping together when he was a freshman and I was a sophomore. We became friends pretty quickly, but the first time we met I was honestly a bit of an ass. I had just come off a successful freshman season and I was a bit arrogant." He paused as a smirk came across his face. "The first time I met Reid, I was getting ready to practice and he came into the arena. He looked like a true freshman, a little bit nervous, and I thought I could mess with him a little. Well, he put me in my place real quick, showing me he was just as good a roper as I was.

"I was a cocky fuck and thought it would be funny to rope his leg as he was running across the arena. Well, I missed and then he got back at me later when he actually caught me, causing me to fall face first into the dirt." He laughed at the memory, and I could tell right away how close they were.

I had to give him shit, though. "Colter Carson being cocky? I could never imagine that."

"Hey, I'm very humble, thank you very much." He feigned offense.

"Sure, you're as humble as my hair is red," I joked, even though I knew Colter was one of the better cowboys. Sure, he was good at what he did, but he didn't flaunt his money or boast about it.

We were about fifty paces away from the small ice cream shop. It was a little kiosk-type shop with mint-colored paint and pastel tables and chairs surrounding it. It was my favorite place growing up.

"Here we are." I gestured to the flag that read, "The Inside Scoop."

"What if I told you I was lactose intolerant?" He looked at me, wringing his hands as though he was nervous.

"Then I wouldn't believe you because I saw you down that milkshake at The Legless Cow. Besides, everyone knows that lactose intolerant people just ignore their lactose intolerance. Ice cream is too good to resist!" I was practically squealing as I peered at the sign to see the flavors they offered, even though I knew exactly what I was going to get.

If there was anything that put me in a fantastic mood, it was ice cream. I might have been cold and reserved most of the time, but ice cream warmed my heart.

"All right, you got me. I do love ice cream, but the real test is what flavor you get. There's only one correct answer and—" he started to say.

"And it's obviously Neapolitan!" I cut him off.

"The answer is very clearly cookies and cream. What kind of person eats Neapolitan ice cream?" He looked at me like I was crazy.

What could I say? Neapolitan was my dad's favorite. He would eat the strawberry parts, I would eat the chocolate, and we would share the vanilla.

"Dad! That's my flavor!" I complained as Dad took a big spoonful of the chocolate part.

"I'm sorry, Sunshine. Here, you can have some of mine." He offered me a bit of his strawberry flavor.

"No, strawberry's gross." I pouted.

"Well, how are we going to settle this then?" He raised his eyebrows at me, knowing what my answer would be. It was my answer every time.

"I get to come to the next rodeo with you!" I giggled. "And I get to ride the horses!"

It was always our way of compromising. I shared my ice cream, and Dad shared his passion with me. No matter how far away the rodeo was, Dad always upheld his promises, and I always got to go with him.

"It's my favorite and that's all that matters."

We were getting closer to ordering. There were only a couple people in front of us.

"Hi! How can I help you today?" the girl working the kiosk asked cheerily. She looked young and overjoyed to be serving people ice cream.

"I'll take a double scoop of Neapolitan in a waffle cone." I beamed and handed her my card then gestured at Colter. "I'll also get whatever he wants."

"I'll have a double scoop as well in a waffle cone, please, but I'll take the best flavor there is, which is cookies and cream." He winked at me.

"I'll have those right out." She looked between the two of us, clearly fascinated by our ice cream debate. She came back a moment later with our cones, and we moved to a table to continue our conversation.

"Give me three good reasons why cookies and cream is better than Neapolitan." I turned to Colter in between licks and crossed my arms.

"Easy. One, there's Oreos, obviously. Two, it's still chocolate, but it's not overbearing or too chocolatey, and three, it's just superior." He lifted a finger with each point.

"Okay, the last one was not a good reason." I rolled my eyes.

"Then you give me three good reasons why Neapolitan is better than cookies and cream," he challenged me, but I was prepared.

"One, it's three flavors in one. Two, it basically tastes like a banana split, without the banana, which is fine because who likes bananas? And three, it's the *perfect* ice cream for sharing. If you don't like a flavor, you can let someone else eat it and there's no arguing about who gets more." *Mic drop.*

"You put up a good case there, Blaze, but I hate to tell you, you're still wrong."

"How much do you want to bet?" I tilted my head, putting my hands on my hips for extra attitude.

"If you can find more people who like Neapolitan than cookies and cream, then I will not only admit I'm wrong but also declare to this entire park that Neapolitan ice cream is superior to cookies and cream, even though it's clearly not true."

"And if I can't?"

"If you can't, then you have to come to the rodeo tomorrow so you can watch me win the damn thing." He winked, and I considered the terms.

It would be pretty satisfying for Colter to tell everyone in this park—there were probably two hundred people here—that he was wrong. And going to the rodeo wouldn't be terrible if I had to go, especially if it meant I could spend more time with Colter before he left.

"You have yourself a deal, Sparky. Be prepared to lose!"

He had a stupid grin on his face the entire time as he watched me go from table to table, group to group, asking people what type of ice cream was better.

"Cookies and cream for sure," a college-aged couple said.

"The only type of people who eat Neapolitan ice cream are old people...and apparently you." A little boy looked me up and down as he expressed his distaste for it.

Even the elderly people had to agree with Colter. "Between the two, I'd choose cookies and cream. But if butter pecan was in the picture I would pick that."

"I would rather have a hot fudge sundae," an older man crooned.

"So, how did that go for you?" Colter raised his eyebrows as I came back to him, feeling slightly defeated.

"Shut up, cowboy." I rolled my eyes.

"It's okay, honey, not everyone can have amazing taste in ice cream."

I raised my eyebrow at his use of "honey." I playfully pushed away from him, pretending I was upset.

"Hey, it was just a joke." He put his arm around me to try to console me, unaware of my sneak attack plan.

"Oh, I know, I just wanted to do this," I teased right before I stuck the remaining scoop of my ice cream smack in the middle of his nose.

"Oh, you're going to pay for that," he roared as he tried to grab my arm and press his ice cream into my face.

I was too quick for him, though, and I raced away, knowing he was about to chase me through this park.

I ran as fast as I could, my lungs burning as I zigged and zagged through people. I was laughing as I ran, my ice cream melting down the cone and onto my hand.

This was arguably one of the best days of my life. I felt free, weightless, like all of my concerns about what dating a cowboy would entail had faded. In the moment, I didn't care what it would mean for me, for us. I forgot about my vow to separate myself from rodeo, forgot about my dad's death. I didn't know what long distance dating a cowboy would look like, didn't know if that was something Colter even wanted, but what I did know was that I didn't want to let him go.

CHAPTER TWENTY-SEVEN

colter

I ran behind Ellison after tossing my ice cream cone in a trash can, slowly catching up to her with each stride. When I finally caught up to her, I wrapped my arms around her, lifting her in the air and spinning her around, causing her melted ice cream to drip all over us.

"Stop. Colter, stop! I'm getting ice cream everywhere!" she squealed and laughed.

What a beautiful sound. I put her down, and she turned around to face me. There was sticky ice cream all over her hair and face, but she still looked radiant with the mid-afternoon sun casting a glow behind her hair like a halo.

"What are you looking at?" She turned her head to see if there was anything behind her.

"Just you."

"Is there something on my face? Come on, Colter, tell me."

God, I loved seeing her get all flustered like this. I mean, there was ice cream on her face, I wouldn't lie about that, but that's not what I was looking at.

I also didn't lie when I said I was only looking at her.

Because I was. I was looking at how her eyelashes perfectly framed her baby-blue eyes—eyes more vibrant than the clearest sky, more sparkling than the waters in the Maldives. The way her nose perfectly sloped, and her lips. She was perfection. If I didn't know better, I would have thought she was sent down from God himself.

"Here." I swiped my thumb across her cheek where ice cream was dripping down, not answering her question of what I was looking at.

"Oh. Thanks." She blushed, seemingly hyper aware of how intimate the interaction was.

I smiled at her, but then my phone started buzzing in my back pocket. *Right on time.* Figures someone would call me whenever Ellison and I were getting closer.

"Colter Carson," I answered the phone as if a stranger was calling, even though I knew exactly who it was.

"Where the fuck are you?" Mikey's voice growled on the other end of the line.

"Out." I wasn't going to tell him exactly where I was, or else I'd be hearing about it for the rest of the day and probably tomorrow too.

"Well, get your ass back to the trailer. It's already four-thirty."

Fuck. It's already been an hour?

"All right, don't bite my head off. I'll be there soon." I hung up the phone before he could say anything else. Since when was Mikey such a stickler for being on time?

"The guys need me," I apologized to Ellison as I stuck my phone back in my pocket.

"I understand," she murmured, even though she looked a little sad. Was she having as much fun as I was then? Was she also dreading the moment I'd have to pack up and drive away from Houston?

We started to walk back to our vehicles, hand in hand, through the park and by the ice cream place we had just been to. I was going to miss this girl like hell when I left in two days.

When we got back to her car and she let go of my hand, I held it out palm up for her. She gave me a quizzical look and I nodded my head to her hand. Reluctantly, she gave me her hand, like she thought I was about to trick her. No funny business here, though.

"I'll see you later." I brought the top of her hand up to my lips.

"Bye," she whispered, getting into her car and shutting the door.

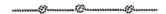

I pulled into the lot where the trailers were parked at exactly 4:58. The boys were standing outside like they had been waiting for me to get back. I had no idea why; they weren't my fucking babysitters. Jake and Reid looked bored, but Mikey? Mikey looked downright pissed. God knows why. It wasn't like we hadn't had to wait on his ass multiple times before because he was trying to pick up a girl.

"Nice of you to show up, Carson," Mikey grumbled, his arms crossed over his chest.

"Did I miss the memo about us doing something today besides going to watch the competition? Because it sure as hell didn't look like you were coming out of your trailer bright and early this morning," I pointed out.

He had likely brought home a girl last night because by ten this morning, he still wasn't up and moving.

"We've been waiting for *you*!" he snapped.

167

The fuck?

Mikey could be an ass, but he usually wasn't like this.

"Watch yourself, Mikey." Reid intervened. He didn't know where I was, but he probably could have guessed I was out with Ellison.

"Yeah, Michael, have a little patience, it might do you some good." Jake smirked.

"Yeah, yeah, patience is a virtue. Well, I have none," he grumbled in response.

"Well, I'm here now, so let's get on with it." I wasn't taking any of Mikey's shit. He wanted me to find a woman down here in Houston? Well, I found myself one. And I wasn't planning on sharing.

He grumbled something I couldn't hear before walking off. I loved Mikey, he was still my brother, but sometimes he could be a giant pain in the ass.

"What's his deal?" I asked Reid.

"Don't ask me, dude. I'm just as confused as you are." He shrugged.

"The girl he was with probably said his dick was small or something," Jake snorted.

"Yeah, either that, or he's meeting a girl *at* the rodeo," Reid added.

We all chuckled as we followed a still-steaming Mikey, who got a little grumpy at times if you messed with his sex life.

We got inside early enough before everything would start that I was slightly annoyed I rushed back here so quickly. If I wasn't seeing Ellison again tomorrow, I would have been much more irritable. I wanted to soak up every moment I got with her.

"Ladies and gentlemen, please join us as we rise and remove our hats—" The rodeo was about to begin as the announcer called for everyone to stand for the national anthem.

I took off my cowboy hat, placing it over my heart. The anthem and prayer were like TV static, blocked out by the sound of Ellison's laugh and the way she called me Sparky.

I hadn't noticed that everyone had already sat down and I was still standing with my hand over my heart.

Jake and Reid were trying to hold back a snicker as I gave them a glare and took my seat. Mikey was off doing God knows what somewhere else, so he wasn't sitting with us.

"This girl must really have you whipped, Colter." Jake elbowed me in the ribs. "I've never seen you like this."

"As long as he's focused tomorrow, that's all that matters." Reid flashed me a grin.

"Yeah, yeah. I'll just remember this the next time you meet a girl. There won't be any mercy for you then." I tried to turn my focus away from the guys and toward the rodeo. They had started the bareback riding.

It was always interesting to watch the other events and see the types of people who were competing as well as their demeanor and attitude. There was usually quite a mixed bag as far as arrogance went. Most of the cowboys were good sports, but occasionally you'd have someone who needed to get off their high horse.

The worst I'd ever seen was somebody getting thrown from a horse because another competitor had messed with their saddle. Apparently, they had beef with each other outside of rodeo and he decided to bring his drama into the arena. Needless to say, he got a hefty fine for it. He was lucky he didn't lose his career, or at the very least get barred from the arena.

There were ten competitors in each semifinal round. The top five from each would move onto the championship. There were some great roping teams competing tonight. Not only were Dash and Wayne competing, there was also a team from Arkansas in this round who had been to the NFR last year. I wasn't familiar with all of the teams, but I recognized a couple of names on the day sheet.

"Look, those guys from Utah that we saw last year in Arizona are on here." I pointed their names out to Reid.

"Damn, I was honestly not expecting that," he replied. That specific team must have improved quite a bit from last year if they were here in Houston, especially in the semifinals round.

A gasp from the crowd broke up our conversation. My head shot up to see what had happened for the crowd to all collectively react like that. By the time I looked up, the rider was already out of the arena, but the instant replay showed that he nearly got stepped on by the bronc.

When it came to sports injuries, rodeo was up there in the ranks of boxing, football, and hockey. Some could even argue that it was *the* most dangerous sport. You risked your life—or at minimum a finger—every time you stepped into the arena.

I never understood how people thought it was animal abuse. If anything, it was *cowboy* abuse. Anybody who has ever met a rodeo family, knows a lick about agriculture, or has been involved in the sport would know these folks cared more about the animals than most people they knew.

The animals being well taken care of was not up for debate.

One of the worst deaths in the rodeo world since Lane Frost had been Levi Merritt. Both were young, with bright futures ahead of them. From the stories I'd heard, they both lit up a room the moment they walked in. The loss of Lane Frost changed the course of rodeo, though, in terms of safety.

Occasionally, there would be scares. But the show went on—it had to.

The rest of the events up until the team roping were uneventful, and then it was time. Team roping. I started wringing my hands, becoming eager for the chute to open —to watch the very thing that gave me such a rush. There were only two things that made me feel like I wasn't so empty, made me feel electrified, as though I had a purpose in life; one of those things was roping.

The first team to rope was the duo from Utah. Although they had made it this far, their technique today looked sloppy. They finished with a time of seven-point-eight seconds. Unless several teams got no time or broke the barrier, they almost certainly wouldn't be moving on.

A couple of teams did get no times for failing to catch their steer. It had to be frustrating to make it this far in the competition just to be unsuccessful at the thing you'd trained so hard to do. Even more frustrating, though, was breaking the barrier. Feeling on top of the world with a great time, just to have ten seconds added on because you got a little too hasty.

Next, the team from Arkansas would rope, followed by Dash and Wayne. Cade and Cameron Maxwell were brothers from a small town outside of Fayetteville. They were both built a bit larger and stockier than Reid and I were, muscles grown from working in a mechanic's shop. They didn't come from a rodeo family, didn't have a legacy passed down to them from their parents. How they ended up roping, I didn't know, but there were all sorts of rumors about it.

Some people claim they had worked on a ranch a couple summers, got good at riding and then tried their hand at roping and were naturals at it. Others say a rodeo legend had met them when he was passing through their town, made an offhand comment about them looking like they could be great cowboys, and then started mentoring them.

Regardless of how they got their start, they were damn good. They were a team that should not be underestimated.

Cade lifted his chin and the chute opened, the steer exploding out of the gate. Despite their size, their motions were expert and smooth, graceful like figure skaters out on the ice. There were no jerks or rough movements. They had the steer roped in an impressive five-point-three seconds.

At last, the team everyone had been waiting to watch geared up to compete: Dash Kingsley and Wayne Marlow. They were a force to be reckoned with in the arena, and they knew it. They held their heads high with pride as they led their horses into their starting points. Dash had a smirk on his face, as if he already knew they were going to dominate the competition tonight.

I'd never met Dash and Wayne, but they got mixed reviews from everyone they'd met. The women were usually the ones leaving sparkling reviews. The men were more fifty-fifty.

Right before they opened the chute, Dash looked into

the crowd and flashed the women his signature smile, the camera picking it up and displaying it on the jumbo screen. I rolled my eyes as a girl a few rows in front of us nearly fainted.

"Get a load of that bullshit." Jake wrinkled his nose.

"They act like they've already won the championship," Reid muttered, a look of contempt on his face. If there was one thing Reid hated, it was people who acted like they were better than everyone else. Not sure how he handled me as his partner in college at times, but he probably tolerated it because he knew he could put me in my place.

"Maybe they think tonight's the championship and they won't show up tomorrow." My retort earned me a snort from Reid.

"Yeah, if only."

We turned our attention back to the arena, right as the chute opened. Kingsley flew out on his horse, roping the horns faster than I'd ever seen anyone rope. Marlow was right behind, catching the feet like he did this in his sleep. I gave Reid a look of half annoyance, half awe as we waited for the announcer to call out their time.

"Ladies and gentlemen, give these young men a round of applause! With a time of four-point-eight seconds, that time is going to put these cowboys at the top of the leaderboard for tonight! Dash Kingsley and Wayne Marlow, folks! Keep the excitement going for them as they take a lap around the arena with the sponsor flag!"

At least we knew who our biggest competition would be tomorrow. A flutter of nerves pooled in my stomach. Reid and I would have to be at the top of our game. These were NFR times that Dash and Wayne were running.

Lord help us if we want to take home gold.

CHAPTER TWENTY-EIGHT

ellison

Today was championship day. Anticipation grew in me the moment I woke up. It had been over fifteen years since I'd looked forward to going to a rodeo this much. I debated telling my mother what was going on as I went through the pros and cons list I had made up in my head.

Pros: She would no doubt be supportive of me, happy even that I was finding my way back to the arena on my own accord. I wouldn't feel like I was keeping a secret from her anymore when I went out to see Colter.

Cons: She would be happy that I was falling in love with rodeo again. It would create a new expectation of going to more of them. She might think I had changed my mind about the sport. She would also know about Colter.

I decided on not telling her, at least not yet. Maybe one day we'd be able to laugh about the time I accidentally caught feelings for a cowboy. Like mother, like daughter. But right now, it would only complicate things more tomorrow and in the days following Colter's departure.

Hell, I didn't even know if Colter and I would continue

to talk. I was secretly hoping the answer was yes, even if it meant I'd potentially have to be the one reaching out constantly. I shuddered a little, thinking about the possibility. Hopefully, it would be equal and I wouldn't come off as desperate.

I was probably just overthinking again. It seemed to be one of the things I did best, besides pushing people away and making sarcastic remarks.

I walked down the hallway into the living room. Mom was sitting on the couch, reading a book with the HGTV channel on in the background. It was rare to see her relaxing on the couch and not being a mom or the owner of the ranch.

"Hey, Mom," I greeted her, and she turned to face me, abandoning whatever book she was reading. It must not have been that exciting if she was able to so easily tear her eyes away from it. Normally, if she was reading, she required zero interruptions, or she flat out didn't pay attention.

"Good morning, sweetie." She smiled, putting a bookmark into the pages and setting down the book. "What are you up to today?"

"Probably will see if anyone needs help around the ranch and then I might go see Isa later tonight," I lied.

"Oh, you aren't going to go see that cowboy of yours?"

Huh?

She had completely caught me off guard.

"What do you mean, cowboy of mine?" I was treading lightly. So much for my plan of not telling her.

"You didn't think you could keep it a secret from me did you?" She laughed. "I know you haven't been going to see Isabelle every day this week."

"How, though?"

"I'm a mother, Ellison. I just know things. Besides, you're not as good a liar as you think. Isabelle was here yesterday morning after you left. Brought over some of those 'kitchen sink' cookies she always makes."

Damn it, Isa.

"Okay, fine. All right, yes. I'm going to the rodeo tonight. He asked me to go. Well, kind of. I lost a bet," I mumbled.

"It'll be good for you. I like seeing you like this." She gave me a knowing look.

"And how's that?" I wanted to know how she knew all of these things.

"Happy." She went back to her book, leaving me speechless.

ACE

Text me when you get inside and I'll see if I can sneak away to find you.

I was almost to the stadium when my phone pinged with the message from Colter. I had decided to leave earlier than normal, getting to NRG Stadium an hour before the rodeo started, because I knew his focus would have to be completely on roping and a small part of me hoped that I would get to see him before the rodeo began.

I pulled into the stadium parking lot, noticing that there were way more cars than I had expected at this time. It was championship night, though, so it made sense.

I strode through the main doors and walked through the sea of people before shooting Colter a text telling him I was here.

I didn't want to find my seat only to sit there for the next hour, so I decided to just walk around the stadium, regardless of how strange it looked. I was on my second lap around when I thought I saw someone I recognized, so I looked away for a split second. By the time I looked forward again, it was too late to stop myself and I ran right into Colter's arms.

"We've gotta stop meeting like this, Blaze." He smirked. "Don't run away from me this time, though."

"Wasn't planning on it," I quipped.

"Good to see you here. I didn't know if you'd actually hold up your end of the bet," he teased.

"Trust me, I keep my promises. Those are sacred to me," I responded.

If there was one thing my parents taught me, it was that you never break a promise. Most promises were made only to be broken, but not mine. Not ours.

"Noted. Where's your seat?" he asked.

I pulled out my phone and navigated to my wallet app to find my ticket. "Um, section 322, row twelve, seat twenty-one," I read it off to him.

"Those aren't bad. How'd you swing that?"

"StubHub." I shrugged. Finding a ticket that wouldn't break the bank was difficult, but I managed to snag one of the last tickets that wasn't in the nosebleeds and wasn't going for three hundred dollars or more.

"Well, if I could, I'd have you right down there with me, in the action seats. So you can be up close and personal."

"Maybe next year." I winked.

"Is that a promise?" He raised his eyebrows at me. I would be a fool to promise him something like that, especially after telling him that promises were something I kept.

"We'll see, Sparks." I couldn't guarantee that, not yet. A year was a long time. Even as his face fell a little, looking like I had just run over his dog or something, I couldn't bring myself to make the promise.

"Stick around after everything is over?" He dropped it, changing the subject to the here and now.

"Yeah, I can do that." I was trying to play it cool, even though my heart was screaming, *Of course I'm going to stay!*

For the first time in years, I was feeling something other than grief. If I was what kept Colter feeling alive, then I didn't know how to describe what he was for me.

"Good. I'll see you in there." He leaned in to kiss my cheek, and the featherlight touch from his lips sent a chill down my spine, leaving the spot warm and burning long after he lifted away.

CHAPTER TWENTY-NINE

She sucked in a breath as I lightly pressed my lips to her cheek. I needed to go, as much as I hated the idea of it, but if I didn't, this entire stadium would see my attraction to Ellison. And as much as I wanted to claim her as mine, sporting a semi for everyone to see was not the way to do it.

I gave her a parting wave and went back to find Reid. It was now about twenty minutes until showtime.

We're going to win this. I repeated the affirmation in my head over and over until I stepped onto the arena floor, finding Reid leaning up against a gate behind the roping chute and boxes.

"You good? Ready for this?" he asked, seemingly knowing I was just with Ellison. If he sensed a wave of distractedness coming off of me, he didn't say anything. He knew that when the time came, I would be on my A game. We trusted each other.

"Ready as I'll ever be, bud." I patted him on the shoulder before leaning up against the fence next to him.

There was this weird feeling deep in my stomach, one that seemed to flutter in and out, but I ignored it.

About twenty minutes later, the lights went low in the stadium and spotlights kicked on overhead. The sound of an electric guitar and drums filled the stadium as the introduction of Cody Johnson's "Welcome to the Show" started to play.

"Ladies and gentlemen, you've been here with us the past nineteen days. You've seen these cowboys and cowgirls ride their hearts out on this arena floor, all for the opportunity to increase their winnings by $50,000 and take home a gold buckle and custom saddle. Let me hear you! *Are you ready for championship night?*"

The crowd erupted in screams and whistles. The excitement was comparable to the NFR.

"Let's get 'er done." Reid grinned.

Waiting was the hardest part. I'd said it before, but it never got easier. With every moment of anticipation, it seemed that both excitement and nerves grew. It was important not to let nerves overtake you, but I had never had any issues with them before.

"All right, folks. We're moving on to team roping. We've got the ten best cowboy duos from the preceding weeks!"

Reid and I were near the end of the lineup. We weren't last; the team from Oklahoma had been given that spot. But we weren't first either, which had been reassuring.

I watched the jumbo screen as team after team roped. *Six-point-two seconds, five-point-five, five-point-nine.* Each was beatable.

"Folks, you've seen them dominate the arena all week.

Help me bring out our next cowboys, from Silver Creek, Montana: Colter Carson and Reid Lawson!"

Hearing our names amplified the sense of dread in my chest that I didn't realize had been lingering.

What is happening to me? Fuck. It was rare that this happened so soon before a competition. If anything, I just had bad dreams the night before or light nerves that I could shake off without any problems. Never anything like this.

I blinked a couple times, trying to clear my vision and make the black dots around the edge of my line of sight disappear. The stadium was suddenly too hot, and my heart pounded in my ears in a painful rhythm.

I'm not sure if I can do this. My brain threatened to shut me down, to throw me into one of those flashbacks that sometimes kept me awake at night.

You're nothing but a failure. Weak. You'll never amount to anything.

I frantically scanned the arena, trying to find something I could focus on to ground me.

It was at that moment that the cameras panned over the crowd and I saw her on screen. Her eyes were trained ahead, focused and hard as stone.

She came here for you.

I couldn't see her from the floor, but that moment the camera paused on her section in the crowd was all I needed to catch my breath and steady my heart rate. My hands were still shaking, but my body no longer felt like it was trying to attack me.

You can do this, Colt. Don't let them down.

I mounted my horse, nodding at Reid and taking deep breaths. We'd done this so many times.

Muscle memory. You are a well-oiled machine. You are two of the best. I repeated the phrases in my head as Reid entered the box and I followed on the left side of him.

Deep breath, Sparky. Ellison's voice played in my brain.

I took a deep breath and looked at Reid who gave me a short nod, telling me he was ready.

This is it. I nodded and the steer was released from the chute.

I raced after the steer, Bullet taking only a couple strides as I swung the rope over my head.

Come on, Carson.

The voices of everyone who believed in me echoed in my head instead of the ones who told me I was a failure. I had my opening and I took it, the loop catching both horns and tightening as I pulled back. My part was done; it was up to Reid now.

Come on, buddy, I willed silently.

Cheers erupted as Reid legally caught the hind legs and we turned to face one another. I jerked my head up to the screen to see what our time was.

"Let's give 'em four-point-five seconds!" the announcer called.

I beamed at Reid as the noise in the stadium became no more than that: noise. The sounds of cheering were dulled, and all I could see was Reid mouthing something, likely celebrating the time. It wasn't over, but four-point-five seconds was a damn good time to beat.

ellison

"Four-point-five," I breathed out. It was the best time of all the team roping competitors, out of any round.

There was one team between them and the last team, the team I knew Colter was worried about. We had texted about them yesterday, when he was watching the rodeo.

ACE

Dash Kingsley and Wayne Marlow are our biggest competition tomorrow, but they are also the biggest assholes I've ever met.

What makes them so bad?

I knew nothing about the other people competing. I guess that's what happened when you alienated yourself from an entire sport.

ACE

They're just arrogant.

More than you are?

ACE

Jeez, Blaze. Good to know what you think of me 😒

They're much worse.

I took the liberty to make a quick Google search. They were the runners up for last year's NFR Average. They were both from Oklahoma, and Colter was right: they were arrogant. There were a few videos of them online "celebrating." I rolled my eyes and typed out a text.

They seem...fun

ACE

I guess that's one way to describe them.

The team before Kingsley and Marlow clocked in at six-point-two seconds. Not enough to clinch a win.

"Our last roping team of the night hails from Stillwater, Oklahoma. They nearly brought home gold from last year's NFR. I know you know them, folks. Dash Kingsley and Wayne Marlow!"

I scoffed at the announcer's introduction. As if they needed more of an ego boost. I'd seen videos of them competing. There was no denying they were good. Dash seemed to be a bit of a sex symbol, too, and I wondered how much of his time was spent riding versus getting rode.

Just looking at him, I already knew we wouldn't get along. He was exactly the type of cowboy that I *didn't* want to be involved with.

Right before starting, Dash looked out into the crowd, like I had seen him do in every video. I would have wanted to focus on the task at hand instead of charming women in the crowd, but that was his prerogative I guess.

A moment later, they were off. Both of them had determined looks on their faces, like they would rather walk through hot coals than lose to a young team from Montana.

Their reputation preceded them. They were fast.

"Four-point-five seconds! Ladies and gentlemen, it appears that two of our teams had the same time when looking at the tenth of a second. We'll need to review the times to determine our team roping champion."

A chorus of, "oohs," and, "ahs," rose through the crowd like waves.

It only took a couple of minutes to review the clock, but it felt like an hour. The camera panned over both of the teams. Colter and Reid looked nervous, while Dash and Wayne looked confident, like they had it in the bag.

"Ladies and gentlemen, our officials have reviewed the times. Colter Carson and Reid Lawson had a time of four-point-five-three seconds."

The arena went quiet, everyone eagerly waiting for the scores for the crowd favorites. The announcer paused for effect.

Just get on with it, I thought as my heart beat rapidly.

"Dash Kingsley and Wayne Marlow had a time of…"

Another fucking pause. I get it, it's dramatic but Jesus.

"Four-point-five-four seconds."

My jaw dropped. They beat them by one-hundredth of a second.

The camera locked on Dash Kingsley as he mouthed something vulgar enough to get him a fine and threw his hat on the ground like a toddler throwing a tantrum. Wayne finally pointed up at the screen, telling his partner off. Dash's temper would be something that would hurt them in the long run, I was sure of it.

All that mattered right now, though, was Colter and Reid. The camera panned over to them, Colter's face still frozen in what I couldn't tell was shock or disbelief or pride or a mix of all three. Reid nudged him, and he followed so they could mount their horses and take their victory lap.

I watched him with adoration as he took off his cowboy hat and waved it around. I didn't think he could see me in the crowd, but as he looked up and smiled, I knew it was all mine.

After the bull riding had concluded, they brought all of the champions onto the arena floor to announce their names one more time and award them their prize money and buckles. A lot of people took this opportunity to exit and get a head start to avoid traffic on the way home. I wasn't too worried about traffic. I was planning on being one of the last people out of the stadium again.

I walked down the steps of the bleachers with the intention of meeting Colter down on the floor. As I was walking, I overheard a deep, masculine voice talking in a not-so-hushed tone.

"Those fuckers from Montana should have never won. There's no way they roped that quickly, this is bullshit. The officials just want to make us look bad because we had made it so far last year."

I continued walking, and the voices got louder. Dash and Wayne were standing next to one of the arena entrances talking shit about Colter and Reid.

They paused their conversation as I walked past, and I could feel Dash's eyes burning into me. One of them, I didn't care who, let out a whistle, and it took every fiber in my body to not whip around and serve whoever it was an uppercut. I wasn't some buckle bunny they could objectify and take home as a consolation prize for losing.

Colter was stepping out of the arena right as I got close enough for him to see me. I couldn't control myself, I ran up to him, straight into his arms, pulling him in.

"You looked good out there, Sparky." I smiled up at him.

"You were my good luck charm." He winked.

"So…" I started, wondering if we were going to address the inevitable. The fact he was leaving in the morning. "This is it, then, isn't it?" I looked away, not wanting him to see the tears that stung behind my eyes, the ones that threatened to betray me and fall. There was no chance I was going to cry over a man—a cowboy, no less.

"Hey, look at me." He cupped my chin gently, pulling my head back toward him, forcing me to look him in the eyes.

"What?" I murmured.

"I meant it when I said I wasn't going to lose you. I may be leaving, but I'm not going anywhere. We'll still talk, if that's something you want."

"Promise?" I hated the way I sounded—childish, like a lovesick teenage girl.

"Promise. You can't get rid of me that easily." He laughed and held out his pinky.

CHAPTER THIRTY-ONE

> We made it to Arizona. Going to be here a few days, then hitting the road again to go over to Las Vegas.

BLAZE

> Good luck, Sparky

Ellison had no idea how much those three simple words meant to me. With Sophie, especially toward the end, it was a battle to leave for rodeos. There were always questions like, "When will you be back?" or "Can't you skip this one?" And when I told her I couldn't because it was my career, she'd end up giving me the silent treatment or demand that every free moment I had was spent talking to her. So it meant the world to have someone supporting me.

The small fear that Ellison could potentially react the same way if we did make our relationship more official did pop up in my mind, but that would just be something we'd have to discuss in depth later. My gut was telling me that she wouldn't be like Sophie, but there was still the small part of me that felt insecure.

A week had passed since the end of the Houston Rodeo. We would be in Arizona for a few days, make the trip over to Vegas, and then go up to Utah. It would be a long month ahead of us before going back to Montana for a short break during the Bucking Horse Sale, and then another month of traveling before the Home of Champions Rodeo in July. We all knew what we had signed up for, though, when we decided to pursue this career.

I missed Ellison. The past week, we hadn't talked much because of how busy the boys and I were on the road and her work on the ranch. We had done our best to keep in touch, sending texts every once in a while to check in, but I didn't want our friendship, relationship, whatever this was, to fall through the cracks just because we weren't in the same state.

At this point, the guys knew how much I liked Ellison and they were relentless in giving me shit for it too. Reid was really the only one who knew about my underlying fear of losing her, though. He knew about my insecurities, my fear of not being enough.

I opened up my phone and looked back at my string of text messages from the past week with Ellison.

Monday

Morning, Blaze.

BLAZE

Hi Sparks

Anything exciting going on?

BLAZE

Not really. Pretty typical stuff. Lots of
repairs. We should be done calving soon
though

She had sent me a selfie of her in the middle of a
pasture with cattle surrounding her. It was a live photo too
and when I held my finger down to play the video, it
showed one of the cows coming up to her phone and
sticking its tongue out to try to lick the screen.

Tuesday

BLAZE

You aren't going to believe what happened
today

What happened?

BLAZE

I started thinking about maybe competing

Wait really?

BLAZE

Yeah, I'm considering it. Who knows
though. It's a little complicated, you know

Her excitement about competing had made me feel
better about my concerns of her potentially not liking me
being on the road all the time. But I still wanted to know
how she felt.

Can I ask you a question?

BLAZE

Uh sure? Is there something wrong?

> No, nothing wrong.

> Does the fact that I'm constantly on the road bother you at all?

BLAZE

No, of course not. You obviously love it and I'm not going to stand in the way of that

Should it bother me? Why are you asking?

> Just curious.

I had been sure that she'd probably ask about it again later, but at that moment, I was content and felt secure in the fact that she would support me purely because I loved rodeo.

Thursday

> Sorry, busy day yesterday. Tell me about your day.

BLAZE

Pretty uneventful. Isa's been trying to get me to go out with her again

> Should I be scared? After all, the last time you went out with her, you met a pretty good looking cowboy.

Her only response was an eye roll emoji, which I had to chuckle at.

Friday

> Goodnight, Blaze.

BLAZE

Goodnight Sparky

I grinned at my phone, knowing these little pieces of her life were more than enough for me. She could give me crumbs for the rest of my life, and I would gobble them up like they were my last meal.

"Ellison?" Reid asked, looking over my shoulder.

"Yeah." I fought the urge to hide my phone or turn off the screen. It wasn't that I was keeping her a secret; no, I would scream my praises for her from the rooftops if I could, but it was nice having some things that were just ours too.

"Tell her I said hi." He was so casual about it, it made me a little embarrassed that I was trying to hide our conversations like I had gotten caught watching porn or something.

CHAPTER THIRTY-TWO

ellison

I waited a little too eagerly for Colter's update on the rodeo in Arizona to come through. I never wanted to text him too much because I didn't want him to lose focus or be distracted because of me. But I had to admit that sometimes not hearing from him for a few days at a time made my heart feel heavy. I'd never been dependent on someone, though, and I wasn't going to start now. Besides, he always made sure to reach out when he was done.

ACE

You there, Blaze?

I'm here

The tiny dots that told me he was typing popped up on the screen. They stayed there for a few seconds and then stopped and started again. *God, Colter, you're such a slow texter.* It had already been three minutes, what the fuck was he typing? Suddenly, the dots stopped popping up altogether.

Um, okay, weird. I started to type out a message asking

him what the hell he was doing, but then his picture popped up on my screen with an incoming FaceTime call.

I accepted the call, and his face appeared on the screen. He had a five o'clock shadow from shaving a couple of days prior and his hair was a bit disheveled, but somehow that made him look more attractive.

"Hey," I greeted him, an amused grin on my face.

"I missed seeing your face. And besides, you know I'm a slow texter so it was easier to call anyway." He laughed.

"You don't have to justify anything. I'm almost glad you called instead of trying to type out a message. I might have been waiting two weeks for you to finally send it," I teased, holding my phone over my face as I lay down on my bed, hair sprawled around me in a mess of curls.

"Ha ha. You're so funny," he joked.

"Well, how did the rodeo go? Did you win another buckle?" Since he hadn't given me an update, I figured I would just ask. I probably sounded like such a buckle bunny, asking if he won. *Pfft, as if that's why I was asking.*

"It went really well. We ended up winning, so that will be good for our standings," he explained, giving me a full recap and not sparing any details. His face was so animated when he got excited. He could tell me a story about what he bought at the grocery store and I would probably be captivated, hanging onto every word.

"That's good! I'm so proud of you!" I really was. I'd seen how hard he worked and I wanted nothing more than for him to succeed. "Hey, so last week you asked me if I was bothered by the fact that you're on the road all the time. But you never told me why you asked."

"Oh, uh." His eyes shifted a little, like he was nervous. "I just have experience with...people...who have gotten upset about me always being gone. People who would try to get me to stay home instead of going on the road."

"You love rodeo, though." I tried to understand where this was coming from. My impression was that Colter's family supported his career and his closest friends were all on the road with him.

"Yeah, I do love it."

"I would never stop you from doing something you love, Colter. Just because I didn't have the best relationship with rodeo growing up doesn't mean that I would ever want you to stop. I hope you know that." My voice softened as I reassured him.

"I know. Thank you, Ellison."

We were silent for a moment, but then Colter cleared his throat and changed the subject. "Did you ever end up going out with Isabelle?"

"Yeah, we did for a little while. Nothing exciting happened, though," I admitted.

"No? Didn't meet another charming cowboy?" He smirked, the corners of his eyes crinkling and dimples deepening.

"Well, actually, there was a saddle bronc rider that—" I started to make up a lie, but immediately Colter's face fell, as much as he was trying to mask it. "No, Sparky. No one could replace you."

"You're not wrong there. I *am* truly one of a kind." He pretended to flip his hair like Isa sometimes did.

I was starting to realize one thing: Colter might have been twenty-six, but he was a kid at heart. Not in an immature way, but in a fun way, a way that made everyone want to be his friend. His charm was magnetic, and his pull reached me even from states away. He always found some way to make me laugh or smile.

"Don't let your ego get too inflated now, you might float away."

"You see, Blaze, my ego already is inflated. Past the point of no return even. You keep me grounded, though." He winked.

Oh, and another thing about Colter? He was cheesier than Kraft mac and cheese.

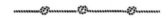

ACE

Heading over to Vegas today. Will let you know when we stop driving again.

Drive safe Sparks

It was late afternoon the next day when I got the text from Colter letting me know he was back on the road. Isa had come over to my house, and we were getting ready to watch trashy reality TV shows for the rest of the day.

"Is that your boyfriend?" She giggled, drawing out the word boyfriend.

"He's not my boyfriend, but yes." I punched her on the arm as I settled into the couch next to her.

"Oh, please, you talk literally all day every day. I'm surprised you two haven't tried to do it over the phone yet. He may as well be your boyfriend, Ells." She grabbed the TV remote. "So, what are we thinking? *Love Island* or an old season of *The Bachelor*?"

"Depends on what seasons of *The Bachelor* are on Hulu," I responded as she flipped to the streaming app.

"We could watch season sixteen with Ben or season twenty-three with Colton. Personally, I wouldn't mind watching Colton hop the fence again." She smirked. "Do you think Colter could jump a fence?"

"Oh my God, Isa!"

Leave it to her to bring Colter into every conversation we had.

I'd bet money that Colter *could* jump a fence, though. And he'd probably look hot doing it.

CHAPTER THIRTY-THREE

> We got to Vegas super late last night. Didn't want to wake you.

I sent off the text to Ellison letting her know we had made it to Las Vegas. We didn't get here until about one o'clock last night because Mikey wanted to make so many stops. Combine that with leaving Arizona in the late afternoon and it made for a long, late drive.

My phone chirped with a message.

BLAZE

> All good. Glad you made it

I was happy that she wasn't upset about me not letting her know I made it *the moment I made it*. Sophie would have had a full-fledged meltdown and started calling everyone I knew trying to figure out where I was. Or she'd rag on me for not having my location turned on. It wasn't that I was trying to hide anything from her, I just never had it on.

We were staying on the Strip and we usually gave ourselves a day before and after all of the events to enjoy

Vegas and have fun. Although my idea of fun was a lot different than Mikey's, especially with his birthday being this week.

Mikey *loved* his birthday. Maybe even more than a child loves their birthday. He no doubt would be hitting up the strip clubs.

Reid, Jake, and I preferred to walk the Strip and Fremont Street and occasionally spend a couple hundred dollars on the slot machines.

It was almost seven here, so it was about nine o'clock in Texas. I wanted so badly to call her, to hear her voice, but she more than likely was working. But it wouldn't hurt to ask.

> Working today?

BLAZE
Actually no, for once. Lol

My heart felt like it burst for a second.

> Alright if I call you?

BLAZE
What? Miss me that much already?

Yes, actually.

"What do you mean you've never seen *Grease?* That's one of the greatest movies of *all time*," I complained.

"I don't *know*, okay!" She giggled, hiding her face with her hands. "Besides, I never pictured you as the kind of guy to watch rom-coms."

"I'm full of surprises, honey." I winked. "Well, that just means we have to watch the movie. I can even send you a playlist so you can learn all of the songs."

"Don't tell me you know *all* of the songs," she groaned, her eyes widening.

"Obviously. You can't watch *Grease* and not know all of the songs." I pointed out. "I was also Kenickie for Halloween three years in a row."

"I don't know who the fuck that is, but okay, Lover Boy." She laughed.

"That's *Dirty Dancing*, but nice try."

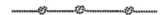

The five days in Las Vegas had some of our best runs, besides the one in Houston. We were consistently getting faster and keeping up our winning streak. I wouldn't admit it out loud to anyone, but I wholeheartedly believed that hearing Ellison's voice, simply talking to her about anything under the moon, contributed to my success. She melted all my stress and nerves away every time we spoke. Calling her, even if it was for five minutes, started to become part of my routine.

I recalled the first time we started the little ritual. It was right before the first competition in Vegas and I was starting to feel the same sense of dread I felt before the championship round in Houston. In a panic, I had instinctively dialed her number straight from my favorites tab on my phone.

"Hello?" she had answered, obviously very confused why I was calling her.

"Hi."

"What's going on? Aren't you at a rodeo right now?" There had been a small hint of worry in her tone.

"Yeah, we're going to be roping soon. But I just wanted to hear your voice," I had mumbled, still trying to ease my rapid heart rate and almost erratic breathing.

"I'm here," she had replied, understanding what I meant. "You're going to be fine. You're going to do great, Colter. I believe in you."

I believe in you. I loved hearing those words come out of her mouth.

"Would it be okay if we did this more often?" I had asked.

"Anything you need. I want to support you in whatever way I can. As long as you don't think I'm being annoying." A breathy laugh had sounded from her end of the phone.

"You could never annoy me, Blaze."

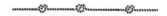

"I'm starting to like this version of you, Carson." Mikey raised his beer bottle to me. It was our last full day in Vegas before we hit the road to head to Utah so we were all hanging out poolside.

"He's definitely more tolerable than you, and he hasn't even been getting laid," Jake quipped at Mikey.

I might not have been getting laid per say, but no one said anything about self-gratification, and I drew my lower lip between my teeth daydreaming about the few times I'd had to jerk off in the shower thinking about how Ellison's lips would feel wrapped around me. I quickly pushed away those fantasies, bringing myself back down to Earth.

"Hey, hey, hey! That was a personal attack, Flynn!" Mikey grumbled. He'd been going out to the clubs practically every night and it appeared to be affecting his performance. Mikey was Mikey, though. He seemed to be the "can't teach an old dog new tricks" type. The "tricks" in question being a steady relationship and not just bouncing around from woman to woman.

"Is it really a personal attack if it's true?" Reid snickered.

"Lawson, just because I have fun with women doesn't mean I'm a bad guy."

"Whatever helps you sleep at night, buddy." I patted him on the back before I got up to go call Ellison again.

I clicked her name and admired the photo that I had snuck of her at the zoo in Houston. She had been looking at the red panda exhibit and she turned around to tell me something, a bright grin on her face. It might not have been a posed photo that most girls preferred, but it was real and it captured the personality she kept hidden from so many people.

The FaceTime call rang a couple times before her face appeared on the screen.

"Hey, Colter, I'm sorry but now's not the best—" she started.

"IS THAT HIM?" a bubbly, feminine voice in the background screeched.

"Isabelle Bennett, I swear if you take this phone from me I will never go out to a bar with you ever—"

The FaceTime cut off.

I needed to meet Isabelle Bennett one day. If not to see what Ellison's best friend was like in the flesh, then to at least thank her for everything she did to bring me and Ellison together.

I'm so ready to be home.

BLAZE

You're almost there

I wish you were here with me. That would make this trip a whole lot better.

BLAZE

I miss you too Sparks

CHAPTER THIRTY-FOUR

ellison

ACE

What would you say to a trip up to the north country?

Depends. What kind of trip are we talking about?

ACE

Oh, you know. You, me, the wide open Montana skies, and this thing we call the Bucking Horse Sale.

How charming. I'll think about it

W*hat the fuck is the "Bucking Horse Sale?"* I thought to myself as I read Colter's text repeatedly. Also, a trip to Montana? I knew he missed me after a month and a half of being apart, but how did he think I was going to get there? My phone buzzed again.

ACE

Please don't say no, Blaze. I spent good money on this plane ticket 😉

Well, that decided it, I guess. I was going to Montana. I was excited to see Colter, there was no denying that, but I was also a little nervous. I would be traveling across the country for this man. I was a fool if I thought this didn't make things between us a little more official.

I was also a little nervous about abandoning my job. But any fears I had about leaving and my responsibilities faded when I told my mother. She practically fainted from happiness, which solidified the trip even more. I didn't realize she wanted me to leave the ranch that badly.

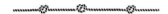

A week and a half after his invitation, and after tying up loose ends back home, I stepped off the plane in Bozeman, which was four hours away from Colter's small town and yet was apparently the closest airport for a direct flight.

Montana was beautiful. It was what I imagined heaven looked like. Texas was pretty, I wouldn't deny that, but truthfully, all of the songs about Montana were right. The skies felt like they went on for miles with a mountain backdrop that not even the world's greatest artist could do justice.

The moment I stepped past the security checkpoint, I saw him. He was leaning up against one of the wooden columns, a bouquet of carnations under his arm and a to-go coffee cup in his hand.

He hadn't noticed me yet, and I was soaking in the sight of him, observing his little tics and habits that most people would ignore. How when he was nervous, he had the tendency to wring his hands together or bounce his leg.

I was about fifteen paces away from him when he finally looked up at me and grinned. He looked at me like I was the only person in the room, and I wondered how it could be possible for someone to see me as perfectly as Colter Carson did.

I would never admit it out loud, but I craved the connection my parents once shared. That almost divine, unconditional love. The kind most people search for their entire lives.

Colter and I might not have been in a relationship, at least not officially, but he had this hold on me all the same.

I couldn't help but smile, seeing Colter look at me in that way. Texts and FaceTime calls could never compare to the real life thing.

I continued to walk toward him, and he met me halfway, pulling me in for a hug. I breathed in his leathery scent, with a hint of cinnamon and musk, that was so perfectly him.

"Hey, Sparks." I held on to him a little bit longer.

"Hey, Blaze." He took my hand and kissed the top of it.

I wasn't one for public displays of affection, but the action alone caused a flutter in my stomach.

"I'm so happy you're here."

"Me too." I eyed the coffee cup. "What did you get to drink?"

"Oh, this is for you." He handed me the cup and the bouquet.

I took a sip. White chocolate mocha. "This is my favorite. Thank you."

"I remembered that's what you got when we went to The Corral together." He smiled, and I practically melted.

He remembered. A coffee order seemed so insignificant, but he paid attention and he remembered my favorite coffee.

"So, how was your flight?"

"It was fine. Got stuck in front of a kid who kept kicking my seat and a screaming baby two rows ahead of me, but you know, that's flying." I shrugged.

"One of the few reasons I choose to drive instead." He chuckled.

We headed in the direction of the baggage claim. I was staying for less than a week, but I still took a suitcase. A bad habit of mine was packing way more than I ever needed. I rationalized it as always wanting to be prepared. Besides, it was Montana after all. Who was to say that in a couple days it wouldn't be snowing? I hoped not at least because the warmest thing I packed was an old Texas Longhorns sweatshirt from college.

I continued the conversation as we started to walk down the stairs. "Why else? Because of the price?"

"Yeah, that too." He ruffled the hair on the back of his head.

I raised an eyebrow, suddenly very curious about his aversion to flying. "Wait, what's the other reason?"

"I...I get a little nervous, okay?" He tried to speed through the admission as fast as he could.

"You're scared of flying, aren't you?" I giggled.

He avoided eye contact with me as his nose crinkled a little. "No..."

"You totally are!"

"Okay, fine. Maybe a little bit. But it's normal! I mean, people have super irrational fears, and flying, I don't think, is that irrational," he rambled.

"Relax, Sparky. I get it." He was kind of cute when he was flustered. "Not everyone can be fearless like me." I winked before I grabbed my suitcase off the conveyor belt.

"All right, this is it." I gestured to my bag.

"Let's get out of here, shall we?" he suggested.

We walked out of the airport and immediately the air felt much colder than what I was used to. It might have been nearing the sixties in Bozeman, but Houston was probably somewhere in the eighties.

A shiver went down my spine, and I shuddered.

"What's wrong, Texas? Not used to this weather?" Colter nudged me as we walked.

"No, Montana, I'm not." I nudged him back, initiating a war between our elbows.

"Don't worry. I can provide enough warmth for the both of us." He winked.

What is that supposed to mean? I ignored his comment, and a few hundred feet later we were at his pickup.

"All right, are you ready for this little road trip?" he asked.

"This'll be the real test of our friendship, won't it?" My eyes widened a little at the thought of being in the car, with Colter Carson, for *four hours* in a place I was completely unfamiliar with. *It's really not a problem.*

"Friendship? If that's what this is, then I'm not sure I have very many friends." Colter winked at me, causing my face to turn red from my choice of words.

We had been in the car for the past three and a half hours and surprisingly our conversation never stalled. It seemed like we would never run out of things to talk about; the topics just flowed into one another.

One moment, we could be talking about country music, and then the next, we'd be talking about Nashville and the favorite places we had traveled to.

"What's your favorite country song?" he asked me.

"'Amarillo by Morning' is one of my favorites. I still can't believe it never made it to number one. It has to be one of the best," I answered. "What's yours?"

"You know that one song? The one that has all of the elements of a perfect country and western song? That one."

"Really?" I was surprised.

"Nah, not really. I mean it does embody country music, though. It talks about drinking, pickups, and prison."

"Ah, yes. And don't forget his mother." I chuckled, thinking about the song. The first time I heard it I had to rewind it to make sure I was hearing everything right.

"Did you listen to the *Grease* playlist I sent you?" His tone suddenly turned serious, like he was a teacher and I was his student.

"Was I supposed to?"

"You're killing me, Ellison. Yes! That was the whole point of me sending it to you. I can't be the only one singing the songs when we watch the movie, I'll get embarrassed." He jutted his lip out and gave me the sad puppy dog eyes.

"I'm sure your ego can handle it."

"Actually, you know what. We still have forty minutes or so. I'll turn it on now." He reached for his phone to switch the music from the '90s country playlist we were currently listening to.

"Great."

What have I gotten myself into?

Forty minutes, and a bad rendition of "Greased Lightning," later, we pulled into Silver Creek. The town itself was tiny. I didn't know if you could even consider it a town, or just a cluster of houses and farms out in the middle of nowhere. Colter's place was on the edge of it, but close enough that you could consider the other houses his neighbors, even though they weren't close together like some of the cookie cutter styles back home.

Colter owned a simple double wide with forest-green paint and a small set of wood plank stairs that took you up to the front door. We parked in the driveway, or well, at least it was kind of a driveway. It was really just a gravel road leading up to the lawn and a small patch of concrete connecting the house and the road. Behind the house was a fenced-in pasture and a barn.

"We have cattle, but they're on a different piece of land right now," he explained after he caught me staring out into the pasture.

"Here it is. Home sweet home." Colter lingered on the end of "sweet" as he gestured to the house. He didn't sound very enthused about it, but he led the way through the front door and flipped on the switch that controlled the ceiling light in the living room, illuminating the space with warm light.

I wasn't expecting his house to look so empty. He only had a few pieces of furniture. The number of cowboy hats on the wall far outnumbered the amount of furnishings he owned. It was the definition of minimalist, maybe even minimalism to the extreme.

"It's…homey?" It came out as more of a question than a statement.

He picked up on my confusion. "I'm never here, so I never felt the need to buy furniture. Why have that kind of stuff when you don't even use it?"

"I mean, that makes sense." I understood where he was

coming from but, at the same time, it made me kind of sad, for reasons I couldn't even explain.

"I guess I've been waiting for someone to decorate for me." He said it casually, even though his words carried much greater meaning and we both knew it.

"Let me give you the tour. Here's the living room and kitchen." He held his arms out in the air for effect. "That tiny little hallway to the left of the living room has the bathroom on the left side and across from the bathroom is my room. And that's the full tour."

"Wow, I hope I don't get lost," I joked.

"I would be impressed if you did." He winked.

How did I ever think I could keep this man at an arm's length away?

We went into Miles City for dinner, choosing to go to a barbeque joint off of the main street. Colter told me his buddies were off doing something else that night but I would surely get to meet all of them the next day.

"They're all good guys," he had told me. "They can just be a lot sometimes, especially Mikey."

"What makes Mikey 'a lot?'" I put air quotes around "a lot."

"He's just, how do I even describe it? He's a bit of a handful. He likes to have fun." Colter was choosing his words carefully.

"I think I'm picking up what you're saying? He's wild," I guessed.

"Think of your stereotypical bull rider persona. Likes women, gets around a little." He fluffed his hair.

"Ah, I see."

"Don't worry, he won't try anything." His eyes immediately got buggy.

"I'm not worried. I can handle myself. Trust me," I reassured him.

"I have no doubt that you can. He's just, he's Mikey."

We finished eating our dinner, making sporadic conversation about what would happen the next day and thinking of things to do for the rest of the time I was here.

Tomorrow was the first day of the Bucking Horse Sale. There were a bunch of different events that would take place, including wild horse races and a rodeo, of course. In the evening, after everything had wrapped up, there was a street dance, which Colter had said was one of the most fun parts.

CHAPTER THIRTY-FIVE

colter

The Bucking Horse Sale in Miles City was world famous. People from all over gathered here in our little town.

I had woken up decently early, despite having stayed up watching movies. Around one o'clock, we decided it was probably best to get some sleep, especially since Ellison had passed out twice already, each time jolting awake and giving me an embarrassed look, especially after she had caught herself drooling on my arm.

I slept on the couch, despite her protests. It had been a long winded discussion.

"I can sleep on the couch," she offered after I had grabbed a blanket and pillow for myself.

"No, you're my guest. I'm taking the couch, you're taking the bed," I insisted firmly.

"Yeah, I'm your guest. That's even more reason for me to take the couch," she argued.

"That's not how it works around here. It's my house, which means we're going by my rules, and I'm not forcing you to have the couch."

"Fine, I guess I'll sleep on the floor then." She crossed her arms as my mouth gaped open with disbelief.

Stubborn woman.

"We might as well both sleep in the bed if that's how you're going to be." I sighed, fake exasperation in my voice.

"Fine." She yawned, satisfied with "winning" the discussion.

After she had fallen asleep in my bed, almost instantly, I came back out to the couch. I just knew that if we had stayed in the same bed, she would have known *exactly* how I felt about her and I didn't want her to feel uncomfortable.

Ellison was still asleep when I woke up, but I didn't want to disturb her. We had time before we had to be anywhere and she probably needed the rest. I went outside to take care of the horses and a couple other minor tasks. When I came back inside, it was almost eleven and she was still asleep.

I wasn't a great cook by any means, but to pass the time until she woke up, I decided I would make breakfast. My plan was biscuits and sausage gravy, with eggs, bacon, and, of course, coffee, even though it wasn't her fancy white chocolate mocha coffee and was just Folgers. I kicked myself a little for not at least buying white chocolate syrup for her, but maybe I would for the future.

This was the breakfast my mom always used to make us when we were kids. Every Sunday after church, we'd come home and have it. Those were some of my favorite memories, back when my parents still loved each other and I was just a care free kid.

I was halfway through making the bacon when the sound of footsteps came out of the bedroom. I had flour all over the front of myself from making the biscuit dough and I had accidentally burnt myself with the bacon grease, but seeing her changed my mood completely.

"Good morning!" I greeted her cheerily.

"What are you doing?" she asked, her voice groggy from waking up a few minutes ago.

"I'm making us breakfast," I responded as I pushed the strips of bacon around in the pan.

"Ooh, what are you making?" She instantly perked up.

"Biscuits and gravy, bacon, and eggs. There's also coffee if you want some. It's nothing fancy, but I've got sugar in the cabinet and milk in the fridge if you need that." I nodded my head toward the coffee pot.

"I will definitely take coffee, regardless if it's fancy or not. I don't discriminate when it comes to caffeine." She laughed as she walked over to pour herself a mug.

My girl does love her coffee, I thought.

"Oh, how do you take your eggs?" I asked because that was something I didn't know about her yet.

It was funny. We knew each other's biggest secrets, opened up the darkest parts of our hearts to each other, yet didn't know how we took our eggs.

"Over easy," she answered.

"That's how I like mine too." I was relieved. I didn't know how to make eggs any other way so over easy was undoubtedly what she was going to get, unless she had said scrambled.

"Anything I can do to help?" She came up next to me, putting a hand on my shoulder.

"Nope. I just want to do this for you."

Ellison was a caretaker, I could tell. She might not have considered herself one, but I'd seen the way she put others before herself, especially her mother, even if it meant neglecting her needs and feelings; she cared about the people she loved.

ellison

I sat down at the dining table with my coffee and watched him cook. He had this natural flow, moving from one side of the kitchen to the other. He hummed as he cooked, a melody I didn't recognize. The house smelled heavenly as the savory smell of bacon and the sweet, bakery scent of homemade biscuits wafted through the air.

His eyebrows furrowed as he focused on cracking the eggs into the pan, and as they sizzled, I imagined a future with this in it. Maybe we'd alternate cooking every morning, or maybe we'd have children who helped us, ones who would steal the bacon right after it came out of the pan and get full before the meal was even done.

It was a crazy thought, I knew that. Yet, with every gesture, grand or tiny, I started to think maybe it was possible.

The timer on the oven for the biscuits went off, and Colter walked over to me with a plate that had two biscuits, gravy piled on top, two eggs, and four strips of bacon.

"Okay, chef." I looked at him with admiration.

"Better taste it before you start calling me that. You wouldn't want my ego to get any bigger." He grinned before he went to make his own plate.

I took a bite of the biscuits and gravy, the taste exploding across my tongue. "Mmm." I closed my eyes and practically moaned. It was probably the best biscuits and gravy I'd ever had.

"Good?" Amusement flickered in his eyes.

"Keep cooking like this, and I may never go back to Texas." I stuffed my mouth with bacon. It was cooked perfectly, not too crispy, but not limp either.

"Don't tempt me, Blaze." He sat down next to me.

After we'd finished eating, I helped him clean. I wasn't going to let him do all of the work himself. We worked as a team, with Colter scrubbing dishes and me rinsing and drying them.

"We make a pretty good team there, Sparky," I said as I dried off the last few utensils.

We might have wasted time teasing each other and splashing bubbles from the sink around, but we eventually got everything cleaned.

"That we do." He checked his watch. "Oh, shit, we've got to get ready to go."

With the time it took for both of us to shower and get ready, we pulled into town around three o'clock, and the streets were already bustling with people. The horse races and rodeo wouldn't start until later in the afternoon, so we spent a good deal of our time walking around and looking at the vendors set up at the fairgrounds.

People were selling handcrafted jewelry, woodwork, clothing, and so much more.

We passed by a booth selling paintings, and I teased Colter, "Hey, maybe you should buy one of these. Give your house a little bit more character."

"Only if you're paying for it," he teased back.

The paintings really were beautiful, though. There were landscape scenes, rodeo scenes, horses, bison, really anything that came to mind when you thought about Montana.

"Colter!" a lady at a booth called out to him as we walked by. When we went over, she stood up and gave him a hug.

"Hi, Susie." He smiled after she stopped squeezing him.

"Is this your girlfriend?" She tilted her head, giving me a warm look.

"Oh—" I tried to correct her but Colter cut me off.

"This is Ellison." He introduced us, and she pulled me in for a hug.

Did he not want me to say I wasn't his girlfriend? I was confused because we'd never really defined what we were. I wasn't in any rush, especially considering I was here for less than a week, but over the past month it had felt like we'd already moved past the point of being just friends. *But what do you want it to be?* My conscience was mocking me again.

"She's very beautiful." The woman took my hand, breaking me out of my thoughts.

"She is. I'm very lucky." He beamed.

If Colter was this proud to be standing next to me and we weren't even dating, I wondered what it would be like to actually be *his*.

"Why didn't you tell her that we're not actually together?" I asked him after we had moved far enough away from her table.

"I don't know." He shrugged. "Just didn't seem important."

"What do you mean?" I asked, confused.

He stopped, facing me so that I was looking up at his face. "I'm willing to be whatever you want us to be. I've been yours for a while now, trust me. I'm leaving it up to you whether you want to be mine."

CHAPTER THIRTY-SIX

colter

I had told her exactly how I felt. Ellison stole my attention from the moment I saw her, and now I wanted nothing more than for her to be my girlfriend. I just couldn't vocalize it. I knew she still had reservations, too, so I was determined to do anything in my power to ease her mind. Putting the power in her hands felt right.

We walked toward the arena where the horse races and rodeo would take place in a little under an hour. I wanted us to get a good seat, so we could be up close to the action.

Reid, Mikey, and the rest of the boys were nowhere to be found, so I shot Reid a text letting him know we would find them after the rodeo at the street dance.

I led Ellison to the grandstands and chose a spot in the middle of the arena toward the front rows.

The stands gradually filled with people who were eager to watch everything unfold. The Bucking Horse Sale wasn't like typical rodeos that had all of the events. There was only saddle bronc riding, and there would be twenty riders vying for the prize money. Tonight, these riders would be some of the best permit riders, but in a couple of days, it would be the top thirty-two saddle bronc riders in the world who would compete for $50,000.

There was also horse racing, and the Bucking Horse Sale was one of two venues in Montana to hold the event. All in all, it was an exciting weekend that allowed people from all over to see what we had to offer here in Montana.

"Folks, you've gathered here from all over the world for the famous Miles City Bucking Horse Sale! Let's get this show on the road and kick it off!"

Shouts from the crowd drowned out the announcer's voice as excitement filled the air. People in Montana were fairly simple. They loved the state, they loved football, and they loved rodeo.

I didn't know a whole lot about horse racing, but it still intrigued me as I watched the jockeys race around the track. Both Ellison and I were practically sitting on the edge of our seats.

"I've never been to a horse race before," she admitted, still watching the action.

"I've been a few times, for this, but I couldn't tell you a single thing about it." I laughed.

The horse racing wrapped up, and they prepared to start the event that I actually knew a lick about, although I didn't compete in it myself. I enjoyed watching saddle bronc riding, even if they caught a lot of shit from bareback riders and bull riders.

I knew that Jake had done some saddle bronc riding back when he was younger, but an injury prevented him from continuing. He was also a bit too tall now, standing at six-foot-two.

Ellison was so focused as she watched the riders that it was hard to imagine a time when she wasn't invested in the sport and had separated herself from it completely. I noticed how her brow furrowed when the rider was having a tough time and how the corner of her lips curled up when one made it to eight seconds. I could spend an entire rodeo watching her reactions instead of the sport itself. It was comparable to seeing a football fan cheer on their favorite team in the Super Bowl.

She caught me looking at her a couple of times and raised her eyebrows at me. She didn't say anything, but I could probably guess what she was thinking.

Being with Ellison was so easy. She was fun and carefree when she was here with me.

After the saddle bronc riding, they had one of my favorite nontraditional events: wild horse racing. Wild horse racing stemmed from the days in the Old West when cowboys would have to break horses.

It consisted of up to ten teams, with three cowboys on each team who were required to saddle up a wild horse and race it around the track. The first team to make it across the finish line would win. It was entertaining to watch, that's for sure.

There weren't any people that I knew competing, although we had tried to sign up Mikey for it one year. It didn't work out the way we had hoped since he never ended up competing; the rest of us weren't going to try to compete with him, so he backed out.

The starting pistol went off, and it was pure chaos as the teams entered the arena. One cowboy would hold the horse's lead rope to make sure it didn't run off. Another would control the head so the horse didn't rear back, and the third was the rider who would saddle up the horse and race it around the track.

Bucking horses were running and dragging cowboys around. A couple of riders were being dragged on their stomachs, holding on to the lead rope for dear life. Laughter erupted around the crowd, and even Ellison couldn't suppress a giggle. I loved wild horse racing. It was always one of the most entertaining parts of the Bucking Horse Sale.

It was still absolute mayhem as bucking horses were running into each other, each team just trying to get their horse calmed down enough to put the saddle on. One team finally was able to get a saddle on their horse and the rider exited the arena, but there were still plenty of other teams struggling.

Finally, the last team got their horse saddled and the riders were off, racing around the track. I shot off a text to Reid poking fun at Mikey.

> Damn, we should have tried to get Mikey to do this again.

REID

Lol if only.

"This is so fun." Ellison smiled, sitting on the edge of her seat and waiting to see who would cross the finish line first.

It ended up being a team of three guys from down in Wyoming, and they celebrated as they got all of the horses and participants out of the arena.

About thirty minutes later, the rodeo had wrapped up with the mutton bustin'—another crowd favorite—and everyone was gearing up to head to the street dance.

CHAPTER THIRTY-SEVEN

ellison

We left the fairgrounds to go to the street dance. We walked since the fairgrounds were only a short distance from Main Street. The street was blocked off from traffic and there was a stage for a live band. It seemed as though the entire town, and then some, had shown up. The road was filled with people. Children were running around while their parents watched from the sidewalks and everywhere people were dancing. The smell of cinnamon fry bread and grilled meat filled the air, and the entire event exuded small town charm.

The band, whose name I had paid zero attention to, started playing a cover of "Wagon Wheel." Even though I had no idea who they were, I was enjoying the music. Colter grabbed my hand to dance. I tried to brush him off to keep walking, but he was already starting to spin me around.

I had to hand it to him, he was a great dancer. It felt natural—effortless—with me predicting his moves but still letting him be in control as a lead—how dancing should feel. It was like we'd known each other for years and not only a couple months. As he spun me around, I could picture myself fitting into his world—this community—more and more.

The song ended, and he pulled me close to him again, instead of letting go of my hands, planting a kiss on my temple.

"Let's go find Reid and the boys, shall we?" He pulled away and started walking in the direction of one of the bars.

We walked into Rudy's, a bar about a block away, and looked around for Colter's friends. I had no idea what they looked like, with the exception of Reid, so I wasn't a lot of help.

"There they are." Colter nodded his head toward a pool table in the back of the bar. There was a group of four guys standing around it.

In addition to Reid, there was a younger looking one, likely around my age, with sandy brown hair. The others were a bit older. One of them was shorter, probably only about five-foot-eight, if that, and he looked to be the oldest with dark hair and a five o'clock shadow nearing on the side of too short. The fourth guy was a bit taller than Colter and had blond hair.

We walked over to them, and they immediately started saying hello to Colter.

"Hey, Colt. Hi, I'm Reid." Reid introduced himself to me, shaking my hand for a quick moment before he walked around the pool table to line up a shot.

I gave him a small smile, but couldn't get my own introduction out before one of the other guys started talking. Loudly.

"Carson, my man. Good to see you. Nice to see you've got a pretty lady with you for once." The short one started eyeing me a little too closely, making me guess that he was Mikey.

"The pretty lady has a name. It's Ellison." I raised an eyebrow at him, unimpressed so far.

"Sorry about him. This is Mikey." Colter introduced us and confirmed my suspicions.

"She's a real firecracker, ain't she, Carson?" Mikey snorted.

Oh, you have no idea. You haven't even seen anything yet. The thought put a smirk on my face.

"This is Hayden." Colter pointed to the younger one. "And this is Jake."

"Pleasure to meet you." Hayden waved from across the pool table.

Jake just gave me a nod of acknowledgment.

"Ah, shit," Reid mumbled as he hit the cue ball into one of the pockets.

"Damn, man. You need to work on your skills." Jake slapped him on the back before lining up his own shot. "My grandma can play pool better than you can."

I couldn't resist a snort at his comment. After Jake went, Hayden made a couple shots, making up for Reid's misses.

"Even if your grandma couldn't shoot better, I'm sure I could." I yawned.

"You think so, Firecracker?" Mikey's eyes piqued with interest.

"Of course. I could definitely at least beat you." I looked him up and down.

"All right, prove it." Reid handed me his pool stick as Mikey lined up a shot. He easily pocketed the shot as well as another. But then he missed, setting up a difficult angle for me.

I pouted my lips, trying to figure out how I was going to swing this.

"What's wrong there, city girl?" Mikey taunted me as I figured out how I was going to make the shot. He clearly didn't know anything about me other than the fact that I was from around Houston.

I pulled back the cue stick and looked Mikey right in the eye as I took the shot, bouncing the cue ball off the cushion to make a bank shot in the corner. "Nothing's wrong." I made another two shots and pointed out the pocket that I wanted the eight ball to go into before sinking it. "And I'm not a city girl."

"Goddamn!" The rest of the boys looked away, snickering as Mikey pursed his lips.

"Rerack 'em, boys." Reid laughed. "I know who I want my pool partner to be from now on. No offense, Hayden."

Hayden just shrugged as the corner of his lip turned upward, a small dimple showing.

"Oh, no, I'm done. I've proved my point." I gave the pool stick back to Reid and sat down.

"All right, well, you tryin' to get in on our game?" Mikey nudged Colter.

"Maybe the next one." He put his hands up before he grabbed my hand and nodded toward the bar. "Let's get some drinks."

We walked over to the bar, and I grabbed one of the empty stools. Colter waved over the bartender and ordered a beer for himself and a tequila soda for me.

"So, those were the guys." Colter chuckled. "Sorry about Mikey."

"I can see what you mean about him being a handful. Don't worry, though. Like I said, I can handle him. I've dealt with worse." I rolled my eyes at the thought of Mikey trying to hit on me.

The bartender brought back our drinks, and Colter closed his tab before leaning against the bar and turning to face me.

"What did you think of the wild horse racing?" he asked me.

"That was probably one of the craziest, most chaotic things I've seen in a while." I laughed. "I enjoyed it, though."

Before Colter could say anything else, there was a crash from the back of the bar and people yelling.

"What the fuck?" He jumped up, putting me behind him. He started walking toward the yelling and gestured for me to stay put.

Like hell I was. I followed closely behind him because, well, I was nosy, and it wasn't like I hadn't seen a bar fight before.

Glass was on the floor, and Reid was pulling Mikey off a guy who was clutching his nose, blood seeping through his fingers.

"Get out of here and don't come back if you're going to act that way!" Mikey snapped at him.

The guy gave him a glare and started walking toward the entrance of the bar, still holding his nose.

"What the fuck, Mikey?" Colter demanded. "What happened?"

"He was talking shit. I put him in his place." Mikey wiped his hands off on his pants, his knuckles bloody.

"You know damn well you could have gotten arrested for that shit."

"The guy was belligerent and saying shit about you. I did you a favor." He shrugged.

"He's telling the truth, Colt. Honestly, I would have done the same thing if Mikey hadn't jumped at the opportunity," Jake added.

"We're brothers, man. I'm not just gonna stand by when someone talks about you like that."

I watched their exchange, honestly impressed by Mikey's loyalty to his friends. Was punching a guy the right way to do it? Probably not, but it got the point across.

"All right, well, we're gonna head out before Rocky over here punches anyone else. I'm not trying to bail you out of jail tonight." Colter put his arm around me and started to lead me out. "Make sure he doesn't do anything stupid again," he directed his friends.

I wondered how many times Colter had bailed Mikey out of jail. Clearly enough times that he didn't want to be the one to deal with him tonight.

We walked down Main Street and passed the band again who were playing an old George Jones song.

Someone in the crowd hollered, "Play 'Free Bird!'" and I had to suppress a laugh.

The lead singer retorted, "No," in between the chorus and the verse and then continued on with the song.

The streets were beginning to clear out more and more as parents started to herd their children home and the college kids funneled into the bars.

"Let's go home, shall we?" He brushed his fingers against mine. A delicate touch that proclaimed the attraction between us—this tension—was more than just that.

Colter drove us home, his hand resting on my thigh the entire way. When we got to the house, he stopped me right before the front door, grabbing my waist and pulling me toward him.

"Colter." His name was no more than a whisper as I looked into his eyes. They tracked from mine down to my lips and back up, reminding me of the afternoon we spent sitting in the back of my dad's F-100 and the dream I had of him. This time was different, though. This was real and I wanted Colter, needed him. I needed him as much as I needed air.

"You have no idea how badly I want to kiss you right now." His eyes were hungry. For me.

"Then what are you waiting for?" I barely got the last word out before he yanked me toward him and crashed his lips onto mine. He tasted like cinnamon and vanilla, and he didn't push me or try to rush. He kissed me slowly, like he was savoring the moment. I parted my lips, inviting him to deepen the kiss.

Weeks of push and pull had led to this. Half of my heart was still begging me to stop before I got in too deep, to rebuild the fortress around my heart, to fill the cracks that Colter had been chipping away at, but the other half was falling willingly.

Before Colter, it was like I was drowning in the loss of my dad and the pressure I put on myself to avoid feeling the same pain that I believed my dad's love for rodeo—our love for it—caused. But being with him made me feel like I could finally breathe again. He was steady when I stumbled, patient when I was stubborn.

He pulled me through the front door, kissing me all the way from my lips across my jaw to my ear and down my neck.

"Are you sure you want this?" he asked me.

I couldn't be more sure of anything at that moment. "Yes, I'm sure."

"If at any point you change your mind, please tell me

and we'll stop." He looked me in the eyes as if waiting for an acknowledgment, and I nodded, not wanting this to end.

He picked me up, wrapping my legs around him as he carried me into the bedroom. After tossing me on the bed, he crawled over top of me.

This time when he kissed me, he wasn't gentle. He pulled on my bottom lip with his teeth, eliciting a moan as he moved one hand up my tank top, running his thumb over my hardening nipple and rolling it between his fingers as he moved his other hand down beneath the waistband of my jeans

He slipped one of his fingers in, causing me to gasp from the sudden pressure. "Mmm, so ready for me. You've wanted this as much as I have, haven't you, baby?"

I grabbed at the cotton fabric of his T-shirt in response, wanting to feel him, the softness of his skin and the solidness of his chest, against me.

His hands retreated from my body, despite my protesting whine, to yank his shirt off and to pull mine over my head, revealing every inch of my chest.

I already knew his body was toned from rodeo and working on the ranch, but there was still a softness to him as I ran my hand across his stomach.

My heartbeat pounded in my ears as he whispered, "Absolutely beautiful," before he made his way down my body, pulling off every last bit of my clothing and peppering my body with kisses as he went. He stopped at my breasts, taking one in his mouth and sucking gently, causing me to arch toward him as a jolt went through my body. This man was slowly destroying me in the best way possible.

He took his time, worshiping me with his mouth and fingers like I was the last woman he would ever be with.

"Colter, p-please," I stuttered, needing more of him.

"What was that? I don't think I heard you." He removed his fingers—making me ache for him, I was so close—and looked up at me, teasing me.

Cruel. So blissfully cruel.

"I need you inside me. Please, I can't take it anymore," I pleaded, hating how desperate I sounded for this man's touch.

"That's my girl." He pushed himself up to kiss my lips, getting off of me for a split second. The pull of a zipper and a tear of a condom wrapper broke the brief silence. A moment later he was back and pushing into me, our bodies connecting in a way I'd never experienced in past relationships.

I'd had sex before, but nothing like this. This was meaningful and unhurried.

Our eyes met as he moved in and out in a steady rhythm, never slowing, even as he leaned down to kiss me.

"You feel so good," he murmured as he started to pick up his pace.

"I-I'm close, Colter," I moaned as a wave of pleasure washed over me. Pressure kept building, and it only intensified as Colter reached down to massage my clit. I tilted my head back, my mouth slightly opening as I closed my eyes.

"Eyes on me, Ellison. I want to watch as you come all over my cock," he ordered as he grabbed my legs and pulled me even closer to him so I could wrap them around his waist. The look on his face was unlike any other that I'd seen from him. His pupils were dilated, eyes full of lust for me and only me.

"Faster, please," I gasped as he slammed into me. "Ah, fuck!" I was nearing my climax as the angle got deeper the more I clenched my legs around him.

"I'm going to come, baby," he rasped as he gripped my hips and pounded into me harder, which I didn't think it was possible.

"Ah, Colter," I moaned, never taking my eyes off him as we both unraveled.

For the first time, I wasn't worried about the future. It didn't matter what happened tomorrow or even in a week. He was mine and I was his, even if just for this weekend. He was *mine* and nothing had ever felt so right.

"You are so perfect to me," he murmured, after we had finished and he had discarded the condom, before pulling me close to him and drifting off to sleep.

CHAPTER THIRTY-EIGHT

Sunlight streamed through the shades as I pulled Ellison closer to me. She snuggled against me, and my mind went back to the previous night. How it felt to finally have her lips on mine, to feel her wrapped around me, but also knowing that we didn't feel the need to rush, despite our desire to be close.

I wanted to bottle up that memory and drink it every day for the rest of my life. With her, I was comfortable, content. I was convinced the universe had created her especially for me, flaws and all, and I would be damned to ever let her go. I might not have felt worthy of love, especially not Ellison's, but she sure as hell was worthy of mine.

My plan for the day was to take her riding—on horses, although who knew what would happen later. I was open to all of the possibilities.

I knew she loved to ride, and I was sure she was probably missing it, since she was away from Texas and her ranch. I was also a little selfish and wanted to see if she was willing to try her hand at roping with me later.

I rolled out of bed, got dressed as quickly and quietly as I could, careful to not wake her, and slipped outside to catch Bullet so I could bring him over to the trailer to saddle him.

It was a beautiful morning. The sun painted the horizon with an incandescent glow that contrasted perfectly with the blue sky. There were only a few clouds streaking across the horizon, and there was a gentle breeze. Perfect for riding.

Bullet was in the pasture with a few other horses, and it wasn't difficult to catch him with the lead. He was looking forward to this.

I had started walking Bullet back to the trailer when I saw her step out of the house wearing bootcut jeans and one of my Wrangler sweatshirts. God, she was beautiful. Her hair was slightly messy and she looked a little sleepy, but she had a giant grin on her face.

"Are you ready to ride this morning?" I called out to her.

"Both of us are going to ride on that one horse?" she asked sarcastically.

I knew she knew better than to think we were going to double up. She'd been around horses enough to know that shit only happened in the movies and cheesy romance novels.

"Of course not. What kind of cowboy do you think I am? There's no way in hell. I'm not risking injuring my horse or either one of us. You've got to go catch your own." I nodded my head toward the pasture where the other horses were.

"You're going to make me catch my own horse too? Wow, romance must be dead," she joked when she passed me, her hips swinging as she walked away.

Ellison Wilson was going to be the death of me.

She came back with the horse I told her to grab, Trigger, who was one of my other roping horses, and started tacking him up. She hummed a little as she brushed his back, but we didn't say anything as we worked.

The thing was, I could sit in silence with Ellison forever if she had asked me to. We didn't need to speak. Being in the same space as her, breathing the same air, was more than enough. And I think she felt the same.

Minutes later, we were riding side by side out in the country, nothing but open fields ahead of us. There were hills way off in the distance, but for the most part, eastern Montana was really flat. I didn't mind it, though. It felt like you could look out on the horizon forever, with nothing blocking you in.

"I can see why you love it here," Ellison murmured, almost too quiet for me to hear.

Truth was, I liked it more because *she* was here. We could be anywhere in the world right now and it would be my favorite place because of her.

"What's your favorite place in the world, Blaze?" I asked. I knew I had already asked her this question before, but I didn't care.

"That field we drove to back in Texas. Haven't you already asked me this before?" she answered warily.

"Have I?" I replied, waiting for her to take the bait.

"Yes, you did ask me, because you said yours was the rodeo arena." She eyed me suspiciously.

"All right, well my answer has changed," I stated.

"To what?" Of course, curiosity got the better of her; it always did.

"Right now, here. Next week, Houston."

"What do you mean? Why?" She was looking at me

with intrigue now, even if it was mixed with confusion and a little suspicion.

"Because, Ellison, my favorite place is wherever you are." For a moment, there was silence, and I worried I had said something wrong.

"Oh my God, you're so cheesy." She drew out the words and rolled her eyes, but the smile on her face was all I needed.

We rode a little further, down into a valley of wildflowers. When we reached the bottom of the hill, I dismounted Bullet and reached my hand out for her to grab.

"C'mon." I beckoned for her to follow me.

"What are we doing?" she asked.

So many questions.

"Just trust me, come on. The horses will be fine, they won't go anywhere." I pushed, still not giving her details. She took my hand, and I helped her down from her horse, even though I knew she didn't need it.

I pulled her close to me and pressed my lips to her forehead before putting her hand on my shoulder and intertwining her other hand with mine. We didn't have music, just the breeze blowing in the grass and the birds chirping in the background, but I still pulled her in to dance in the middle of the open field.

"What are you doing to me?" she whispered.

"Whatever it takes to make you mine," I murmured back.

"I'm already yours." The three words that came out of her mouth were simple, but they made all the difference. I pulled her in and pressed my lips to hers, savoring her sweet taste, wanting to memorize her, etch her into my mind permanently like a tattoo.

We stumbled through the front door after we had taken care of the horses, hands already on each other, desperate and hungry for each other's touch.

I'm already yours. Her words reverberated off my brain, bouncing around my head as I moved over to the couch and pulled her down onto me. I wanted to hear her say it again and again, like a broken record. I didn't think I'd ever get tired of hearing her claim me.

She straddled my legs, her hands moving up my chest as she rocked her hips. Our lips locked, tongues fighting for dominance.

She grasped my shirt, stripping it over my head, so I returned the favor, taking off her shirt and unclasping her bra, freeing her breasts. I pulled away for a moment to look at her.

"What the fuck are you doing?" she protested and placed her hand on the back of my neck to pull me back to her.

"I want you to say it again." I smirked, not letting her move me toward her.

"Say what?"

"That you're mine."

She sighed, looking away for a moment, but then she was back, her eyes staring into mine. "I'm yours, Colter."

I grabbed her thighs then, flipping her so our spots were reversed, her with her back against the couch and me above her. Before she could move, I pulled her legs toward me and lowered myself to the ground so that I was kneeling in front of her.

"W-what are you doing?" she stammered, cheeks flushed and lust clouding her eyes.

I didn't say a word as I reached for the buttons on her jeans, undoing them and pulling them down her legs. Her eyes widened as I started to kiss my way up her leg, not stopping until I had reached the soft skin on the inside of her thigh.

I blew air on the cotton fabric of her underwear and watched as she sucked in a breath. I could feel myself getting hard, my jeans noticeably tighter. She tried to sit up, but I stopped her, squeezing her breast and holding her against the couch at the same time.

"I want to make you feel good, baby." I pushed aside her panties and plunged a finger inside her. *Fuck.* She was already soaked. I pulled my finger out, her arousal coating it, as I grabbed the sides of her underwear and pulled them all the way down her legs, baring her to me.

"Please," she whined.

"Tell me what you need, baby," I teased, running my finger along her entrance but not sticking it completely in. She was practically dripping with anticipation.

"Your mouth," she gasped as I rubbed her clit, eliciting a moan and causing her body to tremble.

I lowered my mouth onto her, working my tongue and my fingers to make her squirm. Looking up at her, my mouth still latched on, I watched as she writhed with pleasure.

"I'm s-so c-close," she stuttered.

I picked up the pace of my fingers, moving in and out, and rubbed circles on her clit with my thumb as she came undone.

"That's it, baby, take what you need." My words were muffled, creating a vibration on her clit that sent her unraveling into her orgasm. The taste of her exploded on my tongue, and I licked up every sweet drop.

She sat up, looking a little dazed, but still had a determined glint in her eye. Pulling me toward her, she tugged on the zipper of my jeans and pulled them down, putting the outline of my erection on full display. Before she could do anything, I moved her so she was lying flat on her back on the couch.

"But I—" She pouted, reaching for the bulge in my boxers.

"There will be plenty of time for that later. Right now, I want to be inside you." I moved out of her reach, pulling my boxers down. There was nothing between us as I pressed my weight onto her, just our naked bodies.

She sucked in a breath right before I quickly stopped, my tip barely touching her entrance.

"What the fuck, Colter?" she growled, reaching for me.

"I don't have a condom," I breathed. *How could I forget?*

"I'm on birth control." She sighed as her hand grasped my length, starting to stroke it.

"Fuck," I gasped. "Are you sure? I'm clear."

Ellison was the first woman I'd had sex with since my engagement. There were no worries there, but as much as I wanted to take her bare, I didn't want her to do anything she might regret later.

"Colter, if you don't fuck me in the next three seconds, I'll do it myself." She clenched her jaw in sexual frustration.

"So bossy. You like to be in control, don't you?" I taunted her, still not giving her what she wanted. Her eyes burned into me with a fire behind them. "Well, with me you're going to have to learn to let go. I'll take care of you, but I'm going to take my sweet time."

She opened her mouth to argue, but before any words could come out, I plunged inside her, giving her all of me.

"Fuck, baby," I groaned as I moved, slowly at first. Her nails scraped my back as she held onto me, gasping for air. "You feel so good."

She whimpered in response, a jumble of curse words and moans.

"Use your words, baby. Tell me what I'm doing to you," I ordered. I wasn't normally like this, but something about Ellison brought out a different side of me, a more dominant side.

"Y-you're," she stuttered.

I was bringing her to the brink and then pulling back before she could find any kind of release.

"I'm what, Ellison?" I pulled out of her slightly, pausing.

"You're fucking me so good, Colter! Please don't stop!" she cried out, begging me to move back inside her.

"Good girl. I love it when you say my name," I murmured in her ear, right before I picked up my pace, thrusting deep into her, harder, faster with every movement.

Her moans got louder as I kept moving, until I felt her tighten around me. I placed my hand on her abdomen, feeling my cock moving inside her, filling her. God, I was so close, I was doing everything I could not to bust right then and there.

"Where do you want me to finish?" I forced out the question through gritted teeth, trying not to come. Even though she was on birth control, I didn't want to assume she was okay with me coming inside her.

"Huh?" She opened her eyes.

"Can I finish inside you?" I asked, pausing for a beat. She simply nodded, but that wasn't good enough for me. "I need a verbal answer, Ellison. Do you want my cum to fill you as badly as I want it to?"

"God, yes. Please," she moaned, and that was all I needed for affirmation as I slammed back into her.

I could tell it would only take a few more strokes for me to come so I leaned closer to whisper in her ear. "Let go, Ellison. Come for me, baby." I nipped her ear right as she came undone, her eyes rolling back. I rode out her orgasm, feeling every wave of pleasure move through her body, before I spilled inside her.

"You're so beautiful." I kissed her forehead, still on top of her, catching my breath. "And. You're. Fucking. Mine." I peppered her neck with kisses every time a word came out of my mouth.

"I'm yours, Colter. I've always been yours." She looked up at me with passion in her eyes, and it took everything I had to not tell her I loved her right there on the spot.

CHAPTER THIRTY-NINE

ellison

I woke up to Colter's arms wrapped around me and our naked bodies entwined together. We hadn't done much the rest of the day, unless you counted the other orgasms Colter had served me throughout the night. I kept waiting for the honeymoon feeling to fade and the dread of this being temporary to sink in, but it never did.

I've always been yours, I told him last night. The old me would have passed it off as being lust and tried to come up with excuses for why I didn't mean it, but every fiber of my aching body knew it was true. I hadn't thought about a single other person since the night at Nectar & Vine, before that even. He had a tight grip on me, and I was done fighting. If he drowned, I was going down with him.

Looking at Colter was like looking into a mirror. He reflected the brightest and darkest parts of me. The main difference was where I tended to blend in with the shadows, Colter shone bright. He put his full heart on display and he was absolutely golden.

I shifted my body and tried to move, but he mumbled

something and pulled me back, nuzzling his face in the crook between my shoulder and neck.

I attempted to move again.

"Mmm, baby," he mumbled.

"I need to get up." I laughed, trying to push him off of me again. My bladder felt like it was going to burst, I needed to get up to relieve myself.

"Mm-no," he complained.

If you aren't going to let me get up, I'm going to make you move, I thought as my hand slid down his body to squeeze his hard length. I looked over my shoulder back at him for a reaction. Nothing. I worked my fingers over his tip, gently squeezing and working the most sensitive part of him.

His eyes shot open, and then a lustful smirk formed on his face.

"Didn't get enough last night, baby?" He grinned, looking satisfied with himself as he let go of my body, presumably to move on top of me.

"Nope." I took the opportunity to slide out from the covers, getting out of bed and leaving him with a bemused look on his face.

"What—"

"I'll be back. I just need to use the bathroom." I rolled my eyes and rushed to the bathroom.

After I was done, I looked at myself in the mirror, a glowing flush on my face, and smiled to myself as I washed my hands.

When I got back into the room, he was lying on the bed waiting for me, pouting like a puppy, his cock still standing at attention.

I got up on the edge of the bed, crawling up to him. "What's wrong, baby? Did I wake you?" I teased, spreading his legs so I could come up between them.

"Yes, and then you left," he groaned as I grabbed his cock, pumping it in my fist.

"Let me make it up to you." I lowered my mouth onto him, swirling my tongue around his tip, the salty taste of him coating my tongue.

He shuddered as I took him deeper, still only going halfway down his length. His hands fisted my hair, pushing me further down, urging me to take all of him.

The tip of his cock hit the back of my throat as I worked up and down, using my mouth and hands in tandem. I moaned a little, the vibrations from my mouth causing him to grip me harder and curse his praises.

"Fuck, Ellison. Fuck you're so good, baby."

I pulled him out of my mouth, popping my lips like I was sucking on a lollipop. I was about to lower myself onto him when the sound of a fist pounding on the front door interrupted us and I scrambled off onto the other side of the bed.

"What the fuck?" Colter muttered.

"I'm coming in, Carson! You two better not be fucking!" Mikey's voice yelled from behind the wooden door.

"For the love of God." Colter rolled his eyes as he got up and put on a pair of shorts, tucking his still hard dick to the side. "Stay here, I'll take care of this," he told me before he closed the bedroom door.

Well, that officially killed the mood. I decided to get dressed for the day, knowing if Mikey was here, Colter and I probably wouldn't have any alone time to finish what I had started.

I was pulling on my jeans when Colter came back into the room.

"Sorry about that. They want us to come by Reid's

place this afternoon. Not sure why he had to come all the way to the house to tell me, but Mikey's nosey," he explained before he flopped face down on the bed.

"Oh, okay," I said, sitting on the bed next to him and running my nails gently up and down his back.

"Baby, you keep doing that and we aren't going to leave this house today. Unfortunately, we do have to leave the house to see them, otherwise I would have had other plans." He groaned as he reluctantly hoisted himself off the bed to go get dressed to see the boys.

Reid lived only about fifteen minutes away, in between Silver Creek and Miles City. He had a big arena next to his house where he and Colter practiced when they were home. It was built before Reid had bought his house, the previous owners having been a rodeo family. Colter mentioned he wanted to build one someday, but until then, the one Reid had was more than enough.

When we pulled up to the metal fence, Colter's friends were already standing around. Before we left we had loaded up Bullet and Trigger, since Colter also wanted me to rope with him, despite my claims that I didn't know how to. I was lying of course. I'd helped with roping the calves many times at brandings.

"Hey, Colter, Ellie!" Reid called out to us after we stepped out of the pickup.

I wasn't going to correct Reid on my name. Usually, I reserved the nickname for the people closest to me—Isabelle and my mom—but I wanted Colter's friends to like me. And I knew from what I had heard about Reid and our small interactions that I could trust him.

"Hey, man." Colter gave him one of those bro hugs, where they didn't fully hug, but they almost did and then they slapped each other on the back.

"Hey." I gave him a smile before he caught me off guard and pulled me in for a hug too.

"You're part of the family now," he whispered in my ear. "Anyone who makes Colter this happy is one of us."

"Carson, come over here!" Mikey yelled at him from across the arena.

Colter grinned at me and shook his head a little before he took off.

"So, how are you liking Montana?" Reid asked as he helped me get the horses out of the trailer and tied up.

"It's definitely not Texas," I joked. "But I do like it here. It's different in a good way."

"Well, I'm glad you're here and I know Colt is too." He looked at me with a genuine smile, but there was something else behind his eyes that I couldn't pinpoint, maybe a tinge of concern. The look quickly faded, though.

We tied the horses to the trailer and then walked into the arena where Mikey, Hayden, Jake, and Colter were all standing in a circle and talking. Mikey was making wild gestures, which seemed to be a norm for him, and the rest of the boys were just listening to him, occasionally shaking their heads with disbelief or amusement.

"And then she stormed out of my house and I haven't seen her since!" Mikey exclaimed as we got close enough to hear their conversation.

"Damn, bro, maybe you should think about not being such a whore," Jake joked as Mikey flipped him off.

"Well, boys, are we going to stand around all day or are we going to do something?" Reid clapped his hands together.

Jake and Hayden walked off, having their own conversation between themselves. I noticed Hayden was a lot quieter than the rest of them, more reserved. I liked him.

"Do you want to rope with me?" Colter asked.

"Do I have a choice?" I raised an eyebrow, and he smirked. *I guess not.*

We tacked up our horses and watched as Hayden and Jake roped together. I learned that Hayden was a team roper but Jake wasn't, so that explained their dynamic. It wasn't that Jake wasn't good at roping—he was because he did tie-down roping—he just wasn't used to roping with another person and being the heeler.

Mikey was the one who opened the chute for the steers because he was solely a bull rider and didn't generally rope.

"Mikey, you gonna get out there?" I called out to him.

"Nah, sugar, I use my ropes for a different purpose." He winked, and I frowned, trying to get the image out of my head.

Gross.

"Mikey! Stop hitting on my girl," Colter scolded him.

"Oh? Your girl? Damn, Carson, that's a new development. Are you sure you agreed to that?" He turned to me, and although I knew he was fucking with Colter, I still got defensive over him.

"Yeah, Mikey. I'm his girlfriend, what's it to you?" I quipped before I could stop myself.

Colter's face lit up, his smile brighter than I had ever seen it, as he came over and wrapped me up in his arms.

"Girlfriend, huh?" he whispered in my ear, and my heart fluttered. "I could get used to that."

He kissed me on the cheek as Jake whistled and Mikey yelled, "Gross, get a room!"

I just laughed, feeling very content as part of the friend group, even if some of them were pure goofballs.

"All right, Blaze, are you ready to show me what you're made of?" Colter pulled me along.

"I don't really have a choice," I grumbled, a little nervous to showcase my roping "skills" in front of these people who did this for a living. They were professionals. I was not.

"You'll be fine, baby. Hell, you could rope circles around Mikey," he reassured me as we both mounted our horses and Reid handed me a rope.

"Have you heeled before?" he asked me, and I shook my head.

We roped calves for branding using head-and-heel instead of heel-only, and I never really learned how to heel. I'd still had plenty of experience roping, but I knew heeling could be difficult if you didn't have prior experience.

"It's a little bit different from being a header." He explained the differences with where to aim and how to throw the rope effectively.

I nodded as he went along, grasping the basics of it fairly easily.

I held the reins nervously. I didn't rodeo; this wasn't part of my lifestyle, showing off my skills to other people. Yet, I found myself wanting to be part of this, no pressure, just having fun.

Colter backed his horse up, and I followed, backing up on the right side of the box. I knew enough about team roping to know how it worked, but I still didn't want to mess anything up, even though there was nothing on the line.

"You ready, baby?" he asked me.

"Ready as I'll ever be?" I tried to say confidently, but it came out as more of a question.

"It's okay if you miss, this is for fun, okay?"

I knew he meant well, but it only fueled my competitive side more.

Colter nodded, and Mikey opened the chute gate. This particular steer was a bit slower than the ones they had during competitions, so it wasn't hard for Colter to catch up to it and rope its horns. I followed fairly closely after him, swinging the rope over my head waiting for the right moment to throw the loop as the steer was still moving. I saw my opening and I took it, catching the legs.

I felt my jaw drop. I couldn't believe I'd actually caught the steer on the first run and was dazed for a split second before I snapped back into what I was doing and dallied my rope.

"Hell yeah, Ellie!" Reid whooped from the outside of the fence. "Now that there, boys? That's a real cowgirl!"

I looked over and saw the corner of Colter's lip turn up in a grin at Reid's comment. Even Hayden and Mikey were smiling and clapping.

"That was pretty damn impressive there, Blaze." Colter rode his horse over to me, getting close enough to peck me on the lips. "Might give Reid over there a run for his money!" he called loud enough for Reid to hear, but Reid just shrugged his arms in response.

CHAPTER FORTY

She was a natural. Watching her out here, roping with the boys, made me happy. It was nice to see her being involved in my life, even if it meant hanging out with the people she least expected to be associating with. I knew she had experience with roping, but I didn't expect her to be able to keep up as well as she did, and that was purely a mistake on my part. She was talented, and I hoped one day she would compete, even if the first couple times scared her to death.

We stood against the fence on the outside of the arena, my arm wrapped around her shoulders, pulling her close to me. I tried not to think about her going back to Texas in a few days, leaving us with a long-distance relationship—a real one—since she had proclaimed herself as my girlfriend earlier.

"What are you thinking about?" She looked up at me with her round eyes, eyebrows furrowed.

"I am thinking about how perfect these last few days have been and how much I want you to stay here." *Forever,* I added in my brain.

"These last couple days have been perfect, haven't they?" She grinned, putting her arm around my waist as we stood there, holding each other and watching as Reid and the boys messed around in the arena.

"Colter! Let's go!" Reid yelled at me.

I kissed Ellison and climbed over the fence. Reid and I hadn't practiced in a couple of weeks. We needed to keep our skills sharp for the next month of traveling that would start in a few days, after Ellison left.

I mounted Bullet, getting him to walk over to the chute, and Reid followed.

"I like you two together, Colter. You're good for each other."

His approval meant the world to me. He knew more about my personal life than anyone and if he thought Ellison and I were good together, then that was more validation than I would ever need.

"Mikey, get over here! Stop texting your woman!" I yelled at him, and he glared at me before typing furiously for a couple more seconds and then running over. "You're like a damn teenager," I teased.

"I don't know if you should be calling me a teenager, Carson, considering I almost caught you and your girl this morning."

Meh, minor detail.

Reid and I lined up as Ellison watched from the sidelines. I looked over at her and her eyes locked on only me.

"Let's go!" I nodded and we were off. I don't know what it was about this particular run, but something felt off. I ignored it, though, as I swung my rope and threw it onto the steer's horns.

I went to dally as the steer turned, and my horse

followed. However, unbeknownst to me, my stirrups weren't adjusted correctly, and my left boot had slipped out of it. With the sudden jolt of the turn, I was thrown from the horse and into the fence, my spine rattling against the metal railing and my skull slamming against the post that stabilized it. A frantic yell rose from the end of the arena before everything went black.

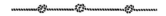

CHAPTER FORTY-ONE

I saw Colter's body lying on the ground, his horse still running as Reid tried to catch the steer to guide it back to the corral. People were yelling and running into the arena to help him, but I was paralyzed.

Shit, shit, shit.

I couldn't move; my feet felt like they were glued to the earth.

At that moment, it was like I was eight again.

Dad's crumpled body lay motionless on the floor of the arena. He was too far away to see clearly, now that the cameras were off of him, but I could still see the blood soaking through his shirt.

The arena was eerily quiet, almost as if it were empty, with only the livestock and horses making noise. Dad's hazer had retrieved his horse and the mounted officials had already gotten the steer back in the corral while first responders carried a stretcher down to take Dad to the hospital.

Mom grabbed my hand, urging me to follow her. Her movements were jerky, panicked, and her hand shook in mine as we hustled down the stairs of the grandstands and toward the exit.

"Mom, where are we going? What about Dad?" I whimpered.

"We're going to meet him at the hospital, Ellie. It's going to be okay," she tried to reassure me, keeping her voice as steady as possible.

At that point, the paramedics had Dad on the stretcher and were carrying him out of the arena toward an ambulance. Their demeanor was urgent, and from that alone I could sense the accident was more serious than Mom was letting on.

We hurried out to the vehicle to try to meet the ambulance at the hospital. I saw a tear stream down Mom's face out of the corner of my eye before she quickly wiped it away. Externally, she was trying to be strong for me, for us, but I could tell that, internally, she was terrified and didn't know what to do. She drove to the hospital faster than I had ever seen her drive. She almost ran a stop sign—she was that determined to get there.

When we got to the hospital, my dad's parents were already there waiting. Grandpa pulled me away from Mom to go sit down in the waiting room. I tried to pull away in protest; I wanted to be with Mom, but I wasn't strong enough.

Before we got too far out of earshot, I faintly heard Mom ask Grandma in a hushed tone, "Where is he? Is he going to be okay?" It was like she didn't want me to listen to their conversation, but I could hear everything.

"They have him in the ICU. That's all we know right now. The only thing we can do is pray the steer's horn didn't pierce his heart," Grandma told her. "They're trying to get him stabilized. I'm sorry, Hanna, they just aren't giving us much information."

"Grandpa, how long is it going to be?" I asked him.

"I don't know, sweetheart. I wish I had an answer for you, but we're just going to have to be patient," he replied.

Mom and Grandma joined us a few minutes later, and we all sat together in the waiting room. The rodeo was still being televised, and they had already moved on to the next events, like the accident hadn't happened and my entire world wasn't about to change.

I counted the tiles on the ceiling, watched cars go by, and watched people leave the hospital. People in wheelchairs, couples with tiny babies, and families with tears in their eyes. I begged God to not let my family be one of the latter. I silently pleaded that Dad would be okay and leave the hospital holding both Mom's hand and mine.

There were only so many games you could play in your head before you started to get anxious and impatient and I was well past the point of being impatient. Time felt like it was moving in slow motion. A minute felt like an hour as we waited for someone to come tell us what was going on.

"How much longer is it going to be?" I pouted. It had only been fifteen minutes but I wanted to see Dad.

"I don't know, Ellison," Mom curtly responded. She was stressed. We were all stressed.

"This isn't fair," I huffed and crossed my arms. I was tired and I wanted to go home and I wanted Dad.

"Let's go take a walk, shall we?" Grandpa offered.

"But I want to see Dad," I protested.

"Well, let's just go walk around and that will pass the time," he countered.

"Fine," I conceded.

He grabbed my hand and we went down the hallway, past a coffee shop and vending machines. The hallway had a sterile smell to it, like it was trying to mask the fact that people died in this place all the time.

Once we reached the end of the hall and couldn't walk any farther, we turned around. It had already been a couple minutes. On our way back, he bought himself a bottle of water and a chocolate bar for me.

"Our little secret." He winked at me, and I gave him a beaming grin.

When we got back to the waiting room, a man in a white coat who I assumed was a doctor was speaking to Mom and Grandma. Mom was chewing on her lip and had her hands clenched together but she was nodding at what he was saying. We made our way over to them, and I politely waited for an update.

"We can go see Dad now, Ellie," Mom said softly.

The doctor guided us through the closed double doors, down a long corridor. After taking a few turns, he gestured for us to enter a small room.

Dad lay in the hospital bed hooked up to machines with bandages on his chest. Even though he looked weak, there was still a glint of mischief in his eye.

Mom entered the room before the rest of us. "You're supposed to aim for the back of the steer, Cowboy," she joked.

He just chuckled at her. "You're right, Baby Blue. You always have been. From the moment I met you, all you've ever been is right. And I love you so much for that." He turned his head to me as I walked into the room. "Hi, Sunshine."

"Dad, are you going to be okay?" My lip trembled a little, and I couldn't bring myself to meet his eyes. It was weird seeing him laid up in a hospital bed, and I didn't like it. I just wanted him to come home.

"I don't know, but the doctors are taking care of me the best that they can," he replied, a little sadly.

I believed him. Dad was always right.

Except for maybe one thing because he had promised me that I never had anything to worry about when he was competing, that he had never been hurt by a steer.

But he was wrong. He had *gotten hurt by one.*

I had seen him bleeding on the dirt and I saw him now, with cords and machines hooked up to him.

"What exactly did the doctor say? Is there anything they can do? There has to be!" Mom asked frantically. "What are we going to do

without you? What am I going to do without you? I need you here with me! I can't do this without you!"

I didn't understand why she was asking those questions. What did she mean by, "What am I going to do without you?"

He was coming with us. He had *to come home with us.*

Tears welled in my eyes. I didn't understand.

Dad ignored her, his focus locked on me. "Hey, look at me."

I looked up at him, my eyes still glassy.

"Listen, when I get out of here, we're going to make sure Mom takes you to Cheyenne one day. You'll love it there."

"Okay, Dad." I nodded.

I had no idea what that meant, besides Cheyenne being the place where Mom and Dad had first met. It had to be special if we were going to go there in the future.

"I love you, Sunshine." He kissed my forehead.

"I love you too, Dad." I hugged him, not wanting to let go.

Grandpa and Grandma came in and said a few things to Dad and then they told me to go with them and give my parents some time alone. I didn't argue because I knew that once they were done talking, Dad would be cleared to go and we would all leave the hospital together. He had to; he was invincible.

I gave them one last look over my shoulder, not knowing it would be the last time I would see my dad alive.

"Ellie! Come here, girl, you look like you've seen a ghost!" Reid called out to me, bringing me back to reality. Everyone was gathered around Colter, trying to evaluate how serious his injury was.

"Is he going to be all right?" I asked as I slowly walked up to the group, trying to keep my expression as neutral as possible. My mind was still clogged with thoughts of that night, and it took all of my focus to keep the sound of my dad's voice from shouting in my head.

"He hit the railing pretty hard when he was thrown from his horse. Enough that he's out cold right now. We're going to run him to the hospital if you want to come," Reid explained.

I hated hospitals. Even if I never had to step into another one again, it would still be too soon. Especially for something like this. But Colter was important to me. And I was going to be there for him when he woke up.

"Yeah, I'll go with you guys," I agreed.

CHAPTER FORTY-TWO

colter

My head was throbbing. And when I opened my eyes to figure out where I was, fluorescent lights made the pain worse.

"Where the fuck am I?" I groaned and tried to sit up.

"Easy there, Sparky. You're concussed, lie back down." Ellison was standing to my left.

"What happened?" I was trying my best to remember, but the last memory I had of the accident was foggy.

"You got thrown into the fence. Hit your head pretty hard. The doctors said you were lucky there was no significant damage." Reid walked closer to me.

"Fuck, man." I didn't know what to say. This was the kind of injury that could have been prevented. The kind that shouldn't have happened. Not at this point in the year.

"It happens, Colt. It wasn't your fault," he tried to reassure me.

It was my fault, though. This could cost us big in the long run. I wouldn't be able to compete, and Reid would have to rope with a different partner. It wasn't always the biggest problem, but competing with someone who you weren't familiar or compatible with could result in a drop in the rankings. We couldn't afford that, especially not if we were hoping to make it to the NFR.

A sense of apprehension rose in me. I was about to fail another person. I had failed Sophie, and now I was failing Reid too. Who was to say I wouldn't fail Ellison next?

I knew if that happened, I would never recover. I couldn't handle letting down two of the most important people in my life on the same day.

The room started to heat up, getting uncomfortably warm. I didn't realize I was sucking in air, unable to breathe, until Ellison was right next to me, holding my hand. I leaned into her touch, her presence starting to quiet the thundering voices in my head.

"Breathe, Sparks," she urged, her voice immediately calming me. "Do it with me. In and out."

"I'm so sorry, I-I don't know what happened." *Fuck, why am I so weak?*

"Colt, I'm sorry, I-I tried to stop her." Jake ran in apologizing, out of breath.

"What do you—" the words fell from my mouth as I saw her walk in.

Sophie.

I had to do a double take to make sure it wasn't just a figment of my imagination, that the injury wasn't making me see things. But no, it was really her. Why was she here? Why now?

"Hi, Colter," she murmured as she walked over to the side of the hospital bed opposite Ellison to put a hand on my arm.

I couldn't pull away before she discreetly dug her nails in and asked with saccharine concern, "How are you doing? Are you okay, *babe*?" She looked directly at Ellison when she called me babe, an icy bite to her tone as if she was claiming territory she had no right to anymore.

I couldn't find any words, couldn't tell her to leave. I just stared at her in disbelief, or perhaps awe, at how calculated she could be.

CHAPTER FORTY-THREE

ellison

I looked back and forth between Colter and the unfamiliar woman who currently had her hand on his arm. She was beautiful. No, she was absolutely stunning. And she was nothing like me. It was like looking at a polar opposite.

She smiled at Colter, and he just stared at her. Confusion and hurt poured through me, and any and all rational thoughts were gone as jealousy creeped up my skin. The room had suddenly warmed to what felt like a hundred degrees and it was as though the walls of the already tiny hospital room were closing in on me.

How could I have been so stupid? It only took one look at them to know that she meant something to him. I mean, she called him *babe*. I just didn't know what she was to him. And I didn't think I wanted to stick around to find out.

I dropped Colter's hand before I pushed past Reid and Jake and stormed out the door. My fight or flight instinct had kicked in, and I wasn't sure I had any fight left in me.

"Ellison, wait!" Colter called after me.

I ignored him. I needed air, space. I needed to be out

of that room and away from whatever sick punishment that was for finally letting someone in.

Was any of it real? My mind was racing through worst-case scenarios. I saw the way she looked at him. The way he couldn't seem to take his eyes off her. He looked at me that way the other night—had looked at me that way the past couple of months—and I foolishly thought I was special, that I could take his words at face value.

That was the problem with cowboys. They came into your life and made you feel like you hung the moon, but they always took off at some point. Heartache was not a question of if, but when.

"Ellie, stop!"

I turned my head as Reid flew out of Colter's hospital room.

"It's not what it looks like."

"Then what is it, Reid? Who is she?" I whirled around to face him before he could touch me, hardening my jaw, despite the lump in my throat. I wasn't going to let this break me.

"She's Colt's ex-fiancée. I have no idea why she's here or what she wants. Please, just hear him out," he explained.

Ex-fiancée?

I blinked, trying to wrap my head around that information. "Why should I, though? I saw the way they looked at each other." My voice broke slightly as I spoke.

Dammit.

He reached toward me, but I jerked away, crossing my arms defensively.

Don't touch me. Please, I pleaded silently.

He took a step back, hurt flashing in his expression for a moment. But then he sighed. "Because, Ellie, you're the best damn thing to happen to Colter in two years. If there's only one thing you believe, then let it be this. Colter cares about you. He's a better version of himself when you're by his side. And I know you care about him too. Otherwise you wouldn't be running away like this."

Colter was right about Reid. He was observant.

"And yeah, Sophie made him happy once. We all thought she was it for him. But then she broke up with him with a text message. She didn't even give them a fighting chance, and Colter blamed himself for every single moment, every single fight leading up to the breakup. He let it consume him, thinking that he had failed—that if he wasn't worthy of Sophie's love, he wasn't worthy of anyone's. But the moment Colter saw you, Ellison, something changed in him."

"Is that enough, though? What if I can't be what he needs? What if I'm not worthy of *his* love?" I was fighting an emotional war within myself.

I knew I was broken. I'd spent so much time over the past fifteen years trying to piece myself back together on my own—fighting my demons outnumbered—and I was tired. Tired of asking myself if what I was doing was enough for everyone around me.

But what if the question wasn't whether I was enough for Colter or whether he needed me? What if the question was whether Colter was what *I* needed?

I already knew the answer. Over the past couple months, I had fallen back in love with rodeo, with the lifestyle I never thought I'd return to.

Deep in my heart, I recognized that I didn't need to carry all of this weight on my own, but for me, it was a matter of letting go and allowing someone to shoulder the burden with me. But letting go and asking for help didn't mean I was weak or had lost control of the situation. Showing someone my vulnerabilities didn't make me someone who needed saving, so why was I still running?

I wholeheartedly believed Colter wasn't going to try to save me. He didn't expect me to be a certain way or try to change me. Time and time again he showed me that he accepted me as I was. That was all anyone could ever ask for, and yet I was still terrified.

"I can't tell you that, but what I can tell you is that the man in that room would walk through fire for the people he loves. He won't force anyone to stay if they don't want to, but he's not just going to give up either."

Love. There was that word—the one that threatened to break everything apart. The one that desired to creep up my stone walls like ivy and cause them to come crashing down to no more than rubble.

"I'm scared," I admitted. I'd never had the type of connection I had with Colter with anyone else. Every relationship I had before now was surface level. I had never let them get so deep.

My first heartbreak came in childhood. I wasn't ready to have it broken a second time.

"I know. But Colter? He's not going to let you go. You can trust him, Ellie." He pulled me into his arms, reassuring me.

This time, I didn't pull away, understanding that Reid was someone I could trust and that his words about Colter were genuine.

I remembered Colter's words from a few days prior. "*I've already been yours for a long time.*" That had to have meant something; he wouldn't have just said that. The realization alone gave me the courage to go back.

"Okay."

You can do this. Just hear him out. You at least owe him that.

I was about to walk into the room when I heard Colter.

"Why are you here, Sophie? What makes you think you can just come back?"

"I'm still your emergency contact, Colter…" I couldn't hear her full response, but Colter was naturally loud.

"You left me once already and I dealt with the consequences, believe me. You could have chosen to come back when I needed you, but you didn't. You abandoned me during the worst year of my life and you have no right to come back now!" He was angry, hurt.

I chose that moment to step around the corner and enter the room just as his ex lowered her voice.

"Yeah, well, I came here to make sure you're okay. It's not like I wanted to, but I was doing the right thing." She noticed me entering the room and began speaking in a normal tone again as she looked me up and down and scoffed. "But obviously you already have someone doing that for you."

"I didn't ask you to come here and you shouldn't have! When you broke up with me, you lost any entitlement to me and any right to care. You need to leave now."

I could tell that it pained Colter to see her here. That it really was unexpected and caught him off guard.

She gave me an icy glare, a look of disgust, as we passed by each other, and then she was gone.

He was sitting up in the hospital bed, his head facing the ground, holding his forehead like the entire interaction with Sophie gave him a worse headache than getting thrown from the horse did. The moment he looked up, guilt flashed in his eyes.

"I'm sorry, Ellison. I had no idea she was going to show

up. And I should have told you about her." Colter immediately apologized when he saw me.

I gave him a sheepish smile. It was my turn to apologize. "I shouldn't have reacted the way I did."

In all honesty, I knew Colter hadn't done anything wrong. Yes, maybe he should have told me about her, but the fact was, all he'd ever done was place his trust in me. He had told me once that he had failed someone, that he blamed himself for what happened. I never thought to ask more about it, when I could have. And he had no way of knowing she was going to show up here. I didn't care anymore that he had never told me anything about her because it was clear from their conversation that she wasn't a part of his life.

"After the breakup, I guess I was so caught up in everything that I forgot to change my emergency contact to Reid. I'm not sure why she felt the need to come here, because she's no longer in my life. I can promise you that. She made sure of it. It's not her decision anymore whether or not she gets to come back."

I looked down at my feet, heat rising to my cheeks as I continued my string of apologies. "I'm sorry I ran. I panicked. I assumed the worst, and you didn't deserve that."

We were throwing each other a lifeline here.

"There was no way you could have known. I never told you anything about her, about what happened between us." He squeezed his eyes shut, pausing for a moment as if he needed to compose himself. "I never told you because the breakup destroyed me. I was scared to tell you what happened because I didn't want you to see me differently. After she left, I was angry, depressed, and I had a drinking problem. I was doing whatever I could to try to numb the pain, even if it meant everyone around me suffered. If Reid hadn't helped me, gotten me back on my feet, I wouldn't be sitting here.

"And I hate that about myself. I hate that I wasn't strong enough, that I didn't fight hard enough for her, enough for myself. I couldn't even keep myself together." His voice had turned gravelly, like it still pained him to talk about it.

I started to tear up, thinking about how selfishly I had run away without considering his emotions, how it might affect him. All my life I had been running, retreating from anything that could cause me or others to hurt. But I was here now, and I wanted to take all of his pain away— reassure him that he was enough and he didn't have to hide. I was his and he was mine, and I wasn't going to run anymore.

He had done so much to make me feel like I didn't have to fight on my own. He had been strong for me, and now it was my turn to be strong for him.

"I'm here now. It's okay, we'll get through this together," I murmured, maybe to myself more than to anyone else.

Healing wasn't linear, I knew that better than anyone. But I also knew that no one should have to feel like they were alone in whatever challenges and struggles they faced. The road ahead of us would be long, with winds and speed bumps, but I knew we could make it. We had made it this far, after all.

CHAPTER FORTY-FOUR

colter

The concussion really threw a wrench in my plans. The doctor prohibited me from competing for about a month. If I was lucky enough, I would be able to come back for the Home of Champions Rodeo on the Fourth of July, one of the largest rodeos in the state, where some of the best of the best would be competing. Competing in that event would be crucial to maintaining my spot in the world standings and making it to the NFR.

Ellison changed her travel plans to stay in Montana with me while Reid and the boys went out on the road. Neither of us wanted Reid to have to stay home and miss out on competing, but I still protested her staying. As much as I wanted her here, I didn't want her staying for this reason.

I kept saying I would be fine and *definitely* wouldn't be practicing while they were gone, but apparently no one believed me, and my girl was stubborn enough that she would have argued with me about it until the end of time.

I overheard her make some calls before we left the hospital.

"Mom, there's been an accident," she'd spoken in a hushed tone. "It's okay, Mom. Colter got a bad concussion. But he can't compete for the next month and no one trusts him not to try to tough it out. The last thing he needs is brain damage."

I puffed air out of my nose at that as she continued.

"I think I need to stay here longer. Will you be okay by yourself?"

Her phone call with her mother went on for a little bit longer, but she stepped away so I couldn't hear unless I really strained my ears. When she came back, she was on the phone with the airline, already switching her flight back home.

"Hi, yes, my name is Ellison Wilson. I had a flight out of Bozeman in a couple of days, but I'm going to need to reschedule my flight. Mm-hmm. Yes, thank you."

I had to admit, I did appreciate her making such big sacrifices for me, but I was supposed to be stronger than this. I wasn't supposed to be the one who needed help from everyone; that was a past me I didn't want to think about anymore.

If anyone could understand how I was feeling, it was Ellison, but I still didn't feel strong enough to bare that piece of my heart to her. She knew about the engagement and a little bit about the drinking problem now, but what she didn't know was how much I still felt like a failure because of it.

Before Ellison came into my life, I wasn't worried about failing because my only focus was on rodeo and Reid and I were successful. But then she came into the picture and raised the bar for me. She added this layer to my life, patched up the parts of me I didn't know I was missing and made me feel more complete.

The boys took us back to my house, and Reid gave me the whole lecture about not practicing or doing anything that could set back my date for getting cleared. A lot of times in this career, cowboys would sustain a minor injury, but the pressure would surmount, and they would let peer pressure, from fans, sponsors, or even other competitors, get to them, ultimately making the decision to compete and causing the injury to be much worse.

"Colter." He looked me in the eyes, his expression hard and stern. "I mean it. *I* need you at one hundred percent. I'm fine without you when you're not at your best. Just focus on coming back healthy."

No pressure, buddy, I thought, but all I did was nod. We would come back from this, it was a minor setback.

Yeah, a minor setback that's costing you thousands of dollars.

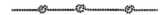

"They're probably branding back at home right now," Ellison whispered to me as we lay next to each other in the dark. "Branding is always kind of a shit show on the Merritt ranch." Her body shook with silent laughter.

"Why's that?" I laced my fingers with hers, brushing my thumb over her index finger.

"It's a miracle if someone doesn't accidentally get branded or shot. Truthfully, though, my mother runs a tight ship during branding, so you wouldn't think things would happen but they do. I don't hold the calves when we brand, so I don't have to deal with accidentally getting branded at least. But I have to deal with men telling me that they can rope better than me."

I could somehow feel her roll her eyes in the darkness.

"Well, that's a huge mistake on their part," I responded.

"Oh, trust me, I know. I can rope circles around them back at home. My horse, Lucille, is amazing. She always knows exactly what to do before *you* even know what to do. But she's a lot of horse, that one. Checks out, though, with me as her rider."

This was how the first few days had gone, both of us whispering in the dark about everything under the sun. I wasn't able to do anything around the house, so we'd just been holed up in my room. Ellison didn't have to stay by my side but she insisted.

"So, when you're not being a badass cowgirl, what do you do back at home besides drive cowboys like me crazy?" I joked.

"Normally, I'd be hanging out with Isa. It gets a lot easier for me to go out and do things when I'm not thinking about the rodeo and my dad being gone. March is just a hard time. I definitely miss Isa, but I wouldn't trade coming up to Montana for anything."

I hated that I was doing this to her, keeping her here when she could be back home in Texas, not wasting her time on me. But another part of me was selfishly happy she was here.

It wasn't until the next week that everything seemed to unravel.

"No, Colter! It's not fine!" Sophie screamed at me, and all I could do was stand there.

I had just been on the road for two weeks and I came home to surprise her before going back down to Wyoming.

"Sophie, please," I pleaded with her. "Let's talk about this."

This was how it had been constantly the last month. These little arguments that resulted in a screaming match between us. They always resolved themselves within a day or two, though. I wanted to believe it was just stress causing these fights.

"What is there to talk about, Colter? You're never fucking here!" She grabbed her roots and tugged on them, her hands on top of her head. I was worried if she pulled any harder she'd rip strands out of her scalp.

"You know why I'm doing this, Soph. Please, baby. I'm doing this for our future, so we can have the house you dream of, so we can have the kids and the dogs."

She was crying now, and I didn't understand.

"I-I just." She sobbed, and I pulled her close to me, her tears staining my shirt.

But then the mood shifted. She pushed me away from her and then suddenly my head smacked against the metal railing of the arena fence.

"Fuck you, Colter." Her voice from one of our fights rang through my mind, and my head pounded, my vision getting blurry.

Black spots dotted my vision and my stomach dropped as though I was falling.

I didn't realize I was screaming, tears rolling down my face, my body slick with sweat, until I felt her holding me in her arms.

W-where am I? What's going on?

"Shh, I've got you. It's just a nightmare. You're okay."

Ellison's voice soothed me, bringing me back to the present as she ran her fingers through my hair. "You're safe. I'm here."

Fuck. I tried to breathe in and out, but the air was getting caught in my throat, causing me to wheeze.

"I-I'm so sorry. You d-don't deserve to see me like this." Self-hatred sank deeper into my bones as I choked out each word.

She didn't deserve this. I didn't *want* to put her through this. This was exactly what I had been so afraid of. My struggles were just that—mine. I shouldn't have had to burden her with them, even if she was the whole reason why I hadn't had the nightmares in the first place.

"How long has this been going on?" she asked.

"Since the breakup. Ellison, *please.* You don't want me to drag you into this, trust me." I tried to push her away, keep her at an arm's length so this struggle stayed my own.

"No, that's not how this is going to work. I'm not going anywhere. Please, just tell me." Her expression was filled with worry, the glow of the night sky illuminating her face and the tears that dotted her eyes.

"I'm sorry. I should have told you. After the breakup, I started getting these nightmares. These flashbacks. The only way I could numb them back then was by drinking." I didn't want to be telling her these things.

"I probably went through two bottles a day trying to keep my mind numb. I couldn't sleep unless I drank because at least at that point I wouldn't even remember falling asleep." My voice shook with the recollection, but she deserved to know. "But they stopped when I met you. B-but the injury and then seeing her again. I-I don't want to b-burden you with my issues, Ellison. I'm s-so sorry."

"You're not a burden." Her voice broke as a tear rolled

down her cheek. "You're so far from a burden, Colter. I'm here. I'm not leaving you."

She just held me in her arms that night. We were two people, broken in our own ways, helping each other piece back together the parts we'd been missing.

I woke up to her fast asleep, still holding me in her arms. She was so perfect, and I was nowhere near the man she deserved. I so badly wanted to be that, I just didn't know how. She deserved someone who wasn't going to use her like a crutch, someone who could stand on their own.

I moved to get up, to go outside and get some air. I needed to think. I sat on the bottom step and put my head in my hands, not knowing what to do or where to go from here.

A little while later, the front door creaked and she walked up behind me.

"Do you want to talk about it?" she asked.

"I don't know," I admitted.

I didn't know *how* to talk about it. Yeah, I had Reid, but I never unpacked all of my trauma with him.

"I know it's not the same, but I've been where you are," she sighed, sitting down beside me. "My dad didn't just die from a rodeo accident. I was there when it happened."

I sucked in a breath, my heart feeling like it stopped, for her, for me, for both of us.

"How did you get past it?" I asked, my voice shaky.

"I haven't. At least not completely." She laughed as though she realized the irony in it all. "I was angry about it for a long time. I was mad at my dad for promising that nothing would ever happen to him, for competing in rodeo while knowing the risks. I considered him selfish for months after the accident. My mom even took me back to Wyoming—to Cheyenne—where they met, and I didn't understand how much meaning that trip had until recently. The truth was, my dad loved rodeo. It was his passion, his life. But he also loved me and my mother more than anything. Nothing can take that away from me."

She looked away for a moment, but then her eyes came back to mine. "I still struggle with the loss of him every day. I keep a strong front for the people around me, my mother especially, but sometimes it feels like the ceiling is caving in on me. Gradually, it's gotten better, though. You're not alone, Colter. You have so many people around you that love you, you just have to let them in."

"I put so much pressure on myself." I sighed. "I've blamed myself for so long for how my relationship with Sophie ended. I felt like a failure—most of the time I still do—and seeing her in the hospital brought up all of those feelings again. I guess I'm scared that with being unable to compete for the next month, I'll end up failing Reid too."

"It's not your fault, Colter. Relationships are a two-way street and Sophie made her choices, you said that yourself. I know it's hard, trust me, but you are not a failure. You are so much more than you could ever imagine. You are everything to Reid and the guys, you just have to be able to see that for yourself. I had convinced myself I would never be a part of rodeo again, a part of this lifestyle, but you've helped me see there's still good in it. These wounds don't heal overnight, but every day, even if you take one tiny step, you get closer. And I'm here for you. I'll always be here for you, like you have been for me."

CHAPTER FORTY-FIVE

ellison

I t killed me to see Colter hurting. If I could have, I would have taken every ounce of hurt in his body and transferred it over to me—even if it meant I broke down as a result.

He soaked in my words, storms behind his eyes. "Thank you," he whispered.

We sat there, on the front steps of his house, for what felt like hours, holding each other and listening to each other's heartbeats and breathing.

He kissed my temple, mumbling, "Thank you," over and over again.

In that moment, I silently promised I would do whatever it took to make sure he never felt alone. That even if I couldn't take away all of the weight on his shoulders, I could at least lighten the load. He might have seemed like a failure in his eyes, but to me he was everything.

If I wasn't sure before, I was confident then. As we sat in silence, I realized I was falling for Colter Carson. The idea of being in love with a cowboy had always seemed impossible to me. But with Colter, I just knew.

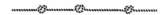

The Fourth of July rodeo was a week away. The doctor had cleared Colter for moderate activities, not competing at full speed, but he was able to ride again and do minor work around the ranch. This brought his spirits up, and over time it felt like the Colter everyone knew was starting to come back.

I knew a lot of it was a mask, that he was hiding a much darker side of himself, but I was there to support him and let him decide how he wanted to move forward on his own terms. I'd experienced people trying to force me into therapy before and I wholeheartedly believed Colter would pursue that route when he was ready to.

For now, I was there to hold his hand when the nightmares came, although they were starting to become less frequent again. I wanted to believe I was prepared when they came, but sometimes my heart still dropped into my stomach when he started shaking and couldn't control his breathing. I did the best I could to ground him and bring him back to me, though, even if it meant just holding him and staying awake watching him sleep until the sun rose.

Witnessing Colter's struggles, knowing what he was also going through, encouraged me to look back at myself and what I'd been through and consider giving therapy another try. I had started to research practices back in Texas that I could reach out to when I got back home.

When I had tried it before, I was admittedly stubborn

and it was hard to connect with people and admit that it was okay to get help. Now, I realized everyone struggles in their own ways, deals with their pain differently, and it was okay to seek out help.

I'd talked to Isa on the phone a few times in the past couple weeks to tell her what was going on and also because I missed her. We had never really been apart for that long; we were practically attached at the hip.

"Hey, babe, how's everything going there?" she had asked one morning after a particularly rough night.

"It's been okay, I just wish I could do more to help him." I didn't divulge all of the details of what he was going through—that was his story to tell—but I'm sure she could sense I was tired from restless nights worrying about him.

"The best you can do is be there for him, Ells. I know it's hard, but you know better than anyone, sometimes you just need a shoulder to cry on. I know he appreciates you being there."

"Thanks, Is. What would I do without you?"

"You'd be perfectly fine, but thanks for the confidence boost." She giggled.

That morning, Colter wanted to go for a ride, just a slow, easy one to get out of the house and get his riding legs back.

"How are you feeling, really?" I asked him as we rode almost shoulder to shoulder down the trail. I checked in with him as often as I could, wanting to see if there was anything I could do to help him.

"Getting cleared to do more things was nice," he answered, but I could sense he was still holding back.

"But?" I pushed a little, but ultimately I wasn't going to make him tell me what he was feeling. I was just encouraging him to talk to me.

"But I'm still nervous about the possibility of not being able to compete and leaving Reid high and dry for another rodeo."

"For what it's worth, you've been following the doctor's orders and you've been getting better every day. We can only hope for the best, but I have confidence you'll be cleared to go," I tried to reassure him, hoping I sounded confident enough.

"Thanks, baby." He smiled, even if it was only a half-smile.

We rode in silence for a while, enjoying each other's company and the mid-day summer air. He showed me all of his favorite spots on the land he owned, and then we decided to ride back.

When we reached the clearing of wildflowers from a couple weeks prior, I was the one who dismounted my horse and went over to him.

"What are you doing, Blaze?" he asked, confused.

"Just trust me, Sparky." I winked, and he got off his horse and followed me. I walked to the middle of the field of flowers and lay down on my back, looking up at the sky.

He followed suit, looking over at me, a melancholy look in his eyes.

"When I was younger, my dad and I used to lay down in the middle of the yard and cloud gaze. We would try to identify the most ridiculous things we could," I explained to him as I pointed up at a cloud shape. "See, that one looks like a bear on its hind legs."

He smiled at me before pointing at the sky. "That one kind of looks like a, uh, bird."

The cloud he pointed at looked more like a blob, but he was getting the idea. We lay there for a while, pointing out shapes and giggling like kids.

"Thank you for that." He took my hand and twirled me around when we finally stood.

We rode back to the house, cracking jokes and telling stories about our college days.

"Reid and I actually met Mikey at a bar." He chuckled as he recalled the story. "He was sitting at the bar by himself and called us over to talk to him. If you could imagine him ten-times worse than he is now, that was him then."

I snorted, trying to imagine an even more outspoken, flirtatious Mikey.

"Somehow, despite us being ropers and him being a roughy, we ended up becoming friends. He gets on my nerves sometimes, but he's as loyal as they come."

I told him the story about how Isabelle and I met and his eyes gleamed with amusement and his personality shone through. Colter was so caring, and sensitive, but in a good way. He felt everything and wore his heart on his sleeve, and I wanted to feel everything with him too.

We sat on the couch after we had taken care of the horses, my head in his lap. He ran his fingers through my hair.

"Colter?" I looked up at him.

"Yeah, Ells?" he asked.

"I'm proud of you and I know you're going to come back from this." I sat up, and he cupped my face with his hands, brushing his thumb over my cheek before leaning in and kissing me with more force than he had in the past few weeks. We had slowed things down since his injury, but his eyes still burned when he looked at me.

"I want you," he whispered into my mouth as his tongue wrestled with mine.

"I want you too," I mouthed back, and he lifted me up, carrying me into the bedroom, never separating our lips for more than a breath.

He laid me down gently on the bed and pulled off my top. I grasped the hem of his shirt, pulling it over his head.

He pressed his weight against me, rocking his hips into me as his hardness pressed against my body. He kissed my lips once more before making his descent, taking his time and stopping at my nipples, taking one in his mouth, lightly nipping it as he rolled the other one in his fingers.

"Fuck," I moaned, arching my back toward him. I was so desperate with want, I was sure that he would be able to feel my wetness through my panties.

He moved his hand down the curve of my waist and tugged on my jeans, pulling everything off in the process and then teasing me, sliding his fingers around my entrance but never giving me what I actually wanted.

"I can already feel how wet you are for me and I'm not even inside you yet," he purred.

I clenched my jaw, as my hips bucked, trying to get him to stop teasing me and do something.

"Patience." He pressed my hips down with his free hand, his other one rubbing circles on my clit before he dipped a finger in and started moving it. "Look at me, baby," he commanded as he worked his fingers, getting faster.

I tried to keep my eyes open, but the pressure was building inside me and I squeezed them shut.

He stopped, causing me to open them again.

"Why are you stopping?" I pleaded.

"I want you to look at me. Don't take your eyes off me or I'll stop," he ordered as he lowered his mouth onto my aching core.

He kept pace with his fingers as his tongue moved in tandem. I kept my eyes locked on him, not wanting him to stop. We made eye contact a couple of times as he looked up, satisfied with my reaction.

"I-I think I'm g-going to c-come," I stuttered.

"Not yet. You come when I tell you to."

God, even after everything that happened he still has such a hold on me.

I couldn't take it anymore, I was so close to orgasming, my moans were becoming more frequent and higher in pitch.

"Please, Colter!" I begged for release.

"What do you want, Ellison?" He looked up at me, still applying pressure to my clit, sending shockwaves up my body.

"I want to come, please!" I cried.

"Such a good girl. Come for me, baby," he praised as I exploded on his fingers.

He took off his pants and boxers, freeing his erection and not giving me any time to come down from my high before he entered me, causing me to gasp for air.

"You're so tight and wet," he groaned as he pumped in and out of me. "Tell me whose pussy this is."

"Yours, baby," I moaned. "I'm yours."

I knew how much he loved hearing it, and he picked

up his pace, leaning down to kiss me on the lips as he lifted my legs onto his shoulder, creating a deeper angle.

"You are perfect, Ellison. I'm close, baby," he muttered as he pounded into me harder until we both came together, his cock twitching as he spilled inside me.

He lay down beside me and kissed my head as he pulled me close, tracing letters on my back that I couldn't make out.

colter

I was in love with her. Completely in love with Ellison Wilson as I traced the letters to "I love you" on her back. I didn't care if it was the wrong time and place to say it, even if it wasn't verbally. I loved her and I wanted the entire world to know it.

She fell asleep, even though it was only mid-afternoon, her soft snores filling the room, and I whispered, "I love you."

I didn't have to be good enough for anyone else, as long as I was enough for her. I could lose every single rodeo from this day forward, as long as I had her in my corner, I was the luckiest man in the world. She made me realize that although rodeo was a big part of me, it wasn't *all* of me. That whatever happened because of Sophie didn't define who I was. All I had left was to tell her.

I kissed her shoulder and got up to call Reid. He answered on the second ring.

"Hey, Colt. How are you?" he asked me like he assumed something was wrong. Reid and I never usually talked on the phone unless it was something urgent.

"Everything's good. I'll be headed to the doctor in a few days and hopefully he'll clear me for the rodeo."

"That's great. We've really missed you out here on the road. Mikey's been driving us crazy." He laughed.

I was itching to ask him what kind of trouble Mikey had gotten himself into and how many girls he had brought back to his trailer. Maybe one day someone would tie that man down, but it didn't seem like it would be any day soon.

We caught each other up on what had been happening the past few weeks. I admitted to him about the nightmares coming back—how they had stopped once I met Ellison and started again when Sophie came back. He didn't say much, but that was the way he was. He was a listener, and a good one at that, but when he knew it was important, he would provide his input.

Before we hung up, I stopped him.

"What's up, man?" he asked.

"I think I love her, Reid. No, I know I love her. And it's both terrifying and exhilarating." I choked out the words.

"I'm happy for you, Colt. I know I've said it before but I do think you two are good for each other. You needed to find each other," he replied before we said our goodbyes and hung up.

He would be home in four days and the rodeo was in six. I was ready for him to come back, to see my best friend in person.

I was dying to tell Ellison how I felt, but every time I came close to telling her, something always got in the way.

The first time we were sitting on the couch, watching a

movie, and she was stuffing her face with popcorn that we had made on the stove. She looked so comfortable—happy to be with me.

"Hey, baby?" I had said right as she put a handful of popcorn in her mouth.

"Mm-yes?" she mumbled, her mouth full of the kernels.

I laughed because her cheeks looked like a chipmunk after they had stuffed their mouths full of chestnuts.

"Hey! Stop laughing at me!" She elbowed me in the ribs.

"That was rude," I joked, reaching for her and tickling her until she squealed with laughter. And then, well, we got so caught up doing other things that I didn't get the chance to tell her I loved her in a different setting than the bedroom.

The next time was a couple of days later when we were riding. Whenever we felt like we needed to get out of the house, we saddled up the horses and took them out, even if it was only for thirty minutes. I had learned riding for leisure, without the pressure of competition, was one thing that helped me clear my head of any dark, intrusive thoughts. It was what I loved after all, it made sense that it was a healthy coping mechanism for me.

We were at the top of a hill, the view of the countryside laid out before us. The land appeared to shimmer with the setting sun, dazzling with flecks of light.

It felt like the right time to tell her. "Ellison, I—"

"Race you to the bottom!" she cried out, already taking off, her hair blowing in the wind behind her.

My competitive side came out, and Bullet and I took off after her as she laughed the whole way down the hill.

Then it was the day Reid and the boys were set to

come home. They weren't supposed to get to the house for a few hours, so I had plans to tell her how I felt. I was anxious to tell her, my hands a little shaky and my mind locked on her.

My final doctor's appointment was tomorrow and it would be the deciding factor of whether or not I would get to compete with Reid, but I wasn't even thinking about that. It was only Ellison. She was the sun in my galaxy and right now everything revolved around her.

"Are you nervous?" she asked me, placing her hand on top of my knee as my leg bounced.

Yes, but not for the reason you think.

"For tomorrow? Or the rodeo?" I asked, drawing this out, even though all I wanted to do was scream at the top of my lungs that I loved her.

"Yeah, both," she replied, drawing circles with her thumb.

"A little bit. Um, but, there's something I've been wanting to tell you," I murmured.

"Okay, what's up?"

"I've been wanting to say this for a while, but I—" Maybe the universe didn't want me to tell her I was in love with her because, right on cue, a pickup horn blared and the boys pulled up in front of the house.

Ellison shot up, rushing over to the door as Reid, Mikey, Jake, and Hayden all piled out.

"You guys are back early!" She gave all of them hugs. Crazy to think a month ago, she was a stranger to all of them and now they accepted her like she was family.

"Yeah, surprising, huh?" Reid chuckled and flicked his eyes to Mikey. Usually, when we were on the road we were late getting back home and it was almost always because of Mikey.

"Glad to have you home, buddy." I hugged him. *Even though you ruined my moment with Ellison.*

We ended up going into town to get lunch, and the boys told us about the rodeos they had gone to while they were on the road.

"The one in Arizona was fine," Reid explained. "But the header I got paired with wasn't the best."

"Well, of course not, bud. The best was back here at home," I joked with him, feeling more like myself every day.

Reid laughed with me but continued his story, telling us that he ended up placing third, which still won him money and would keep his standing in a good spot, luckily.

"Unfortunately, Kingsley and Marlow were at the one in New Mexico and they were talking shit." He rolled his eyes before Mikey cut in.

"Yeah, I almost got in a fist fight with one of 'em over it, but you'd be proud of me, Carson, I held back."

I had seen some of the interviews that Kingsley and Marlow had done. None of them were particularly friendly and most involved them making little digs about me not being tough enough to continue to compete. Ellison tried her best to prevent me from reading or watching them, but it was my reputation that they were talking about.

"I shouldn't have to congratulate you on having self-control, buddy," I said sarcastically, but I still had to chuckle.

"What did you get up to while you were home?" Hayden asked. He didn't talk about himself much, or really talk much at all, but he was a great kid. Always cared about the people around him and checked up on everyone to make sure they were doing okay.

"I'm not sure if I want to know what those two were up

to." Mikey wiggled his eyebrows as he made the suggestive comment.

Ellison's cheeks flushed as she pushed around her food. "We didn't do much. Watched movies, went for rides." Her voice trailed off a little as she realized how that might have given Mikey ammunition to poke fun at us.

I gave him a glare right as he opened his mouth to make a comment, and Ellison fired, "On horses, you jackass."

A couple hours later, we were back at the house, sitting on the front lawn, drinking beers, and talking about life like we always did. It was our usual tradition, except it felt even better having Ellison sitting on my lap, listening to her banter and joke around with the guys like she'd always been a part of our lives.

CHAPTER FORTY-SEVEN

ellison

C olter had been cleared to compete in the Fourth of
July rodeo, and the day had finally come.

We all drove to the arena the night before so Reid and
Colter could get in some practice runs the next morning.
He was nervous, I could tell. He was even more nervous
when Dash Kingsley and Wayne Marlow pulled up.

"What the fuck are they doing all the way up here?"
Reid grumbled, clearly not pleased that they were here.

The thing about the PRCA was that you could
compete in rodeos anywhere. There were different circuits
throughout the nation and while cowboys had to designate
a home circuit, they weren't restricted to only competing in
those rodeos.

"I have no fucking idea. Probably to get in our heads."
Colter rolled his eyes.

Dash stepped out of his pickup truck, wearing too-tight
jeans and a shirt that was probably worth more than me.
He seemed like the type to flaunt his wealth and indulge in
expensive things.

"Well, well, well, look who's here." His eyes flicked to

Colter as he talked to Wayne. "Looks like the golden boy decided to actually compete. Heard about your injury. What a shame you weren't able to rope this last month. Leaving your roping partner high and dry, were you?" he taunted Colter, clearly looking for a reaction.

"He's got that girl with him too, Dash." Wayne ran his eyes up and down my body, and I gave him a look of disgust.

"Sugar, you can do so much better than this one." Dash walked up to me. "Why don't you come ride with the big guns, not some little cowboy from middle of nowhere Montana who can't even toughen out a little head injury?"

"I would rather shove a pineapple filled with glass shards up my ass than do anything with you." I batted my eyelashes at him as I said it and then immediately curled my lip as I rolled my eyes and looked away.

"Easy there, Firecracker." Mikey pulled me back as Dash muttered, "Fucking bitch."

"You're in my state right now, Kingsley. Stay away from my girl and don't speak about her like that again or you'll be lucky to make it to the NFR!" Colter was close to grabbing his collar before Reid got in the way and pulled him away.

"Be smart about this, man. They're just trying to get in your head. Don't do anything you'll regret," he warned.

"Good luck out there, boys. You're going to need it." Dash sneered, satisfied with the response he got from Colter, and then he and Wayne were gone.

"Don't worry about them." I walked over to Colter, putting my hand on his shoulder, trying to make him focus on me and not the assholes who were currently driving away. "This is your state, your rodeo. You guys will be fine."

Colter and Reid absolutely were fine as they ran their practice runs. If you didn't know Colter hadn't been competing for the last month, you wouldn't have been able to tell. His movements were still smooth, and they were clocking impressive times for being out of their groove.

That was the importance of having a strong bond and connection with your heeler, though. You could be away from each other for a month, or even longer, but the moment you roped together again, it was like you'd never been apart.

The day of competition came. This was one of the largest rodeos in Montana and showcased some of the best in the state as well as some out-of-state competitors. I wasn't sure why Kingsley and Marlow were here, especially since they were from all the way in Oklahoma and there were rodeos closer to home that would get them decent money, but I had to believe it was to get into Colter's head after they had lost to them in Houston.

The rodeo kicked off with an explosive energy, and the events seemed to pass by in a blur. Hayden roped with a random partner from out of state and they did well, clocking a five-point-five run. Jake was also competing in the steer wrestling and it took all of my will to not look away, but I watched the entire thing without having a flashback or feeling like I might pass out.

Finally, Dash and Wayne would compete, followed by Colter and Reid. Their rivalry was gaining popularity, especially after Houston and Colter's injury. Both teams had fairly good positions in their world standings and it was likely that the NFR average championship would be between them.

The tension in the air was palpable as the Oklahoma boys geared up to rope. Dash did his same stupid routine of looking out into the crowd and schmoozing the women, but he didn't have quite the effect that he was hoping for here. When he didn't get the attention he craved, he rolled his eyes and actually started to focus on the task at hand.

Their final time was four-point-eight seconds.

CHAPTER FORTY-EIGHT

colter

S weat pooled on my forehead and back as I watched the teams before us. I was doing my best to control my breathing and not panic, but there was a lot of pressure riding on this performance. All eyes were on me as I came back from my injury. I couldn't fail. There was no room for it at this point.

I must have been breathing hard because Reid leaned close to me and gave me a pep talk.

"Colter, listen to me. We're going to be fine out there. This is exactly like every other rodeo we've been to. Don't focus on Kingsley and Marlow. Don't focus on the cameras. Focus on what you know how to do best."

I nodded, gulping down a mouthful of air.

"I believe in you. The guys believe in you. Ellison believes in you."

"Ellison believes in me. I can do this," I said and breathed in and out. I looked up into the crowd, exactly where I knew she would be. She was such a calming presence for me.

"All right, folks. Our next team consists of a couple of

cowboys from your home state. They won big at the Houston Rodeo earlier this year and they're back to show us all what Montana tough means. Let's help them out here! Your cowboys from Silver Creek, Montana: Colter Carson and Reid Lawson!"

I took a deep breath before getting on the back of my horse and riding it into the arena. Reid gave me an encouraging nod as we walked to the chute.

The roar of the crowd was deafening, all of them cheering for my return from my recovery.

You've got this. Do it for them, for Ellison, for yourself. I pounded the statement into my brain over and over, getting myself into the mindset that whatever happened today, I would continue to fight as hard as I could for our spot at the NFR.

Reid entered his side of the box, and I followed behind him, keeping my shoulder warm by swinging the rope over my head a few times. My heartbeat pounded in my ears and never ceased, not when I nodded my head for the steer to be released from the chute and not when my horse took off after it.

The voices of every person who doubted me rang in my ears, threatening to cause me to lose my focus. They all repeated the same things.

You're a failure.

You'll never measure up.

You've missed too much to be successful this year.

But then a new voice rang out, one I'd heard for the last few months.

I believe in you.

That was all I needed to zero in my focus on the steer ahead of me as I threw my rope and caught the horns. The next part was the part I had dreaded for the past month, but my boots were secure and there was no way I would slip. I dallied my rope and turned the steer for Reid who was right behind us.

He caught the steer successfully, and we finished, turning toward each other as the announcer called out our time of four-point-six seconds, enough to beat out the team from Oklahoma by a hair.

Fuckers. That'll show you, thinking you can come into our state and throw us off our game. I internally boasted our win over them.

Dash Kingsley and Wayne Marlow didn't matter anymore, though, as we took our victory lap around the arena and I looked out into the crowd of fans, smiling and cheering for us. There was only one person who I looked at, though, as I rode around, her smile captivating me—capturing my heart—just like the first day I met her.

ellison

I raced over to him as he exited the arena, sweat slicked on his forehead but a huge grin on his face. He was back. My boy was back and nothing could stop him. The win tonight would keep him in a great position for world standings, so he still had a likely chance of making it to the NFR.

"You were amazing out there, Sparks." I hugged him.

"Thank you, baby." He squeezed me tighter, like he never wanted to let go.

"Carson! Come here!" Mikey yelled out to him, and I

pulled away to let him go take care of whatever it was Mikey needed. We still had plenty of time.

"I love you." He grabbed my hands and pulled me back so I was facing him.

"W-what?" I blinked, not sure if I heard him correctly.

"I love you, Blaze." He tilted my chin up so I was looking directly in his eyes. "I'm in love with you. I love the way that you challenge me and motivate me. I love how understanding and caring you are and how you make me feel like the luckiest man in the world. You make me forget about every past failure in my life, every insecurity, every doubt. Because you see me for me, Ellison. And I love you. I love you so much."

"I love you too, Sparky."

Colter Carson was everything. He was a best friend, a son, a brother, a rising team roper, and a cowboy from Montana. But most importantly, he was mine. My entire world had changed in the past three months, but I knew we didn't have anything to worry about. I was absolutely carefree as I pulled him toward me, Mikey and the boys be damned, and kissed him.

Colter and I? We were exactly where we needed to be.

CHAPTER FORTY-NINE

ellison

FIVE MONTHS LATER: THE NATIONAL FINALS RODEO, LAS VEGAS, NV

L adies and gentlemen, welcome to the final night of the Wrangler National Finals Rodeo!" The announcer's excitement was contagious, and the entire arena was erupting in a chorus of cheers. The NFR was the final event of the year. Every moment, every trial throughout the year had led to this.

"Hey, Sparky?" I smiled at Colter. He was about to run off so he could meet Reid and be ready to rope when the time came.

"Yeah, Blaze?"

"I love you. Give 'em hell." I wished him luck right before stealing a kiss.

Everyone was here to support Colter and Reid. Isabelle was sitting to my right and my mother to my left. Mikey, Jake, and even Hayden were also here. Even though they themselves hadn't qualified for the NFR, they wouldn't have missed the chance to cheer on their brothers.

The events went by in a blur. The boys had done extremely well throughout the entire week. They looked natural out there, as though they had been on this national stage their entire lives. This last day was muscle memory for them.

Dash Kingsley and Wayne Marlow ended up screwing themselves over for the NFR Average Championship by securing themselves a no time and a barrier violation in the previous rounds. I took satisfaction in thinking it was karma for all of the hell they had put Colter and Reid through. I kept my mouth shut every time we passed by them, though.

After the bull riding, they would crown the new NFR Champions and World Champions. One winner would be crowned based on average scores throughout the ten-day rodeo, and the other would be based on overall winnings throughout the entire year. Both would take home gold buckles and a fair amount of prize money.

"Ladies and gentlemen. The time that you all have been waiting for has come. It is time to crown our new NFR and World Champions!"

The anticipation in the arena was palpable. It was unlikely that Colter would win a World Championship with the month he was out for his injury, but he and Reid had a good chance at winning the average.

They announced the first few events, bareback riding and saddle bronc riding. Cheers erupted from the crowd as their favorite cowboys' names were called. There was only one name I wanted to hear, though, and my palms started to clam up as I waited for the announcer to call out the winners for team roping.

"Your NFR Average Champions for team roping are…" The announcer paused for effect. "Colter Carson and Reid Lawson!"

I didn't hear any of the other names or events. The world seemed to pause, the people a blur around me and the cheers and voice of the announcer nothing but background noise.

He did it! We did it!

The boys all hollered for their friends, Mikey howling, "I knew they would do it!"

Isa looked out into the arena with a starstruck look in her eye, and it made me wonder if there was something going on with her and Reid.

When Colter stepped out of the arena, I ran up to him and leapt into his arms. "I'm so proud of you." I planted a kiss on his cheek.

"Wow, Ellison Wilson and public displays of affection? Are you sick?" He acted surprised.

"Don't get your hopes up too much, Sparky. Really, though. I'm so proud of you."

Colter had fought tooth and nail to get here and all of his work had paid off. He was one of the best cowboys in the world tonight.

"I couldn't have done it without you. You are my guiding force, my motivation, my fire. This win wasn't only for me and Reid tonight. It was for you too, baby."

I rolled my eyes with amusement at his declaration. He had always been the sentimental one of the two of us.

Normally, I would call him a cheese ball or something of the like, but the truth was I was happy to be his. I wanted to experience every win and loss, every high and low. I didn't need to know what came next to know that he was meant to be in my life, no reservations, no hesitations.

My mother walked over to me and Colter, and I called out to her.

"Mom! This is Colter." I started to introduce them. She was smiling, but her eyes were glassy so I paused. "What's wrong?"

"Nothing's wrong, El. I'm just so proud of you, you know." She sniffed and wiped a tear from her eyes.

I looked at her with a confused look. Colter had won an NFR Championship and she was about to meet him for the first time. She knew how important he was to me and she knew about our relationship, so why was she crying?

"Mrs. Merritt, it's so nice to meet you." Colter took off his hat and extended his hand.

"It's wonderful to meet you too, Colter. Please, call me Hanna." Instead of shaking his hand she pulled him in for a hug.

After their embrace, Colter motioned that he was going to go talk to Reid. Presumably to give us some space to talk.

"Are you going to tell me what's wrong now?" I asked, a little concerned. Did she not like him?

"Oh, hon, there's nothing wrong. I can see how happy you are and I know your dad would be so proud of you. He never wanted you to blame rodeo, this lifestyle. I did everything I could to help you get there, but I also knew you needed to come to terms with everything yourself, on your own time, and you have," she started to say. "I've seen the light come back in your eyes when you're with him. You both needed each other in your lives. And I'm so happy you've found him. He reminds me a lot of your father, you know."

Now I was the one who was crying. My mouth couldn't form any words, so I just nodded and pulled her in for a hug.

"Thank you, Mom," I whispered.

I looked over at Colter and Reid, their faces bright with excitement at winning their first NFR championship. Their careers would only go up from here as they were full of promise and still in the early stages.

I thought about what my mom had said, about Colter, about my dad, and about rodeo, and it hit me. She was right. Rodeo had been the thing that my dad and I both loved. When he died, I thought my love for it had gone with him—that I'd never be able to feel that joy again. But I was wrong. I was so wrong.

Grief was a funny thing. It made you feel like you'd never get back the pieces of yourself that you'd lost. That you'd feel their absence like a cavity in your chest forever. And in a way, it was true. But even in an injury, your organs shift to fill the space that was left behind. The loss of my dad would still be there, but other things—trust and love—had shifted to fill the void his death had created. It took meeting Colter Carson to realize that.

I wouldn't have had it any other way.

epilogue

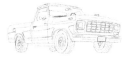

ellison

ONE MONTH LATER

The air was cold, at least cooler than usual, as I walked around the ranch. The weather was gloomy, as if even the ranch was mourning my departure. After the NFR, Colter had asked me to move to Montana with him. It was hard, leaving my mother and the place I'd grown up in, but she encouraged me to go. She said it was time I did something for myself instead of sacrificing all of me for everyone else, and for once I didn't fight her on it.

Isa had cried, mostly from happiness, but I told her she could come visit me whenever she wanted—especially because I had an inkling that she had a crush on a certain heeler—and that I would come home as often as I could.

It was a bittersweet moment as I made my way to the shop, opened the garage door and headed to the back corner like I had done so many times. One last drive before I moved fifteen hundred miles away.

However, when I got to the pickup, pulled off the tarp, and climbed in, I noticed something new. There was now a letter on the dash, sitting next to the photo of my parents and addressed to me in chicken scratch handwriting. I took a deep breath and opened it, not knowing what I would find.

Ellison, my Sunshine, the light of my life,

I bought this pickup after I married your mother a couple years ago. Baby blue, just like your mother's eyes, and now yours. I never thought there would be anything in the world that I could love more than your mother, rodeo, and this truck. These pieces of my life that seemed insignificant to others, but were everything to me.

But then I had you. And now, nothing is more important to me. Nothing could ever replace a father's love.

I can only assume I've been restoring this pickup for years now, maybe with you by my side, but the time has finally come.

This truck is now yours. Cherish it; love it as I have. But know that no amount of my love for this vehicle will ever compare to my love for you.

You will always be my little girl. I love you so much.

Daddy

THREE MONTHS LATER

It had been only a few months since Reid and I won our first NFR Championship. The excitement of the win, however, was overshadowed by my excitement to have Ellison with me in Montana full-time.

The moment she moved up to Silver Creek, she redecorated the whole house. Honestly, redecorated might be an understatement. She fully decorated it, making it feel more "homey." I didn't know if she realized that it didn't matter whether we lived in a mansion in the hills or a shack in the woods, my home was wherever she was.

This trip back to Texas was a bit of an impromptu one, especially since we had just been there for the Houston Rodeo. I made the excuse that Ells should visit her mom and Isabelle, but I didn't tell her why I wanted to come to Texas too. She would find out soon enough.

It had been a little over a year since I met Ellison. A year since she had completely stolen my heart and refused to give it back. I was perfectly fine with that, though. She could have my heart and every single one of my days for the rest of my life. The final thing I had left to give her was my last name.

Back in Houston, I had asked Hanna for her blessing to propose to Ellison. She said yes with tears glistening in her eyes but a knowing look on her face. She had supported our relationship from the get-go because she had experienced a love like ours once.

Now there was one more person to ask.

Ellison and I had been to Levi's grave together a couple times before. He was buried in the hills behind the Merritt family ranch, watching over them. I'd gotten to know the man that Levi was in Ellison's eyes, even with how young she was when he died. I could only hope that I would live up to the standard Levi Merritt had set for me.

It looked like it was going to rain, the sky a deep bluish gray with storm clouds rolling in. I needed to do this quickly before it started pouring so that Ellison wouldn't wonder how I got drenched.

I drove the gravel road carefully, watching for holes and animals. Very few people came to this end of the ranch, so the road wasn't always maintained. Once I parked, I began the hike up to the top of the hill to where a cross and grave marker stood. When I got to the top, I looked around, taking in the view and preparing myself for what was to come. It had started to rain lightly, but I had time.

I knelt to the ground, next to the stone, and pulled out the tiny velvet box that held my future. Inside was the original ring that Levi Merritt proposed to Hanna with. It was stunning, with a silver band, hidden halo, and oval-cut gemstone, but it paled in comparison to Ellison's beauty.

I took a deep breath, and spoke the words that I had thought about carefully for the past few months, "Hi, Levi. I wish I had gotten to meet you because I know how important you are to Ellison. I came here because I have a really big question that I need to ask her." I thought back to a year prior, to running into her at the bar and doing everything I could to have her in my life.

"From the moment I saw her, I knew she was special. I fell in love with her the moment she showed me the pickup you had started to restore because I could see how much she loved and looked up to you. Well, I actually fell in love with her way before that, but that was the tangible moment in time I can remember thinking I wanted something more with her. I know I would never be able to replace you, and I would never try to, but if you give me the chance, I'd like to ask her to marry me. I promise I will protect her, and that I can and will love her enough for both of us." I finished my speech, even though I knew I wouldn't get an answer.

However, a moment later, as if willed by a higher power, the rain stopped and the sky started to clear, revealing a beautiful baby-blue sky streaked with the pinks and oranges of a sunset.

I'll take that as a yes, then. I smiled to myself. I gave one last look at the cross and stone, and looked up toward the heavens.

"I won't let you down."

closed door modifications

For those who want a reading experience without explicit sexual content (or for those who want to easily find the spice), here are the chapters that include open-door scenes. Please note that each of these chapters include explicit sexual content that is fully consensual.

If you would like to skip the spice, please note the starting points in parentheses that will provide you with the best reading experience. Skipping the entire chapter will cause you to miss out on important scenes and plot points.

- End of Chapter 37 (spice starts on page 231 at, "He picked me up, wrapping my legs around him as he carried me into the bedroom.")
- End of Chapter 38 (spice starts after the scene break on page 238)
- Beginning of Chapter 39 (for closed door, start reading after the scene break on page 246)
- End of Chapter 45 (spice starts after the scene break on page 282)

acknowledgments

The Pieces We've Lost wouldn't have been possible without the love and support of so many people. So much has happened in the past year, and so many of you have impacted me and this book in such a positive way. Words cannot fully describe how blessed I am, but I'm going to try.

First of all, thank *you*, dear reader, for taking the time to read my debut novel. For taking a chance on me and on Ellison and Colter. I've always been a reader, but actually publishing a book hadn't crossed my mind for years. If you told me two years ago my childhood dream would one day come true, I wouldn't have believed you. But here we are, and I am so grateful.

To my parents, you have provided me with the greatest example of what love is, both with your love for each other and your love for me. Thank you for fostering my love for reading, even if it meant spending $50+ every time we went to Barnes and Noble. Dad, you are my hero, my biggest fan, and I will always be your little girl. Thank you for all of the made up stories about horses and kings when I was younger, even if you were just trying to get me to shut up for once and go to sleep. Mom, for always being a phone call or text message away, and for giving me advice, even when I claim I don't need it.

My best friend, my other half. You are my guiding force, my motivation, my other spark. I wouldn't be here without you by my side. Thank you for loving me, growing with me, and supporting me through whatever crazy ideas I have. For always letting me read excerpts and scenes to you, giving your honest opinion *ahem, taxidermy*, and being encouraging and believing in me on my best and worst days, even if that means just being a hand to hold or a shoulder to cry on.

Brad and Sandie, for welcoming me into your life and world with open arms. For loving me as one of your own and pulling this farm girl into the ranching/rodeo world. I know there's no convincing you to not read this book cover to cover, so let's just not talk about the contents, okay?

Callie, Taylor, Jasmine, my Likewise girlies: Isa and Sam, Sydney S., Raquel, and so many others, for keeping all of the details of this book a secret, even when I wanted to spill all of them, being almost as excited as me—if not more—for it to be released, being my hype girls and friends, and most importantly, wholeheartedly believing in *The Pieces We've Lost.* I'm so happy that one little corner of the internet brought us together.

To all my author friends I've met throughout the past year and a half, especially Alex, Elle, Sydney A., and Peyton; thank you for your continual encouragement, advice, and support. You've made this process feel a little less lonely and overwhelming, and for that I am so grateful.

To my incredible beta readers for helping make this book the best version of itself. Your feedback, comments, and encouragement are invaluable to me.

My editors, Andrea and Caroline, without you this book probably would have been a mess of grammar and punctuation issues, not to mention all my repeated words and sometimes weird way of explaining things. Andrea, your attention to detail is immaculate and your ability to catch things I didn't even realize were in *my own story* is amazing. I'm so glad we've become friends through this process, even if you went to the ~~less~~ superior Montana college (wink).

To my street team and the early promo team, thank you SO much. You have no idea how much your support means to me. Every review, post, and recommendation you make has a huge impact, and I cannot express my gratitude enough. I attribute a lot of my growing success to you. I love you all.

To my ARC readers, even though I'm writing this prior to you having the book, I am so thankful that you decided to take a chance on my debut novel and deemed it worthy enough to want to read it early.

Finally, to the Bookstagram community, thank you for being a place where I can escape reality for even just a moment. Without Bookstagram, this story would have never made it to the page.

thanks for reading

If you enjoyed *The Pieces We've Lost*, I would greatly appreciate if you left a review on Amazon, Goodreads, or any other platform!

For more updates on The Road & The Rodeo series and the H.K. Green Universe, subscribe to my newsletter.

about the author

H.K. Green is a contemporary romance author based out of Montana, writing raw, emotional stories that will break your heart then put it back together.

Inspired by real-life, relatable challenges, her books feature found families, a healthy dose of sarcastic banter and emotional angst, strong female leads, and the men who'll do anything to give them the world.

When she's not writing, she can be found curling up with all kinds of books, hanging out with her rescue animals, going to rodeos or her family's farm and ranch, and spending time with her real-life book boyfriend.

You can connect with H.K. Green on Instagram and TikTok @authorhkgreen and learn more on her website at www.authorhkgreen.com.